TEXAS PANIC!

HARRY HAINES

Mayhaven Publishing

This novel does not depict any actual person or event.

Mayhaven Publishing, Inc
P O Box 557
Mahomet, IL 61853
USA

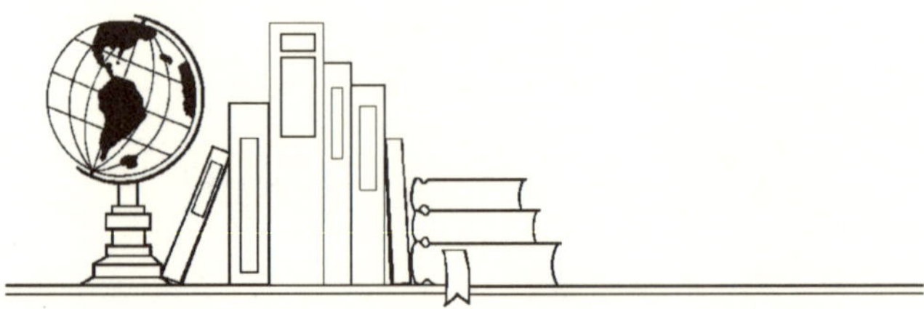

Cover Design and Photo: Steven L. Mayes

Library of Congress Control Number: 2009923249
First Edition—First Printing 2009
ISBN 13: 978 1932278606
ISBN 10: 1932278605
Printed in Canada

To Charlie Ball, CEO Emeritus of the Texas Cattle Feeders Association. I wish he could have lived to see how much he helped me with this story.

Prologue

A cow is found with symptoms of a disease that's invariably fatal in its human form. As a result, world markets close to local exports, jeopardizing the future of an entire industry. Despite the best efforts of producers, beef disappears from the national diet as panic grips the public, the media launches a frenzied inquisition, and reason is forgotten.

Impossible?

No. It's exactly what happened in Great Britain in the 1980s.

In order to understand this bizarre time in British history, one has to first recognize that encephalitis—an infection of the brain—has a number of variants found under the term encephalopathy (in-*seff*-a-lop-a-thee). These variants have different names that relate to the animals in which they were first identified. For example, encephalopathy in sheep is called scrapie; in deer and elk, it is chronic wasting disease or CWD; and in humans Creutzfeldt-Jakob disease or CJD.

Documentation of the disease can be found in medical history for at least 400 years. However it was not until the twentieth century, when scientists began to compare brain samples under a microscope, that a connection was made among the variants. The unifying characteristic was a pink sponge-like appearance of clear holes in the tissue. This is where the term "spongiform" came from. So, when the disease became rampant in cattle, it was called bovine spongiform encephalopathy, or BSE. The largest BSE outbreak in history occurred in Great Britain in the closing years of the twentieth century. The British press coined a new name for the plague—they called it "mad cow disease."

Several factors contributed to the seriousness of the outbreak and exacerbated its impact. The first was an error in judgment by both the government and the cattle industry—they conspired to hide the problem. The resulting loss of public confidence created an opportunity for the sensation-hungry British press. This was the health scare with everything—a gruesomely exotic background, unknown dangers, bungling bureaucrats, and a common food item found in virtually every home. When a self-proclaimed expert said, "BSE would make AIDS look like the common cold," the British public was ready to believe the worst.

Hundreds of thousands of infected carcasses entered the food chain and led to the discovery of a new variant of CJD (the human form of the disease). Called vCJD, it attacked young people and produced a terrifying inevitability: an Alzheimer-like decline into complete mental incapacity followed by certain death. Scientists traced the new vCJD to people who had eaten infected beef.

Politicians, too, were guilty of stoking the flames, albeit with the best of motives. To restore confidence, there could be no question of half measures. Only the mass killing of millions of cattle—at a cost of untold billions—would satisfy. The spectacle of killing and burning so many animals only fueled concern. At its peak one thousand new cases of BSE were reported each week.

The country's panic reached its apex in 1996 when McDonald's of Great Britain, the country's largest consumer of beef, ran full-page ads in all major newspapers stating the following, "From Thursday, March 28th, we will be selling Hamburgers, Big Macs, and Quarterpounders made only from non-British beef." The sale of local beef fell to zero. British cattle, once regarded as the finest in the world, became worthless.

All of this is history. The year 2004 was the first without any new cases of the disease in Great Britain. And as of this writing, the British are now eating more beef than in pre-BSE times. But a valuable lesson has been learned—when the whole world is watching, someone had better make sure the media gets it right.

Just ask any member of the Texas Cattle Feeders Association.

CHAPTER 1

Christmas Eve, the Texas State Bank,
3400 Coulter Avenue, Amarillo, Texas

I felt the news hit Texas like a death knell.

On December 23rd, the repercussions of a single case of mad cow disease, found in a small town near Spokane, Washington, dominated the national news in both broadcast and print media. Cattle prices on the Chicago Board of Trade dropped the limit. A shudder went through the cattle industry as ranchers, cattle feeders, beef packers, truckers—even veterinarians like me—began to worry about their livelihood.

Those who financed the production of beef could see the handwriting of disaster even more profoundly. The news jolted us all, but the most scared were the bankers. Especially those in the Texas

Panhandle where one-third of the nation's fed-beef was grown.

Brandon Williams, president of the Texas State Bank, called and asked me to stop by for a cup of coffee. I knew what he wanted—reassurance. Unfortunately, there didn't seem to be much available, but I agreed to come and would do my best at hand holding, at least figuratively.

Brandon's secretary greeted me with a worried look. "Dr. Masterson. Have a seat, and I'll tell him you're here."

She disappeared into the president's office. I sat and picked up two newspapers to scan the news of the day. The first, a December 23rd issue of the *Amarillo Globe-News*, displayed a headline in bold, black letters, six inches high. It read MAD COW IN U.S. For the second time I reviewed the story of a single cow imported from Canada and the report that our country now banned all Canadian beef—a classic example of too little, too late.

The second, today's edition of the *Wall Street Journal*, offered a smaller headline, CATTLE INDUSTRY IN NOSEDIVE, but a more chilling forecast of the financial implications. I had read only the first paragraph when the secretary interrupted.

"He'll see you now," she said. "May I get you a cup of coffee?"

"Yes, please," I replied. "Just black."

When I entered his office, Brandon's appearance startled me. He looked terrible. And though he's only a few years older than I—early fifties—it seemed as though he had aged ten years. Fleshy bags hung below both eyes, and his face resembled something you might see on ice in a fish market. For the only time in our twenty-five-year friendship, he failed to stand and greet me with a handshake. Instead he blurted out, "You tracking cattle futures?"

At first I didn't know how to take such an inane question.

Everyone in the cattle business was tracking the bad news, minute by minute. I thought he might be joking, but when I studied his face, he looked deadly serious. "Down the limit, and then they suspended trading," I replied.

"Thank God for the Christmas break," he said. "Just one more day of blood-letting, and then they close until Monday, January 5."

I nodded at his mindless, obvious remark.

"May or may not make any difference," he muttered.

"How much will this affect the bank?" I asked.

"Cattle loans are more than 50 percent of our business."

"So if cattle prices go to hell, they take the bank with them?"

He nodded. "Certain bankruptcy."

Our eyes met briefly, then he turned and looked out the window. I guessed why he faced away—he didn't want me to see the moisture in his eyes. Discretion told me to give him some space, wait, let him restart the conversation.

As we lapsed into a momentary period of silence, my thoughts turned to Brandon and his bank. Unlike most other local financial institutions that, during the past two decades, had merged with national giants like Bank of America, Citi-Bank, or Wells-Fargo, the Texas State Bank chose to remain small and independent. They advertised heavily about their "home-owned" status, and folks like me chose to do our banking with them because we liked the idea. The possibility of an exotic bovine disease creating bankruptcy had never entered my mind.

Until now.

"Seems ironic that everything we've worked for should come to this," Brandon said.

I struggled to think of something supportive. "In the 1980s, we survived hoof and mouth disease," I said. "We'll lick this, too."

Brandon swung his chair back so that he faced me. He attempted a smile that failed as he shook his head and said, "Dr. James Robert Masterson, the ever-optimistic veterinarian."

"No, just trying to be realistic."

The secretary came in with two cups of coffee. She handed one to me, gave the other to Brandon, and said, "Ted Austin's here. Shall I ask him to wait?"

Brandon poured a packet of sugar into his cup and stirred. "What does Austin want?"

"TCFA business, I think," she answered.

At the mention of the Texas Cattle Feeders Association, I scooted to the edge of my chair, a gesture of leaving. "Brandon, we can talk about this later."

"No, stay," he replied. "It might be good for the three of us to put our heads together."

Theodore Austin, Executive Director of the TCFA, was my neighbor and close friend. It didn't require scientific deduction to guess why Ted had come to see the bank president. Cattlemen needed money.

Brandon gestured to his secretary. "Ask him to join us."

A moment later my neighbor took the other chair and brought more doom and gloom into the ambiance. "I'm here on behalf of some of my members." Ted named a half-dozen cattle feeders—all men I knew—whose animals I treated.

"And?" Brandon sipped his coffee.

Ted looked from Brandon to me, back to Brandon. "This is about their personal finances."

Brandon shook his head. "Hell, everybody knows what it's

about. Cattle prices are falling like a rock."

"They want me to ask you if the bank's going to foreclose. A few more days like yesterday, and their collateral will be worth less than what they owe the bank."

Brandon slumped back in his chair, the scowl on his face deeper. "Suppose the bank took their herds. If we foreclosed on all the loans where collateral fell into receivership, what would the bank do with hundreds of thousands of worthless cattle?"

Ted had no answer.

Neither did I.

An ominous quiet fell over the room as we each let our thoughts probe the coming disaster.

I felt compelled to say something. "It's just one cow, imported from Canada."

"True."

"And it's in Spokane, Washington, at least two thousand miles away."

"So?"

"So, it'll blow over if we let it."

Brandon sipped his coffee. Again, he turned away and spoke to the window. "When you say *we*, who are you referring to?"

"Ted, you, me, the cattle industry."

"What about the government?" Ted asked.

"Especially the government."

Brandon swiveled back, and we locked eyes. Then he frowned, as though in deep thought, and very slowly, he shook his head.

"You forgot about the media," he said. "They'll never let it go."

CHAPTER 2

At home, two miles north of Bushland, Texas

Through a haze of sleep, I thought I heard a phone ringing.

It rang again, louder. My wife Maggie punched me. "It's for you."

"How do you know?" I mumbled.

Another ring.

"At two o'clock in the morning, it's always for you. Answer the damn phone."

I fumbled for the light. The answering machine started, "We're unable to come to the phone right now, but you can leave a message. Wait for—"

"Hello," I said, my voice low, raspy.

"Brandon's dead."

I recognized the voice of my friend and neighbor, Ted Austin. "What?"

"His wife called. She found him on the kitchen floor a few minutes ago. Mary Sue and I are driving over to their house. Would you and Maggie go with us?"

"Sure."

"We'll pick you up in ten minutes."

Before I could say anything, he'd hung up. I struggled to sit on the side of the bed. Gently I shook Maggie's shoulder to make sure she was awake. "That was Ted. Brandon Williams is dead. He and Mary Sue are going to the house and asked us to go with them."

No sooner had we pulled on some clothes when Ted's pickup stopped in our driveway. His white Ford had a club cab, so Maggie and I climbed into the second seat. "Tell us what you know." I said.

"Practically nothing," Ted replied. "When Nancy called she was crying, sobbing, incoherent."

"But she said Brandon was dead?" Maggie asked.

"Over and over."

"Did you get any details—how it happened?" I asked.

"Look," he replied, an unmistakable frustration in his voice, "all I know is that a hysterical Nancy Williams called and kept repeating, 'Brandon's dead, Brandon's dead.'"

We made the rest of the ten-minute drive in silence.

The Williams home, located in northeast Amarillo in upscale La Paloma Addition, had a police car and an ambulance parked in front, red and blue strobes flashing, the front door open. On a cool December night, temperature in the forties, the four of us hurried in to find Nancy Williams lying on a sofa in the living room, sobbing, a female EMT working to console her.

Maggie and Mary Sue went to her side.

Ted and I found two policemen and another EMT in the kitchen. A body, stretched out on the floor wearing pajamas, robe, and slippers, lay in a pool of blood. I assumed it was Brandon, but with the side of his head blown away leaving such a disfigured, bloody mess, I could not be sure. A handgun lay nearby.

My first reaction was to throw up. I clenched my teeth, turned away, and tried desperately to fight the nausea.

Ted didn't fare as well. He rushed over to the sink and heaved.

One of the uniforms approached me. "I think it would be best for you and your friend to wait in the next room."

I nodded and stepped away, relieved to distance myself from the grotesque scene. A moment later, Ted and the two policemen joined me in the dining room.

"You know the victim?" one of the officers asked.

Ted wiped his face with a paper towel and nodded—a gesture for me to answer.

"I assume it's Brandon Williams. Texas State Bank. He's the president."

The next hour flew by in a jumbled rush. A medical examiner officially identified the body. Police questioned Ted and me. The EMTs gave Nancy a sedative. Ted and Mary Sue arranged for her to go with them to their home and rest. Maggie packed an overnight bag for Nancy. Five of us crowded into the Austin's pickup and left.

Back at our house we started making phone calls. Maggie and I took turns calling the Williams family, bank employees, neighbors, the church, anyone we could think of. With each call we asked for help. A son who lived in Chicago agreed to contact family, the bank's vice-president said he would call employees, their minister knew the best way to notify church members. By the time the sun peeked over the pasture to the east of our house, we had set in motion a network of support.

Christmas Day, normally one of the most joyous times of the year, dragged on and on, and became a wrenching experience of unremitting grief. Finally, that evening, as Maggie and I prepared for bed, she hugged me and quoted Shakespeare's passage from Hamlet, " . . . sleep . . . and by a sleep we end the heartache . . ."

A somber Christmas passed.

Christmas Day came on Thursday.

Friday, the family gathered.

Saturday and Sunday, we grieved. Maggie took food to the Williams home.

Four days later, on Monday, December 29, I served as a pall-bearer at the funeral.

Authorities ruled Brandon Williams' death a suicide. The *Amarillo Globe-News* reported it "a result of his depression over anticipated financial problems in the cattle industry." But a black cloud hung over us as each day slipped by, and I held my breath, waiting for the other shoe to drop. Along with everyone else in the cattle business, I braced for the worst, not knowing what to expect.

On the dreaded January 5, the day the Chicago Board of Trade opened, like almost all of my colleagues in Texas cattle country, I found that I had committed a huge error in judgment. The grisly, spectacular suicide of Brandon Williams caused me to expect a national reaction against beef, a response paralleling that of the British in the 1980s.

It didn't happen.

CHAPTER 3

A year later, The Big Texas Steakhouse, 7701 I-40 East, Amarillo, Texas

Brandon Williams had it wrong. Tragically, he took his life believing that the media would build the story—of a single cow with a horrifying disease—into a national panic. He wasn't the only one. Every cattleman in the Texas Panhandle, at least every one that I talked with, expected a continuous reporting of "mad cow problems" until it developed into a ruinous financial disaster. What happened instead was that the media moved on to other stories, and "the Washington cow" fell from the news.

A major cause of the story's disappearance was its timing. When the cattle markets closed for their annual holiday-season break, that temporarily halted the Chicago Board of Trade and their daily reports of cattle prices. With no values, there was no trend to report. Even more importantly, people kept eating beef all through the next ten days, and when the markets reopened in January, demand continued. The normalcy of the situation—cattlemen selling beef, packers producing beef, consumers eating beef—completely squelched any sensationalism about the impact of a sick cow in the state of Washington.

The story died.

So it was, exactly twelve months later, on January 5, the anniversary of the opening of the Chicago Board of Trade, Ted called, told me he had big news, and insisted on treating me to a steak dinner. I had arrived at the restaurant just as the sun fell below the western horizon, found us a table by the window, and watched as another white Ford pickup pulled into the restaurant's parking lot. In West Texas almost everyone drives a pickup, and 90 percent of them are white. However, the distinctive logo for the Texas Cattle Feeders Association painted on the door, a tan colored silhouette of a cow's head, told me this one belonged to Ted Austin.

Ted walked up and carefully placed an envelope face down on the table. Then he stood there staring at me, the smirk on his face silently daring me to guess the significance of the document—its message or its contents.

"Well, Jim Bob, how's your day?" he asked as he pulled out a chair and seated himself across from me.

I hate it when friends play the game of *I know something you don't*, so I ignored his banal question and gave the most flippant response I could think of. "Cattle futures are up," I replied.

"Really?" His grin broadened to the point it threatened to crack the skin.

I smiled back, waiting silently. He and I both knew this wasn't news. TCFA tracked cattle prices closer than a heart doctor checks blood pressure during surgery.

The envelope continued to lie there, untouched, its presence looming like an impediment to our continued friendship. Ted looked back toward the restaurant entrance and the hostess station.

"I've asked Congressman Stanley Young to join us," Ted said as he checked his watch. Then he turned away, again scanning the entrance area.

"Ted, what's going on?" I asked, an edge to my voice.

"There he is," Ted replied, disregarding my question. He stood and motioned with his hand.

I looked across clusters of tables and recognized the representative from the Thirteenth District, a tall, lean Texan, wearing a white Stetson. As he weaved his way toward our table, the thunk of his cowboy boots on the restaurant's wooden floor caused people to turn and stare.

I stood, and Ted started introductions.

"Stan, I'd like you to meet Jim Bob Masterson, the creator of the renowned test for mad cow disease."

When I stuck out my hand, I had to crane my neck to make eye contact. I'm five-seven, he must have been six-eight. "Congressman, my pleasure," I said.

"Dr. Masterson, we're mighty proud of you and your research." His hand was so huge it completely enveloped mine. "Ted tells me you're the nation's number-one authority on this disease."

I struggled for a response. "Ted's my P.R. man. I have to pay him five dollars every time he says that."

Young chuckled.

"And in West Texas everyone calls me Jim Bob."

"In the thirteenth district, all the voters call me Stan."

The three of us took our chairs, and I relaxed a bit. Whatever the reason for this occasion, Ted was going all-out for my benefit. I decided to play along.

Stan pointed to the envelope. "That the letter?" he asked.

Ted nodded. "Yup."

"You told him?" Stan looked toward me.

"Nope. I waited for you."

A waitress came and stood at our table, notepad in hand, interrupting our conversation. "Everyone want the special?" she asked.

"What's the special?" Ted asked.

"Our twelve-ounce, U.S. prime, Angus T-bone, cooked over mesquite. Comes with baked potato and house salad."

The three of us agreed and took turns responding to her questions for drinks, potato toppings, and salad dressings. Then came the all-important query about how we wanted our steaks cooked.

"Rare," said Ted.

I nodded. "The same."

Stan hesitated and then replied, "Throw it on the grill just enough to keep it from mooing."

Ted rolled his eyes.

In West Texas, everyone orders a good steak rare but this was over-the-top. I looked down to avoid the embarrassment of acknowledging Stan's faux pas. But in so doing, my eyes were once again drawn to the damned envelope.

The waitress left. I looked up.

"Time for the moment of truth?" Ted asked as he and Stan

locked eyes.

"You're paying for the dinner," Stan replied. "Go ahead."

Ted handed me the envelope. "I believe you'll find this interesting."

After a quick glance to see that the return address was Stockholm, Sweden, I opened the letter and started reading:

Theodore Austin, Executive Director
Texas Cattle Feeders Association
5501 West I-40
Amarillo, TX 79106

Dear Mr. Austin:

Thank you for your letter supporting the nomination of Dr. James Robert Masterson for the Nobel Prize in Medicine. His work in the development of the "Masterson Screening Test" for Bovine Spongiform Encephalopathy (BSE), or what is commonly known as mad cow disease, will be carefully considered.

As you know the examination of nominees is a thorough and lengthy process. It is expected that . . .

CHAPTER 4

The Big Texas Steakhouse, 7701 I-40 East, Amarillo, Texas

"You sneaky bastard, why didn't you tell me you'd nominated me?" I asked.

Ted held up both hands in mock defense. "Wasn't me. The British Agricultural Ministry submitted your name. They only asked me for a letter of support."

"You could have told me," I said.

"No, I had to agree to keep it quiet."

I shook my head. "I . . . I don't know what to say."

"Don't say anything. You haven't received it yet. This is only a nomination."

"But still . . . what an honor . . . just to be nominated."

"The Brits say you speeded their recovery," Ted continued.

"And that without the Masterson Test, they'd still be years away from a return of their beef market."

Stan cleared his throat. "I'm afraid I have some bad news," he said.

The waitress brought our salads. When she left Stan continued, his voice reflecting the stern look on his face. "I had a long talk this morning with the American Ambassador in Stockholm."

Ted cocked his head and frowned. "He's not going to help us with Jim Bob's nomination?"

"On the contrary," Stan responded, "the ambassador's found a way to quietly approach the committee chairman at the Nobel Headquarters."

"What did he find out?"

"The inside information is that the committee will likely defer their consideration of Jim Bob's nomination."

"Defer?" Ted asked. "What does that mean?"

"They feel the Masterson Test has not yet stood the test of time. They want us to submit his nomination again in a couple of years."

"Hell, it's been used on thousands of cattle in the U.K.," Ted roared. "Not one case has ever been misdiagnosed."

"Yes, but—"

"But what?"

"But the gold standard is still the old analysis of brain tissue," Stan replied calmly. "When the new cases in Mongolia were reported last year, the Chinese wouldn't accept Masterson Tests. They insisted on the slaughter of suspected animals and microscopic scanning of cerebellum samples."

With the shake of his head, Ted slumped in his chair, a frown of disappointment covering his face.

"Back to the Nobel committee," Stan continued. "As I said, the ambassador thinks we should give it a couple of years."

Our steaks came, momentarily halting conversation.

We cut into them, and I took my first bite. In my opinion nothing can compare to a big, thick, Angus T-bone, cooked on mesquite—especially if it's grilled just enough so that its center is still juicy blood red. Mine was perfect.

Ted's cell phone rang.

Stan and I continued to work on our steaks while Ted talked. I watched as his facial expression changed to dour, hard-faced concern. He rose, walked away from our table, and stood in a nearby corner, his back to us.

"Wonder what's up?" Stan asked.

"Looks like bad news," I replied.

He nodded and took another bite of bloody red beef. Silently we continued with our meal while Ted talked for several minutes. Finally he returned, his face now grim.

"What's happening?" I asked.

"Jim Bob, we have a problem." He didn't touch his food.

Stan and I stopped eating—waiting for him to explain.

"On their six o'clock newscast, Channel 2 reported a case of mad cow disease at the Sagebrush Feed Yard."

"Oh, no," Stan gasped.

I laughed.

Ted looked at me, angrily. "Jim Bob," he said, "this is serious."

"It may be serious for a couple of days," I said with a smile. I knew the report was a mistake.

"Masterson, this is no joke," Ted continued, his voice growing louder. "They have a *videotape* of a cow in convulsions in Sagebrush,

Texas." People at nearby tables turned to look.

I chuckled and continued to cut my steak. "There has never been a case of mad cow in Texas. Never." I plopped a big bite in my mouth. It was delicious.

CHAPTER 5

Driving west from Amarillo to Bushland, Texas

I had a problem. And it wasn't bovine spongiform encephalopathy, or BSE, or mad cow disease, or whatever name the American public gives it. The incident reported at the Sagebrush feed yard was, I felt absolutely sure, a false alarm. The disease has to come from an infection transferred from an infected animal or its remains. Since practically no West Texas cattle operations bring in stock from areas of the world where infected animals exist—Asia, Africa, or Western Europe, and those few that are imported are rigorously tested—I couldn't see how we could have an outbreak. Impossible.

My problem was I'd promised my wife Maggie I would go with her to Dallas where our daughter Liz was to compete in the regional auditions for the Metropolitan Opera. As so often happened in our marriage, I had a conflict between work and family.

But cattle testing needed to be done immediately. The fact that our trigger-happy news media reported symptoms in a West Texas feed yard was enough to create panic. While I felt confident it would quickly prove to be a false alarm, each day these spurious charges went unchallenged would cost the cattle industry millions. Obviously the two-day testing process had to be started without delay. And to avoid any questions about scientific legitimacy, the procedure would have to be done by the area's most highly recognized expert.—me.

I dreaded the confrontation with my wife.

Margaret Smith Masterson, Maggie, gave up a lot to make our marriage work. A New York City girl, she moved to Bushland, Texas, population 1,307, to make 640 acres of cattle pasture into our home on the range. Maggie has a small frame. Because of her undersized pelvis—she's only five feet, two inches, one hundred and ten pounds—the birth of our daughter twenty-four years earlier almost cost Maggie her life. The doctor said no more pregnancies. I willingly had a vasectomy, but this meant that our only child, Elizabeth, became Maggie's central focus.

Liz, as we called her, brought a beautiful voice into our family dynamics. We first recognized this fact at the Bushland Elementary Christmas program when, at age six, she sang a solo that brought down the house. This tiny little girl, one of the smallest children in the first grade, belted out "O Holy Night" in big, pure tones that filled the school auditorium. I don't know much about music, but even a dummy like me could tell our daughter had a special, God-given talent. Fortunately her mother knew what to do and made sure Liz got the best musical training available. For the next eleven years our daughter took voice and piano lessons, attended summer music camps, and made occasional trips to "the city," as we called New York, where she received coaching from the best teachers in Manhattan.

When time for college arrived, it seemed only natural that Liz should go to Juilliard, and this brought another factor into the picture. Her maternal grandmother, Katherine Barrington Smith, lived in New York. Over the years, my mother-in-law and I had been at odds—to say the least—over family matters. In the beginning, Katherine disapproved of her daughter's choice of a matrimonial partner *and* the move to Texas. Katherine openly voiced her opinion that the marriage probably wouldn't last and repeatedly offered Maggie the option of "moving back home" if things went awry. Maggie suggested I stay out of it and let her handle her mother. Most of the time I was only too happy to do so.

That night however, I worried about the implications. Liz's auditions for the Met were of great consequence to her future, probably determining whether or not she became a professional singer. We'd had the dates on our calendar for months. I had promised to be there.

When I walked in the door, Maggie was waiting for me. "Mother called. She wants to fly to Dallas and go with us to the auditions."

My stride broke, and I stood still. "Fine," I said.

"Be nice," Maggie replied. "Remember, Liz is her only grandchild."

"I said 'fine.'"

"But I could hear the way you said it."

"Okay, let me try again," I continued. "Fiiiiiine, I'd love to have the old battleaxe there."

"Jim Bob!"

"Seriously, I think this may be a good thing."

"Really?"

"We need to talk," I said. "Something's come up."

She backed up, her face settling into a *don't-you-dare* mask. "No. You promised."

"Have you watched the news?"

"No, I told you Mother called," she replied. "Since then I've been on the phone to Dallas, trying to get a reservation for her at our hotel."

"Some idiot accused Sagebrush Cattle Feeders of having a case of mad cow."

Maggie's body tensed, and her voice went up in pitch. "Dr. Masterson that is no excuse for failure to meet your responsibility as a father."

When she calls me *Doctor,* that tells me to get ready for a confrontation. I took a moment and thought hard for a way to present the situation from an objective viewpoint. "The Texas Cattle Feeders Association won't see it that way."

"To hell with TCFA. They have other veterinarians."

"Maggie, try to see their side. They need the highest level of mad cow expertise."

"And Liz needs her one and only father," she fumed, tears welling in her eyes.

"This will be over in two days. Then I'll fly to Dallas."

"That's what you said about her senior recital—"

"Maggie, please."

" . . . and a dozen other times." She pulled out a Kleenex and wiped her tears.

"I have no choice," I pleaded. "These people are counting on me."

"I'm not asking for me. This is for our daughter. She's counting on the support of her father."

"I know, and I'll find some way to make it up to her."

We paused—a moment of silence when two sides come to the inevitable choice of escalation versus capitulation. I held my breath. Maggie let hers out.

"Besides, I'll have to listen to Mother's gritching about you."

I breathed a sigh of relief and softened my voice. "You can handle your mother."

"Sometimes I think she may be right." Maggie wiped a tear with the back of her hand. "Maybe I shouldn't have married a cowboy."

I pulled her to me and kissed her, a long passionate kiss that filled me with desire. I started unbuttoning her blouse.

"No—not with a man who loves cows more than his daughter." She stomped away.

Damn.

Chapter 6

The ranch house, two miles north of Bushland, Texas

We call it "our ranch." Actually it's nothing more than a house and a barn sitting on 640 acres of grassland. Maggie designed it. I chose the location. Situated on a bluff overlooking valley-like pasture that slopes down to Deer Creek, a small tributary that eventually becomes the South Canadian River, our house has a feeling of isolation we both love. I especially like the opportunity to run a small herd of about two dozen Black Angus. Our bedroom has twin glass doors—what my wife calls "French doors"—that open out onto a patio on the east side of our house. On that December morning, the sun peeking over the horizon and our cattle grazing on the lush, green pasture, "our ranch" gave us a pastoral scene worthy of a Gainsborough painting.

Maggie packed her bag, a big suitcase filled with her finest clothing and enough shoes to outfit a battalion. I tried to think of an upbeat parting statement.

"Just two days and I'll join you in Dallas," I said.

"Famous last words?" she asked.

"Hey, you can count on me."

"Jim Bob, this audition is a really big deal for Liz. She needs to feel your support, to know that you think it's important."

"I couldn't agree more."

I gave her a card with a half dozen phone numbers and a quick summary of where I'd be for the next forty-eight hours. Then I gave her a warm hug, kissed her, and headed out the door to load a few things into my white Chevy Suburban. Driving away from the house, I pressed the button for the satellite phone.

"Onstar ready," the phone replied.

"Ted Austin," I said, instructing the phone to dial the pre-programmed number. I could hear the connection and the familiar ring.

Ted picked up. "Jim Bob, that you?"

"I'm leaving home now. Be at your place in five minutes."

"Ready and waiting," Ted replied. "I'm on the other line with Paul Edwards."

"Tell him help is on the way." I pushed the button to disconnect.

Ted has the 640 acres next to mine. I drove north on the blacktop a mile to his mailbox and turned in. Fifteen years ago we'd purchased these two sections of grassland, divided the property into two small ranches, and built our homes. The fact that we neighbored—raised our families next to each other and shared a common interest in ranching—gave us a friendship that brought us close together in times of adversity. This morning, as we faced a false charge of mad cow, I especially appreciated having a colleague go with me as we prepared to meet the challenge.

He stood in front of his house, waiting, his face grim. When I rolled to a stop, he tossed a small bag and a briefcase into the back seat and climbed in front with me.

"Come on, neighbor," I said, smiling. "Lighten up. We both know there's no BSE in this country, let alone in the Texas panhandle."

Ted's forlorn look clashed with my smile. "You don't have the TCFA membership calling you every five minutes."

"In forty-eight hours, you'll have such good news to report you'll be the man of the hour."

"Forty-eight hours?" he asked. "I thought you could do your test and have the answer today."

"I can."

He thought for a moment. "But you don't think they'll be satisfied with a Masterson test?"

"Just like the Chinese, Edwards and his TCFA buddies will demand a microscopic examination of the brain tissue."

"It seems so unnecessary to sacrifice the animal."

"Animals." I emphasized the plural.

"How many?" Ted asked.

"At least a half-dozen, maybe more."

"Damn. Are these full-grown, twelve-hundred-pound cattle?"

"Of course. BSE only occurs in animals that are three or four years old—or older. These have to be heifers and bulls from Paul's cow/calf operation."

"Probably worth a thousand bucks an animal."

"At least," I replied.

"Ouch," Ted said. "You're estimating six thousand, maybe

more, just to confirm the legitimacy of the Masterson test?"

"Have you heard about cattle futures?" I asked.

"Yeah. This morning the Chicago Board of Trade was down the limit and suspended trading."

"Sounds like a great opportunity to buy."

"How much have you invested?" Ted asked.

I didn't answer directly, instead switching to another question. "Do you think the futures market will drop again tomorrow?"

"Absolutely."

"I think I'll wait a couple of days and then invest as much cash as I can put my hands on."

"You're investing everything?" Ted asked.

"It's a sure thing," I replied.

CHAPTER 7

Driving north from Amarillo on U.S. Highway 287

Sagebrush, Texas—a tiny, dusty, wide spot in the road—should have faded away into oblivion like dozens of other small communities in West Texas. With the coming of the twentieth century and the age of the automobile, travel distances shrank. Farming families gravitated to larger communities. The reason Sagebrush survived—post office intact was due almost entirely to the business acumen of one man, Paul Edwards.

Edwards recognized the efficiencies of cattle feedlots in beef production. After World War II, when the cattle industry shifted from grass-fed to grain-fed operations, he took a small feedlot and expanded. Through superb business insight and unfailingly accurate financial judgments, Sagebrush Cattle Feeders, Inc. became the largest feed yard in the world.

The seventy-one-mile drive from my house to the Sagebrush feed yard took a little more than an hour. I parked at the headquarters trailer, which was located to the windward side, the southwest corner, of the feedlot. That day its location didn't matter. No one cared about the smell. About twenty people with long faces gathered outside the office. Two men, who looked especially grim, walked over to my SUV to greet Ted and me. I recognized them both—Paul Edwards, the famous owner, and Donald Norton, his staff veterinarian.

I smiled. "Come on, you guys," I said. "We all know this is a false alarm."

"Easy for you to say," Edwards grumbled. "You don't have your financial livelihood on the line."

"Have you heard about cattle futures?" Norton asked. "They dropped the limit and then suspended trading."

My smile became a bit forced. "And when they come back up, some smart investors are going to make a lot of money."

"Jim Bob, how can I help you?" Edwards snapped, obviously anxious to change the subject.

"Let's take a look at your suspects." I tried to hold onto my smile as we got down to business. "The sooner we prove the absence of BSE, the sooner we can all get our lives back to normal."

"Don, you show him," Edwards said, deferring to his vet.

"This way." Donald Norton pointed toward a path between the pens.

I walked along with my fellow veterinarian. Paul and Ted came with us. The twenty or so onlookers followed. I noted the group included three TV camera crews from Amarillo.

"We've isolated the cattle with symptoms," Norton said.

"They're in this first pen." He gestured to a small fenced area with a loading ramp.

The pen contained only six animals. We stopped at the railing and, as cattle observers always do, put one foot on the bottom rail. At first the cattle appeared normal, standing in the far corner, somewhat frightened by the presence of so many humans. Norton asked two of the feed yard cowboys to move the herd from one side of the pen to the other.

When the cattle moved, their symptoms became obvious. One cow tottered and swayed, as if drunk. The poor animal could hardly stand, let alone walk. It staggered. One leg went out, then a second as it tried to maintain balance. After a few faltering steps, it went down. I sensed a noticeable reaction from the crowd, some shaking of heads, a murmur or two, and whispered conversations. With TV cameras rolling, I felt my first doubt as a cold chill rippled down my spine. Something *was* wrong.

"Don, we need to get started," I said.

"We're ready," he replied.

"I'll take blood samples now and have the results for you this afternoon."

"Paul and I have talked this over. We'd like you to do both tests."

"You know brain tissue is required for the old test."

"We understand."

"It needs to be taken from the posterior of the brain, near the brain stem, under the cerebellum," I said.

"We'll open the skull. Would you do the extraction of the sample?" he asked.

"Sure, but I want the tissue sealed in airtight bags."

“We expected that,” Norton replied. “We’ll label the samples from each animal.”

“How will you destroy the carcasses?”

“Incineration.”

I nodded.

He gave orders to his crew, and, one by one, the hapless animals gave their lives to medical science. First, blood samples were taken for the Masterson Test. Then I watched as the cattle were herded into the feedlot’s slaughter facility and killed by electrocution. After I removed a tissue sample from the brain, Don had each carcass dragged off to the incinerator. By noon we had six blood samples and six brain samples, all carefully labeled and iced down in a Styrofoam cooler.

I had hoped we could avoid the media. No such luck. As we approached my SUV, we were surrounded. An attractive, twenty-something blonde elbowed her way in front of the others and shoved a microphone in my face.

“Dr. Masterson, what do you think?”

“I think we’d do better if you’d back off and let me speak to everyone at the same time.”

Chastised, she momentarily seemed at a loss for words.

“I’ll take one question from each,” I said. Then I pointed to a young man at the back. “You first.”

He brought his mike and stood beside me, his cameraman placed strategically about six feet away. “What should we expect?” he asked.

“First, let me remind you of an important fact,” I answered. “We’ve never had a case of BSE in Texas.”

“BSE?”

"Bovine spongiform encephalopathy, what is commonly referred to as mad cow disease."

"But there's always a first time for everything," the reporter interjected.

"True, but I don't see how this could be it," I answered. "Someone else's turn." I nodded to a beautiful, Hispanic-looking brunette standing on my left.

"When will we know the results of your lab work?" she asked.

"We have two ways to identify the disease," I replied. "The first is a blood test, and the results will be available late this afternoon. The other is a microscopic examination of the brain tissue. That test requires twenty-four hours to prepare the sample, so the entire procedure will take at least two days, sometimes longer." I turned back to the aggressive blonde. "Next?"

"Dr. Masterson, why is everyone making such a big fuss over this disease?" she asked.

It was a loaded question. She knew it. I knew it. I paused for a moment to weigh my answer. Even though it would scare people, I decided not to waffle, to soften my answer, or to try to deflect the cold hard facts.

"Because there is no treatment," I said. "Humans or cattle, once you get it, you will die."

CHAPTER 8

Driving south on U.S. Highway 287

Ted and I left the Sagebrush feedlot in silence and headed back toward Amarillo. As we drove south through Dumas and then into the openness of West Texas ranch country, I sensed Ted's apprehension. In the fifteen or more years of our friendship, he'd never looked so depressed.

"A penny?" I asked.

"My thoughts aren't worth that much," Ted replied.

"Humor me, and I'll double the price."

He heaved a big sigh and turned away to stare out the window. After a lengthy pause, what I've sometimes heard referred to as pregnant, he looked at me and asked, "You still don't think it's BSE?"

"Ted, it couldn't be. You and I both know the disease has to come from somewhere. Infected prions don't mutate or appear spontaneously."

"How do you explain the symptoms we witnessed this morning?"

"Pretty scary, wasn't it?"

"Terrifying. And I looked at you. When that first heifer went down, you reacted. That scared me even more."

I shook my head, a gesture of apology. "Sorry, I couldn't help myself. I reacted emotionally, without thinking."

"So, are you thinking now?"

"You bet. And let me reassure you—we do not have BSE."

"Then how do you explain these symptoms?"

"I'm not sure, exactly, but I've read that other neurological diseases have physical indicators similar to BSE. I think listeriosis is one, but I'll have to do a bit of research to be sure."

"Can you use these tissue samples to test for it or for other diseases?"

I looked at my watch and chuckled. "You're giving me twenty minutes to make an on-the-spot diagnosis for listeriosis?"

For the first time that morning, Ted smiled. "Sorry. Guess I'm too close to the panic button."

"You and all the other cattlemen in West Texas."

"And evidently some investors who purchase cattle futures."

"Which would be practically everyone in the cattle business."

"So, are you still going to invest a hunk of money in futures?"

"Of course," I replied. "It's a sure thing." I reached over and punched him on the shoulder.

"Before or after you process your blood samples for the Masterson test?"

"There's no hurry." I answered. "And we'll have results this afternoon."

He punched me back.

We drove on in silence, but I sensed a change in Ted's demeanor. His face appeared less apprehensive and his posture more relaxed. I was ready to change the subject, to tell him about my daughter's audition in Dallas, when his cell phone rang.

"Hello," he said.

I could hear only one side of the conversation, but apparently the caller was Congressman Stanley Young.

"We have the samples," Ted said. "He'll do his blood test this afternoon and complete the brain scan tomorrow."

Ted paused, listened, then turned to me. "Stan wants you to phone him as soon as you have your results."

"Sure," I answered.

Ted went back to his phone conversation. "Jim Bob says he'll call you." Then he held the phone for a long time, listening intently. "I'll tell him." After a few words of closing, he punched off the phone and turned to me.

"The feds are making a big thing of this. Stan wants you to send your samples ASAP to the National Veterinary Services Laboratory in Ames, Iowa."

"I expected that," I said.

"He wants you to FedEx them this afternoon."

"We'll do it first thing."

"And he doesn't want you to release the results of your tests. He wants the NVSL to handle all testing results with the media."

"Too late," I said. "I've already told the Amarillo TV stations I'd give them the Masterson test results this afternoon."

"Jim Bob, I think you should honor his request."

"Sorry, I don't agree. We know the news will be good. If we hold it back, it just makes the media think we really do have mad cow disease in Texas."

Ted didn't like my answer. And, as he always did on those rare occasions when we disagreed, he clammed up. We rode in silence for several minutes. Finally, in a much softer voice, he said, "The prudent thing would be to call Stan before you give your test results to the media."

"Of course. I've already agreed to call him. I'll tell him what I plan to release and to whom."

Our conversation ended as we pulled into the parking lot at Masterson and Associates Veterinary Services. Already I could see several vehicles from the media. One car was marked "Amarillo Globe-News." Another carried a sign that read "KGNC, News-Radio." Two TV stations had brought trucks with tall antennas for remote broadcasting.

"Ted, would you fend off the media?" I asked. "Tell them it'll be three or four hours before we'll have anything."

"I'll try, but they'll want to talk with you."

"Tell them I'm busy." I grabbed the ice chest with the blood and tissue samples and walked toward my office with my head down. Several reporters approached me, but I walked straight past them. Ted lingered in the parking lot, trying to answer questions. Inside, I went directly to my lab, closed the door, and started to work.

The "associates" in Masterson and Associates were Ida Mae Campbell, my secretary, and Fred Johnson, my tech assistant. Ida Mae was fiftyish, a grandmother, a woman who grew up on a West Texas farm and loved animals. Fred was half her age, a rodeo enthusiast who dropped out of college to pursue the roping and broncobuster circuit. Both were good employees, and that day, with all the media circus and pressure for test results, I really appreciated their dedicated service.

Fred knew the procedures for the Masterson Test and had gone through it numerous times as a demonstration. Today, for the first time, he started assembling the equipment for a "real" analysis. While he prepared the lab—Ida Mae and I divided the blood and brain tissue into two sets, one for us and another to be sent to Ames, Iowa. She had packaged and shipped laboratory samples to the NVSL on many occasions, so I turned the procedure over to her and went back to join Fred. Together we had the pressure cookers underway in less than an hour. I left him to monitor the equipment and went to my desk to read up on listeriosis.

Research is one of my favorite things—for me it's almost recreational. With the coming of the Internet and the availability of databases like NEXUS, MEDLINE, and especially the Texas A&M Vet School's information, I now had an almost unlimited source of scientific knowledge. Comprehensive answers to any and all questions about listeriosis and similar maladies came easily. And sure enough, I found many of the symptoms were the same as BSE. Article after article told of mistakes that had been made where vets like me had misdiagnosed the malady with terrible consequences.

The afternoon hours flew by. I was feeling good and patting myself on the back when Fred came into my office with a look of terror on his face. "I've prepared the specimens and have them ready to be scoped," he reported, nervously.

"And—"

"You're not going to like this."

He and I had done this many times—preparing samples for

demonstrations for my clinics. But I'd never seen him react this way.

"What's the matter?" I asked, beginning to feel that cold chill racing down my spine again.

"Come look," was all he'd say.

We had purchased slides of actual BSE from British authorities so that we could show what the disease looked like and make comparisons with samples from our local, disease-free animals. Fred led the way to our lab counter where he had set up two microscopes, side by side. I assumed we were going to do the usual comparison.

"The tissue samples from Sagebrush are on the left," Fred said. "The second scope."

I climbed up onto the stool, bent over, and placed my eye on the microscope eyepiece. Instantly I recognized the pink-tinged, sponge-like tissue as a classic, textbook-perfect example of bovine spongiform encephalopathy. Even though Fred hadn't specifically said so, I assumed I was looking at one of the British slides.

I shifted over to the second microscope and sucked in my breath. It was identical.

CHAPTER 9

Masterson and Associates Veterinary Services Inc.

"Damn it, Fred, you've mixed up the slides," I shouted, the anger in my voice bitterly criticizing him. Immediately, I regretted my outburst. The next few moments were among the most problematic of my life. I looked away, tightened my jaw, and tried to reign in my emotions.

Ida Mae came to the door, peeked in, and hesitantly asked, "You guys okay?"

"We're fine," I snapped. "Just a little problem with the test samples."

"What can I do to help?" she asked.

"Nothing," I said. "We'll handle it."

She looked at Fred.

He nodded.

After an awkward moment, she backed out of the room and closed the door.

Fred made eye contact with me, a pleading look.

"Sorry, but this is really important," I said, the intense edge still in my voice. "We can't afford *any* screw-ups."

I expected Fred to make excuses. He didn't. Instead he whispered four words. "I have a suggestion." His manner of speaking and his body language deferred to me as though I were a bomb, ready to explode.

"What's that?" I asked, breathing heavily, still convinced he didn't fully understand the consequences of his mistake.

"Let's go back to the pressure machines and have you prepare new samples."

"God damn it, Fred, that's your job," I yelled. Not as loud this time, but again demeaning him in no uncertain terms.

"Please, just this once." He made his voice even softer.

I looked at him, shook my head, and reluctantly responded with the only word I could think of that would extricate us from my temper. "Okay." Slowly, I let out my breath and led the way back to the pressure cookers.

I found the lab samples inside and still warm. Resenting every move, I pulled on a pair of surgical gloves, picked up sterile tweezers and a scalpel, and slowly gathered a tiny sample of the processed remains. We took it to the shaving appliance and sliced off a half-dozen strips, each one less than 1/5000 of an inch thick, so thin they looked transparent. Next we took our stack to a staining processor where the machine automatically mounted each sample on a sterile piece of glass and coated it with a light stain so it could be viewed through a microscope. We did that six times and then carried our samples back to one of the scopes where Fred had been working.

When I looked at the first slide, I couldn't believe it.

I switched to a second slide.

Then again, and again, until I had gone through all six samples.

Reluctantly, I turned to face Fred.

"Sorry I yelled at you," I said. "Please accept my apology."

Fred looked at his shoes, and then met my gaze. "Is there any doubt it's BSE?" he asked.

Once more I put my eye to the microscope and carefully scanned the slide. The pink-tinged, sponge-like tissue looked exactly like a page from my textbook. "I can't believe it, but there it is."

"I hate to ask," Fred said, speaking respectfully, "but is there any chance a Masterson test might give a false positive?"

I shook my head, but I couldn't force the words out. In my heart of hearts, I knew my test gave accurate results, but if I said it aloud to Fred, I was proclaiming to the world that we had a disaster on our hands. A long minute of silence dragged by. I decided to wait, to let someone else say it.

Finally, as if Fred already knew the answer, he moved on to another question. "So what're we going to do?"

I wanted to say that we'd pass the buck. What I said was, "We'll do the scanning of the brain tissue tomorrow. Then we'll wait for a report from the National Veterinary Services Lab. We'll probably get their report in two days."

"You going to tell anyone about these results?" Fred asked.

"I promised Congressman Young I'd call him," I answered.

"What about all the people outside?"

"Stan said only the feds can give a report."

"They're not going to like that answer."

I thought about it for a few moments. Then I called Ida Mae into the lab, and the three of us held a conference. I stressed the need to maintain a positive, upbeat appearance. No worried looks. Smile like today was just another day. Refer all questions to the feds.

Then I lied.

And I did my best to make Fred and Ida Mae believe it. "This may be a false positive," I said. "Tomorrow we'll scan the brain tissue. That's the *real* test."

Whether or not they believed me, they acted as though they did. We practiced our smiles, and then, together, the three of us went outside to the parking lot to face the newspaper, radio, and TV reporters, where I gave an academy award performance. I smiled. I joked. And I pounded away at one basic truth—the feds had ordered me not to release any testing information.

Fred was right—they didn't like it. But after about twenty minutes of "no comment" smiles and an impenetrable stonewall about the Masterson test, the media got tired, packed up, and left.

Ida Mae went into the front office, to the telephone.

Fred went back to the lab to prepare for tomorrow's testing of the brain tissue.

I went to my desk and called Congressman Stanley H. Young.

"Cut to the chase," Stan said. "What'd you find?"

"We have two possible answers," I replied.

"Lay it on me," he insisted, his voice curt, harsh.

"The blood test was positive, which means, one, we have BSE, or two, the Masterson test ain't worth shit."

Stan didn't respond.

After a few moments I asked, "You still there?"

"Yeah, I'm here."

"We sent the brain tissue and blood samples to Ames. They'll have everything by ten-thirty tomorrow morning."

Again he hesitated.

I decided to wait him out.

Finally, he asked, "Jim Bob, do broadcast and print media in Amarillo suspect the results of your blood test?"

"No."

"But they are aware that you've completed it?"

"Yes, I told them I had, but that's as far as it went."

"Have you given your results to Paul Edwards, to Ted Austin, or to anyone else?"

"No."

"What about your employees?"

"They can be trusted."

"I'm going to need a few days to figure how best to handle this."

"I understand."

"And you could be wrong?"

"Stan, I'm not wrong about this," I said, emotion gripping my stomach, my voice tightening into a whisper. "We have six animals confirmed and no telling how many more at the largest feed yard in the world."

CHAPTER 10

Masterson and Associates Veterinary Services Inc.

That night I didn't go home.

Fred and Ida Mae left at five o'clock, our usual closing time. I moped around, processed another set of congealed blood tissue samples—with the same result—and spent a couple of hours rereading British publications detailing how they mishandled their BSE outbreak in 1986. About nine o'clock I ordered pizza. When it came, I took one bite and found that I had no appetite. So I went to my desk and pulled out the bottle of Chivas Regal I kept hidden for special occasions.

I intended to have one small drink, just enough to relax and help me face the trials and tribulations expected tomorrow. But one small glass of scotch led to another, then another, and then one more. By one o'clock in the morning, I was in no shape to drive home.

The cot and sleeping bag stowed in the bathroom attached to my office were there for emergencies, for those occasions when I needed to stay at the office to monitor lab experiments or other work that demanded continuous attention. In the five years since the construction of my "new" facilities, I'd rarely used them, only twice that I could remember. On both these previous occasions, the sleep-in had worked well.

Not this time.

I tossed and turned and cursed myself for not having driven home to spend the night. After hours of thinking about the future, about the ramifications of how the government would react to the situation, I finally dropped off, somewhere around three o'clock in the morning. The next thing I knew, Fred was shaking me, his hand on my shoulder.

"Your wife's on the phone," he said.

"What time is it?" I asked.

"Seven."

I staggered out of the sleeping bag and picked up the phone on my desk. "Good morning."

"I called the house last night and left a message," Maggie said, her voice scolding me for my lack of response. "I tried again this morning."

"Sorry." I started to explain, but before I could get the words out, she cut me off.

"Why is it that I'm the one who always has to initiate these conversations?"

"Maggie—"

"You never call me, and now you won't even *return* my calls."

"I'm trying to—"

"You don't know anything about Liz's audition, and—for all she knows—you don't even care."

The words stung. I didn't know, and that fact caused a wave of recriminations to sweep over me. I was now wide-awake, struggling to think of what to say. "How's she doing?" I asked.

"Liz won the first round and is singing in the semifinals tonight at eight o'clock."

"Wonderful. Tell me about it."

"They've reserved seats for us on the front row," Maggie continued. "All of the families will be seated together, and they've scheduled a reception after the performances for us to meet the judges. It's a black tie affair."

I thought about the tux hanging in my closet and the last time I'd worn it—a wedding where Liz sang.

"What time is your plane?"

I hesitated, trying to think how best to break the news.

"You want me to meet you?" Maggie asked.

"I can't come."

The click sounded like a rifle shot. The dial tone that followed tore at me and hurt worse than being hit with a bullet. Maggie was right—I should have called.

I searched my desk for the list of phone numbers she had given me. When I found it, I called Dallas and gave the hotel operator her room number. Maggie answered.

"Let me explain," I said.

"I don't want to hear it," she snapped.

"Maggie, please."

"The only thing I want to know is when."

"When?"

"When will you be coming?"

"As soon as I can," I said.

"All of the other families are here and proud of their sons and daughters."

"That's not fair. You know damn well I'm very proud of Liz."

"Then why in the hell aren't you here?"

"I'm trying to explain."

"Your actions speak so loudly, I can't hear what you're saying," she paraphrased the familiar cliché.

"Maggie, that's unfair," I said again, struggling to keep my temper in check.

"No, it's your lack of support for your daughter that's not fair," she countered, her voice breaking.

Was she crying, now? Suddenly, I felt deflated, drained. "Let me speak with Liz," I said, softly.

I could hear her struggle for control, but Maggie managed two words. "She's asleep."

"Tell her I love her."

Maggie broke down and sobbed, openly.

"And please tell her I'll be there just as soon as I can."

The crying continued until she hung up.

I didn't know what else to do, so I showered, shaved, put on the same set of clothes I'd worn the day before, and went to the lab where I found Fred hard at work.

"Sorry about making an ass of myself yesterday," I said.

"That's okay," Fred replied.

"Okay for me to make an ass of myself?"

Fred smiled for the first time in two days. "You know what I meant."

"Better get ready for it," I replied. "I have a feeling we're going to see the worst side of everyone in the cattle business."

"So you think we really do have mad cow?"

I shrugged. "Doesn't matter what I think. We have to let the science speak for itself."

"That mean you're ready to look at brain tissue?"

I paused for a few moments before answering. And my mind scrolled through possible repercussions—all of them bad. "How long have you had it soaking?" I asked.

"Since one o'clock yesterday," he replied. "It's probably thoroughly pickled by now."

"Fred, if there ever was a time *not* to take shortcuts, this is it."

"Of course. And I understand. But that doesn't keep me from being anxious."

"Let's give it at least twenty-five hours before we slice it, just to be sure."

Fred nodded.

What Fred failed to understand was that I wanted to put off the test as long as possible.

CHAPTER 11

Masterson and Associates Veterinary Services Inc.

That morning Ted Austin started the parade of visitors. As usual, he walked into my lab without knocking. "Where've you been?" he asked. "I called your house last night and again this morning."

"Here," I answered. "You had breakfast?"

"Yeah, but I'll go with you if that's the only way I can talk to you."

We got in his pickup and drove to the International House of Pancakes. I picked up a copy of the *Amarillo Globe-News* from the rack by the door, and, once seated inside, scanned the headline—MAD COW DISEASE IN AREA FEEDLOTS?

"You ducking me?" Ted asked.

"You and everyone else," I replied.

"I came to see if you'd speak with the media."

"The feds won't let me."

"Jim Bob, these rumors are killing us." He pointed to the newspaper. "A few more headlines like this, and we'll be out of business."

The waitress took our orders. Banana-nut pancakes for me. Coffee for Ted.

"You believe our beef is safe?" he asked.

"Of course," I replied.

"May I quote you?"

"Sure, I want to help."

"We need a headline tomorrow that reads, 'Noted Vet Says Texas Beef Is Safe.' Using your name would be the best thing we can do."

"Glad to be of service."

"I'll call the editor." Ted pulled out his cell phone. "He'll have a reporter at your office within the hour."

I paused. "Ted, I can't do that."

"Why not?"

"The feds have *ordered* me not to release information to the media. You can do it. Or if you want an interview, send a reporter to see Congressman Young or one of the government vets."

"The newspaper tried. No deal. That's why they called me."

"Ted, why don't you do the interview? You're the TCFA's executive director, the area's spokesman for the cattle industry."

The waitress brought my pancakes and Ted's coffee.

"You don't get it, do you?" Ted's voice was brimming with irritation.

"I think I understand perfectly. The *Globe-News* wants to sell newspapers."

"So?"

"So they think they'll sell more papers if they have people in the cattle business pontificating about mad cow disease."

Ted shook his head and then took a sip of coffee. After a pause he said, "They want experts, not businessmen like me."

"You're not just a businessman," I scoffed. "You're one of the leading authorities in the cattle business."

"With a vested interest."

"Hell, everyone in West Texas has a vested interest. This is cattle country."

"Jim Bob, quit beating around the bush. Are you gonna help us or not?"

"The feds have told me I can't talk to the media."

"What can they do to you if you do?"

"Jerk my license."

"They wouldn't do that. You're the most famous vet in Texas, a nominee for the Nobel Prize."

I laughed. "Hey, fame didn't help Martha Stewart." Then I took a forkful of pancakes.

Ted sipped his coffee, a scowl on his face. Over the last fifteen years, as friends and neighbors, we'd always been on the same side of beef issues. Though I'd heard rumors of viciousness in his fighting for the cattle business, I'd never had to face him in a confrontation. I hoped we could find a way to avoid a conflict between us.

Ted shifted the conversation. "You ran the blood test yesterday?" he asked.

"Yeah. And we're getting ready to run the test on brain tissue this afternoon."

"If I promise not to tell, would you share the results?"

"No."

"One word, Jim Bob, I'm the guy who backed you for the Nobel."

"Yes, and a friend who also knows that the feds are breathing down my neck."

"You've never held back on me before."

"You're my best buddy. You don't really want me to risk my license?"

"No one would know," he argued.

I gave him a pointed glare. "I'd know."

He stared at me in a way I'd never seen before. My friend and neighbor who had stood with me through the ups and downs of the Texas cattle business, through good times and bad, in what I have heard referred to as "thick and thin," now studied me with angry eyes and a hurt expression on his face while I finished my pancakes. He sat in uncomfortable silence for a few moments.

When I looked up his face softened. "Jim Bob, I understand," he said.

I smiled with tight lips. "The NVSL is only two days behind me with their tests." I picked up the check and led the way to the cash register.

"I know. Stan told me he's working with them."

"Good. We both know our congressman wants to get reelected, and that he'll do everything he can to help cattlemen."

"Of course."

"Nothing to worry about, right?" I asked.

Ted didn't respond, and we started the drive back to my office with another uneasy silence. Sitting beside him in the passenger seat, I struggled to think of conversational ways to rebuild our rapport. "Liz is in Dallas at the Met auditions. She made the semifinals."

"I know," he replied. "Story's on the front page of the entertainment section. Page C-1."

While he drove, I looked through the morning paper and found the article. It had a small headline and a photograph.

"Congratulations," Ted continued. "I know you and Maggie must be proud."

"Thanks," I said. "I appreciated your calling my attention to this article. I might have missed it."

"Keep it," Ted said.

"I really should be there—"

"Jim Bob, you're needed here. You're not thinking of leaving at this critical time?"

"Why not? The feds won't let me say anything."

"Yes, but you're our most knowledgeable vet. Hell, the test has your name on it. People are counting on you. If you left town to go hear some opera singing, even if it is your daughter, folks would never let you forget it."

"So you think I shouldn't go hear Liz?" I asked, at war with my conscience and hoping Ted would understand.

"Seems to me that's obvious."

He let me out at my front door and drove away without a goodbye. So much for understanding and moral support. I wished I hadn't mentioned the Metropolitan auditions.

Ida Mae met me with a stack of pink phone messages.

"The NVSL's number is on top," she said. "They've already called twice this morning."

I took the stack of slips and glanced through them.

"And the FBI's regional office in Lubbock called. They asked for an appointment this afternoon."

I grinned. "Wonder what they want?"

"Jim Bob!" Her brows narrowed toward her nose.

"Sorry, guess that's not something to joke about."

Ida Mae, still frowning, continued. "And Paul Edwards is pushing Fred and me about the test results."

"What did you tell him?"

"What you told me to say. That he should contact the feds. And I tried to give him phone numbers."

"But—"

"But he wouldn't take them. He said he wants to talk with you."

The phone rang, and she picked it up.

I went back to my desk and counted the pink slips. Only nine o'clock and I already had thirty-two calls to return. I went through the stack a second time and picked out three: the NVSL, Congressman Young, and Paul Edwards.

I called Ames, Iowa.

CHAPTER 12

Masterson and Associates Veterinary Services Inc.

"It's a call from a woman named Katherine Barrington Smith," Ida Mae said.

"I didn't catch the name," I said.

"She says she's your mother-in-law."

"Really?"

"Katherine Barrington Smith. And she's very determined to speak with you."

"Thanks, Ida Mae. I guess I'd better take it."

Ida Mae gave me a look that said, yes, I think you'd better.

I punched the button for line one and said, "Good morning, Katherine."

"Jim Bob, I know you don't like for me to bother you at work, but—" She paused for effect.

"Katherine, I don't think you've ever called me at work before."

"These are special circumstances. I can see that your family needs you."

"I appreciate your concern."

"You should. Your wife and your daughter feel that you don't care about the auditions, about them. They desperately need you to show your support."

I felt my voice tense. "They've told you this?"

"They don't have to say it. I can see it in their faces and read it in their actions."

I let her answer linger for a moment. "Katherine, I'd like to ask your help," I said, softening my tone.

"I'll do what I can."

"Ask Liz to call me." I gave her my cell phone number.

"Does this mean you're coming tonight?"

I closed my eyes and took a breath. "Tell Liz I love her and that I'll do whatever she thinks best."

"Good for you, Jim Bob. I've always known you put your family first."

We said our goodbyes, and I wrote the date on my notepad. September 15, in the twenty-sixth year of my marriage—my first compliment from Katherine.

I picked up a pink slip and began the painstaking process of returning calls.

The NVSL people expressed their appreciation for my cooperation.

Paul Edwards, the billionaire owner of the world's largest feedlot, expressed his disappointment for my lack of cooperation.

You can't please everyone, I philosophized, dialing Congressman Young. Stan wasn't in.

Fred came by to talk. He had everything ready to run the tests on brain tissue. All we had to do was wait for the appropriate time. Together, we decided on two o'clock. He offered to pick up some hamburgers for lunch.

My cell phone rang, and I leaped for it.

"Daddy, I saw you on TV last night."

"Really?"

"CBS News. They showed a woman interviewing you at a feed-lot. She asked you why everyone was so worried about a few sick cows."

"So, what'd you think?"

"I thought your answer was gripping."

"You saw this in Dallas?"

"National news. You said, 'Cattle or humans, you get it, you will die.' Is that true?"

"Unfortunately, yes, it is."

"Your quote was the headline in this morning's *Dallas Morning News*."

"Really?"

"My dad, the headline maker."

I could see we needed to change the subject. "How's the voice?"

"Never better."

"If you win tonight, what happens?"

"They give me $10,000 and a free trip to New York to sing in the finals."

"Wow. Liz, that's fantastic."

"It'll be in Lincoln Center with the Met orchestra." She said the words with a simple plainness that came across without a hint of braggadocio.

As I thought about my little girl on the stage of one the world's most renowned music halls, an indescribable rush came over me. "When?"

"I don't have the date. Next month sometime."

"Get me the date. I promise I'll be there."

"Daddy, I haven't won, yet."

"But you will. You're a winner."

"And you're the world's biggest flatterer."

"Wrong," I said. "I'm just your number one fan."

"I know," she answered.

"I love you, and I'll be pulling for you tonight."

"I love you, too, and I understand why you can't come."

"How did I get so lucky as to have the world's most understanding daughter?"

"Must be in the genes." She laughed and hung up.

Fred brought lunch. Nothing like a big, thick sandwich with two beef patties to bolster one's spirits. It seemed almost ironic that we were chowing down on the very meat we were preparing to examine for a deadly disease. Neither Fred nor I gave it as much as a passing thought.

At two o'clock we went to the lab and put on our gloves.

Together, in silence, we prepared the slides. We did it slowly, by the book, with the utmost attention to detail.

As usual, Fred had set up two microscopes to do comparisons.

I slid up on the stool and looked at the British sample. Then, with the image fresh in my mind, I scooted over to examine the brain tissue from Sagebrush on the second scope. Slowly and carefully, I placed my eye on the eyepiece and took a long time to scan each slide.

It gave me a sense of history.

In spite of the fact I knew what to expect and that this lack of surprise made the actual experience anticlimactic, I felt a twist in my stomach as I viewed the pink, spongy, textbook-perfect example of bovine spongiform encephalopathy. Slide after slide showed the same, unequivocal proof of the disease.

There was no question. We had six confirmed cases of BSE in Sagebrush, Texas.

And no telling how many more.

Fred was dying to look. I gave him my place at the scopes.

Ida Mae slipped into the room, closing the door behind her. "The FBI's here. She wants to see you."

"She?"

"Christine O'Shay." Ida Mae smiled. "Today the long arm of the law comes with a skirt."

Ida Mae opened the door, and in walked one of the most beautiful women I'd ever seen.

Chapter 13

Masterson and Associates Veterinary Services Inc.

Chris O'Shay flipped out an ID. Black leather with a plastic window, just like the ones I'd seen on TV. She showed it and, I think, expected me to take only a quick, superficial glance. Instead, I grasped the lower part and for a moment, we both held the identification wallet as though we might lapse into a game of tug of war. She stood at the front of my desk—I by my chair on the other side.

"May I?" I asked, indicating my wish to examine it.

"Certainly," she replied as she released her grip. Her face was a gorgeous mix of surprise and annoyance.

I took my time.

She looked around the room, drumming her fingers on my desk.

"I've never seen one of these before," I said.

She held out her hand, commanding the return of her property. "Not that much to see."

"You don't look like an FBI agent."

"Please," she said, "I've heard all this."

"If you don't mind, I think I need to check."

"Sure, call Dr. Raymond Underwood. I'm here at the request of his office."

I recognized the name of the AVI, the area veterinary inspector. When those of us in the Texas Panhandle cattle business refer to "the feds," we're usually talking about Ray Underwood. I picked up the phone and buzzed my secretary. "Ida Mae, would you get the AVI for me, please?"

Fifteen seconds later she buzzed me back. "Guess who just walked in the front door?"

"Send him in," I replied. I locked eyes with the FBI. "You knew Dr. Underwood was coming?"

She nodded.

"You didn't tell me."

"You didn't ask."

I don't like to be surprised by a sandbagger, and I sensed that this stunningly beautiful woman might be one, an expert in withholding information in order to gain advantage. While I took measure of my thoughts about her, Ida Mae opened the door, and Ray walked into the room.

We shook hands and took chairs around my desk.

"Dr. Masterson wants you to vouch for me," she said.

"I think you'll have to admit," I jumped in, "Agent O'Shay doesn't look like your typical fibbie."

"Okay, you two," Ray said. "Time to drop this *doctor* and *agent* bullshit. We're all on the same team, and I don't want anything but first names—Chris, Jim Bob."

"Okay by me," I said.

"Hey, I like the sound of Jim Bob," she responded. "Add a shotgun and a six-pack, and he'd be the spittin' image of a real Texan."

"Chris." Ray said her name sharply, a rebuke.

She responded with a smile. "Relax, Ray. I'm being transferred to the Los Angeles office. Two more days and you won't have to put up with me."

Ray rolled his eyes. "Chris, we need you," he said.

"Sweet of you to say, but you'll do just fine with the next agent. Maybe *he* won't mind the smell." She fired the pronoun like a bullet.

"Washington's sending someone brand new?"

She nodded. "Not my choice, but that's the word from headquarters."

"This is a big case," Ray said. "No time to break in a rookie."

"To Washington this is another case of hoof and mouth disease. We provide backup—you run the investigation."

"So, the FBI sends us someone new on the job, while experienced agents do something important like arrest an illegal with a pocketful of marijuana."

"Hey, that's our job, too."

"And if a BSE epidemic in cattle country sets off a panic that results in a multi-billion loss in America's beef industry, that's not your job?"

"No. Sick cows are the USDA's responsibility."

"But where did the epidemic come from?"

"You're the cattle experts."

"Chris, let me help you," Ray said. "BSE doesn't happen spontaneously. It has to come from an infected animal or its remains."

"So?"

"We need your help in finding where this infection originated."

She lifted one perfectly shaped eyebrow. "You want me to trace cows?"

"We want you to help us trace the infection," Ray said. "And to hold accountable those responsible."

"Fine, I'll do all that I can in the next forty-eight hours," she replied. "You have any clues? Any suggestions about where to start?"

"You're looking at him." Ray nodded his head toward me.

"Wait just a damn minute." I sat forward. "I don't know anything."

Ray laughed. "Hell no, he don't know nothin'. This poor ignorant sonofabitch was just nominated for the Nobel Prize. He wrote *the* book on mad-cow, even had a cow test named for him. The *Washington Post* called him 'the world's leading expert' on the disease."

Chris looked at me with both eyebrows raised. "Really?"

"You don't have to investigate the test," I said.

"*Start*," Ray exclaimed. "She asked for a place to *start*."

"Fine, I'll give her a copy of my book to read," I said.

"Don't be a horse's ass," Ray said, his voice louder.

Chris chuckled.

"Sorry," I said. "Just trying to be a *real* Texan."

"And Chris," Ray continued, "I'll see if I can get Washington to extend your assignment here in West Texas until we investigate this outbreak."

"Ray, no. Don't you dare do that." For an instant her eyes met mine, and she gave me a look that would scorch ice.

I chuckled. I loved that Ray's comment irritated her and bit my tongue to keep from laughing out loud.

"Listen, both of you." Ray leaned forward in his chair. "We need your cooperation. You know that a BSE outbreak here in the heart of cattle country would be a disaster. People need your help." He stood.

Chris and I stood.

"Can we count on you?"

A couple of moments passed while I thought of Liz and the auditions. "Sure," I said.

"For how long?" Chris asked.

I could see she was holding her breath.

"As long as it takes," Ray answered.

She winced. "I already have an apartment leased in L.A., and the moving van is coming day after tomorrow."

"Chris, would you give me an honest answer to a straight up question?" Ray asked.

"Sure."

"Are you, or are you not, the best *man* for the job?"

Chris shook her head and smiled. A sardonic little smile, signaling that she knew when she'd been had. "Underwood, you are a true S.O.B."

He paused for a moment; just long enough to let the ignominy of the moment bring closure to our conversation. Then, without a word, he turned and walked out the door.

Chris and I sat down.

Damn, she was beautiful.

In a voice so soft I could barely hear her words, "Where do we start?" she asked.

CHAPTER 14

KLLO, Channel 2, Amarillo

Chris and I took chairs at the newsroom conference table. The female TV reporter looked young. Very young. High-school age.

"Anyone ever comment on your youthful appearance?" Chris asked.

"I'm almost twenty-five, and I have a degree in journalism from West Texas A&M University." Her voice reeked of defensiveness. I could almost see the hackles rise.

"When you get a little older, you'll feel differently about looking young."

"So they say," the TV reporter replied, a scowl on her face "You came to inquire about my age?"

"No," I said. "We heard you're the reporter who broke the mad cow story."

Immediately, the young woman's face lit up, and her demeanor changed. "Yeah, my first big story."

"I understand CBS picked it up, and it made the national news."

"With my byline," she said. "CNN aired it on Sunday and CBS on Monday." I could see a sense of pride in her face.

"Would you tell us about how you found it? I believe you stated that the original videotape was made by someone with a personal camera."

"Yeah, an amateur video," she said. "But that's how a lot of big stories start. The best tapes made on September 11th came from people using their home cameras."

"True," I said. "But could you tell us how you found the tape? Where did it come from?"

"A woman brought it in."

"Really?" Chris said, and proceeded to take over the interview. "Describe her."

"Nothing special," the reporter said. "White T-shirt, jeans, and sneakers. Very average looking woman. Average age."

"Average?"

The reporter smiled. "You think I look like a high-school student, don't you?"

Chris nodded. "Youthful."

"Well, this woman could have been late twenties or early forties."

"White, black?"

"Olive complexion and black hair. Hard to tell."

"Hispanic?"

"I don't think so. We have a lot of Hispanics in this area and she looked and sounded different."

"Middle Eastern?"

"Maybe. In fact, the more I think about it, she spoke with a funny, non-Texas accent. Not like an Hispanic with colloquial English."

"What did she say?"

"She asked if I knew anything about mad cow disease."

"And you said—"

"Not much."

"Then what happened?"

"She told me that in the 1980s, the British had 35 million cases, and that it was an epidemic."

"What else?"

"She told me about the symptoms. Said that when she visited the Sagebrush Feedyard, she saw cattle that looked like they had the disease."

"Did you believe her?"

"I agreed to look at her tape."

"When?"

"Immediately."

"Did you?"

"Yes. Right after she left."

"Why didn't you have her watch the tape with you?"

"I tried," the reporter said. "But she was in a hurry."

"Did you get her name, address, ID?"

"No."

"Don't reporters usually get names of their sources?"

The hackles rose again. "You're here to criticize?"

"Absolutely not. We appreciate what you're doing to help us."

"I've had more than enough flak from my boss, from the networks, from everyone else. I don't need you telling me I should've interrogated the woman." Whatever rapport Chris had established was now gone, the defensive attitude back at full tilt.

"We understand," Chris said, trying to mollify the confrontation. "We thank you for all this information."

"What can you do for me?" the reporter asked. "This needs to be a two-way exchange."

Chris hesitated. "We'll call you when we find something."

I decided I should try to help. "This is a big story, but it's going to get bigger. It'll be to your advantage to have us on your side."

The reporter slumped back in her chair and seemed to be thinking over the possibilities. She looked at Chris, then at me. "I don't know if I can trust you."

"We don't know if we can trust *you*," I said.

"How long have you been working here as a TV reporter?" Chris asked.

"Almost a year."

"I've been with the FBI for over fifteen, and for the last three, I've been the SAIC. This is the only time I've ever offered a reporter 'first contact' on a case." Chris smiled. "This is a sweet deal. You'd do well to take it."

"What's SAIC?"

"Special agent in charge," I interjected. "She's the boss. You're talking to the head of the Lubbock Regional Office of the Federal Bureau of Investigation."

The young reporter looked at Chris, eyes wide. "I'm sorry, it's just that you don't look like a chief agent."

"*Touché*," I said, with a chuckle.

Chris stifled a laugh. "And you don't look like the TV reporter who just broke the network's biggest story."

The reporter smiled and held out her hand. "Sometimes it takes me a while."

Chris shook it. "Deal?"

The reporter nodded. "Deal." She turned to me.

I shook her hand.

"What do you want me to do?" she asked Chris, her smile now bigger and warmer.

"Tell us everything you can about the woman who gave you the tape."

As she did, Chris and I made notes. Then Chris made an appointment for the reporter to meet with an FBI artist and develop a drawing of the woman.

"What'd you think?" I asked, in the car, driving back to my office.

"I think we reinforced a valuable lesson for a young reporter," Chris said.

"That she should've gotten an ID?"

"And more importantly, a video of the woman who gave her the tape."

Chapter 15

Masterson and Associates Veterinary Services Inc.

I called the National Veterinary Services Laboratory.

One of the vets, a friend with whom I had worked on a number of occasions, told me he had the results of their Masterson test. As I expected, all six blood samples tested positive for BSE. He said the NVSL high brass were planning to run the brain tissue tomorrow, probably around eleven o'clock in the morning. He didn't spell it out in so many words, but I got the strong impression that the government didn't believe the results of their own testing.

A few moments later the phone rang. Ted Austin pumped me mercilessly for test results.

I resisted.

Finally, he gave up and changed his line of questioning. "When will the NVSL release their findings?"

"I don't know," I said, which was the truth. "But I wouldn't be surprised if it came tomorrow afternoon."

That seemed to satisfy him, so he switched to talk about TCFA's advertising blitz. "We're spending a major part of our war chest."

"How much?" I asked.

"One million, five hundred thousand."

"Wow."

"It's not enough," he said. "That's a thirty-second spot on the three major network news programs, plus radio ads on national news for a week."

"Ted, that sounds like a lot."

"It's not enough to sway public opinion. We're working to build a coalition."

"With whom?"

"With everyone. With the National Cattlemen's Beef Association, with all the state groups. And all the related state and national groups who will be affected—the truckers, the railroads, the grain associations, the dairy groups, the meat packers, even the grocery stores."

"You've been busy."

"Next we're going after the restaurants."

"Such as?"

"McDonald's, Burger King, Wendy's, Outback, Western Sizzler, you name 'em, we're asking them to share the burden."

"What's the response?"

"Pathetic," he answered. "They have no idea what this is going to do to them, to their businesses."

"Maybe you're overreacting."

"I don't think so," he said. "Look at England in 1986."

"But this is America. We have much better regulations for our beef industry."

"That's our story," he said. "We're going to do our best to tell it."

"When will you begin your campaign?"

"We've already committed TCFA funds to an ad agency, but the major campaign, the big money, won't start until after the feds make their announcement about BSE."

"You don't know that we have it."

"Jim Bob, I can read between the lines," he said. "Cattle futures have been down every day since the networks aired your interview and your bombshell about 'you get it, you will die.'"

"At that time I was sure we didn't have it."

"At that time?" he asked. "Meaning you've changed your tune?"

Too late, I realized he'd tricked me. I paused and thought furiously about what to say next.

Ted pressed on. "Why don't you go on national TV and say that you're sure we don't have BSE?"

"I can't call CBS, ABC, or any of the networks and say, 'Hey, I want to be on your program.'"

"Okay, let *me* call them," Ted said. "I'll set it up."

"Besides," I continued, "you know the feds won't let me."

That stopped him. But I could hear heavy breathing, the breath of intense anger. My friend—my neighbor of many years—was so angry with me he couldn't speak. I struggled to find conciliatory words. "Ted—"

"You sonofabitch. You've caused a multi-billion dollar loss, and now you won't do anything to help us."

"Give me a chance," I pleaded. "I'll do everything I can to help."

He hung up and left me with a dial tone.

For the next few minutes I wallowed in self-pity. If only I could take back those words at the Sagebrush Feedyard.

Just as I thought things were as bad as they could get, in walked Chris O'Shay with an angry look on her face "You son of a bitch," she said, her chin stuck out and her eyes blazing. Her hostility came at me like a bulldozer. I could tell she was determined to get even, to make my station in life worse.

I grinned. "Welcome to the club," I said. My friendly response obviously bumfuzzled her. "Everyone's calling me an S.O.B. Soon I'll be getting the son-of-a-bitch-of-the-year award."

"You stupid jerk," she said. "That phrase is not intended as a badge of honor."

Her anger caused my grin to widen. I couldn't help it.

"My boss in Washington called," she shouted. "I've been reassigned to this smelly hellhole until your sick cow stuff blows over."

I laughed. Not a chuckle, but a genuine West Texas guffaw.

Chris' face turned red from her perfect chin to her high cheekbones. I could almost see smoke coming out her ears.

"How long's this bullshit going to take?" she asked—clearly, no pun intended.

I stopped laughing and tried to look serious. "The mad cow epidemic in Great Britain ran from 1986 to 2004, about eighteen years."

"Jesus." She plopped down in the chair in front of my desk. The pink flush of her face turned white, her anger dissipated into a look of despair. She reminded me of an innocent victim on a lawyer TV program where the accused just learned she'd been sentenced to eighteen years in prison.

I felt sorry for her.

"It wasn't me," I said. "I had nothing to do with this."

"Ray Underwood?"

"Obviously."

"That bastard."

"Hey, he said you were the 'best' man for the job. And he's right. We need you. This case's too big for a rookie."

"If you're trying to make me feel good, forget it."

"Okay," I said. "But I have some good news whenever you're ready for it."

"I'm not sure I can take any more of *your* good news."

"You need to know that our situation is far different from the epidemic in Europe. No way it could take eighteen years to resolve itself."

"How long?"

"How long will it take us to figure out what went wrong?"

"*Us*?"

"We're in this together."

For the first time, she smiled. "You and me against the sick cows?"

"Yep."

She took in a breath, a sort of hesitant two-step process. Then she let it out, a long, audible release. To me it sounded like a sigh of resignation.

I picked up two cups, set them on my desk, and poured hot coffee.

Chapter 16

Sagebrush, Texas

We pulled up to the headquarters trailer at Paul Edwards' feedlot. That day the wind came at us from the north, and even sitting inside my Chevy Suburban, the pungent feedlot odor hit us with an overpowering force, but when I climbed out of the truck, the smell of a half-million cattle almost knocked me over. I looked back at Chris.

She sat in the front seat of the Chevy and returned my gaze.

I went around to her side and opened the door. "You coming?"

"Not if I don't have to."

"But you do."

"And to think I almost made it to California."

"There have been olfactory studies that demonstrate the human sense of smell becomes dull and loses its sensitivity to a particular odor after twenty minutes."

"That's a lie. And even if it were true, I don't think I can stand this for twenty minutes." She climbed out, rolled her green eyes, and held a Kleenex over her nose.

I slammed her door shut and started walking toward the office. "You'll look better to these cattlemen without the tissue."

"Jim Bob, has anyone ever told you you're too damn helpful?"

I ignored her sarcasm and together we entered the headquarters of Sagebrush Cattle Feeders Inc. For a multi-billion-dollar corporation—the largest cattle feeding operation in the world—their office looked surprisingly humble. Two secretaries sat at parallel desks. One of them recognized me.

"Good morning, Dr. Masterson," she said.

I answered and gestured toward Chris, pleased to see that she no longer covered her nostrils. "This is FBI Agent Christine O'Shay. We'd like to see Paul. He's expecting us."

The secretary made a quick call, then stood and asked us to follow her down the hall. As we came to the last doorway, I could see Paul Edwards sitting at his desk with an angry look on his face. Chris and I entered.

"Jim Bob, how does it feel to be the number one asshole in the cattle business?"

Chris answered, "He likes it."

I ignored his rebuke and her comment. "I'd like you to meet Chris O'Shay. She's the FBI's chief for this area—their SAIC."

"If you're here to close us down, you're too late. I've called every slaughterhouse in the area. Nobody's buying. I couldn't sell a single head."

Chris ignored his diatribe and extended her hand. "I've heard a lot about you, all high praise."

Paul stood slowly and with obvious reluctance shook her hand. Next he gestured to the chairs in front of his desk. "Have a seat." He ignored me, and for the first time in the fifteen years I'd known him, he failed to offer coffee. "What's the bad news today?"

"We'd like to help," Chris said.

"Help?" he snorted, and glared at me. "I don't see how I can stand any more help from this guy."

"Say the word, and I'll leave," I offered.

"Wait," Chris said. "Mr. Edwards, to turn this around, we'll need Dr. Masterson's help."

"He started it," Edwards yelled. "Look out these windows. Two days ago those 490,000 head of prime beef were worth $1,000 a head, average. That's at least $490 million. Today, two days after the good doctor made his little speech to the TV cameras, I can't sell a single animal. Hell, I can't even give them away."

I started to rise, to get out of my chair and leave the room. Chris put her hand on my arm, stopping me. "So what's your strategy?" she asked. "Are you going to do anything to fight back?"

I sat on the edge of my chair, waiting to hear his response.

"What can I do?" he asked. "Even worthless cattle have to be fed. Every day that passes puts me a quarter-million farther in debt."

"Investigate," Chris said. "Look for the cause of the disease."

"Ma'am, you don't seem to understand—the cattle have already been stampeded." He shook his head in a gesture of antipathy. "I've spent a lifetime building my business. Now the banks tell me it's worthless. You're a nice-looking lady, and I'm sure you have good intentions, but you're a couple days late and about a half-billion short."

"Let me ask again," Chris continued, "are you going to do anything?"

He slouched back in his chair. "Yeah."

"We're here to help," she said.

He got up, walked to the window, and looked out. To the north, as far as the eye could see, the three of us gazed at pens of cattle. Then, as he surveyed his business, Paul Edwards poured out his soul.

He told us how, almost fifty years ago, he'd raised a small herd of cattle on grass and sold them at average prices at the Amarillo cattle auction. Then he heard about cattle feed yards in California where grain-fed cattle brought top-dollar prices. He shipped a few head on trucks to the west coast and made a better profit. That led to a decision to build some pens, buy corn, and feed his own cattle. It worked, and with the savings in transportation, his profit margin increased. He expanded. Other ranchers brought their herds to his feed yards and everyone made money. Paul Edwards wisely reinvested his profits. He hired nutritionists to study weight gain, veterinarians to supervise animal health, and computer experts to track profit margins. A half-century of hard work made Sagebrush Cattle Feeders the biggest and most successful operation of its kind.

Then he turned, and with a proud expression, he told us about his fight with disease. "In the 1980s we had a go with the hoof and mouth epidemic."

"I remember," I said. "I was in vet school in College Station, and everyone saw the cattle business going down the tube."

"We almost did," he replied.

"So, how'd you beat it?" Chris asked.

"We tracked the infection. Killed a hell of a lot of animals. Eradicated the disease."

"Big losses?" Chris asked.

"We took a hit," he answered. "But we had some government support, enough that we survived."

"And you set up procedures to vaccinate against a recurrence of the disease?" I asked.

"Twenty years and we're still free of H&M," he said. And for the first time that morning, he smiled.

"Cattlemen banded together?" I asked.

"We always do."

"What about now?"

His face changed. We locked eyes for a moment, and I had the impression of a bull, pawing the dirt, getting ready to lower his head and come charging. In a way he did—he came back and sat in his chair. Only this time he leaned forward, elbows on his desk, a determined look in his eye, and said, "If I'm going broke, I'll go down fighting."

Chris pulled out a drawing of the woman who brought the videotape to the Amarillo TV station. "Would you copy this and pass it out to all of your employees?"

"Sure." Paul looked at the sketch, unimpressed. "Who is she?"

"That's the problem," Chris answered. "We don't know."

Chris explained about our interview with the Channel 2 reporter, and that she had met with an FBI artist who made the drawing. "We think this woman knew something about your infected cattle."

"If so, she's our best lead as to where the disease came from," I added. "We need to find out how she happened to be here at your feedlot with a video camera."

"If anyone remembers her, ask them to call me on my cell phone, day or night." Chris gave Paul her card.

The meeting ended much better than it started. We all shook hands. Paul actually smiled as he walked Chris and me down the hall to the front door. And I thought Chris seemed more at ease . . . until we stepped outside and headed toward my Suburban. Then she held her nose with her right hand and raised her left to look at her watch.

"It's been more than twenty minutes," she said.

CHAPTER 17

Dumas, Texas

We left the feedlot and drove ten miles south to Dumas, population 14,000, where we stopped for lunch. I headed for K-Bob's, the quintessential West Texas steakhouse, only to find the parking lot full. After circling it twice, someone finally pulled out, and we edged our way into the empty space. Inside the restaurant, Chris and I took a booth, and we both ordered the house specialty, a chicken fried steak with mashed potatoes and gravy.

"You're going to miss this in California," I said.

"You don't watch The Orchid Show, do you?" she asked.

I looked around to see if anyone listened. Apparently no one heard Chris mention the women's talk show host.

"Best not to bring up that name in cattle country."

"The Orchid Show?" She said it in a loud, clear voice. Several people seated nearby turned and looked.

I reached for my glass, held it to my lips, and took a long, slow drink of water. People continued to stare. "Chris, what do you think about the weather?"

"I think the weather's just fine." She gave me a puzzled look.

"I've heard that we may get rain next week."

"Jim Bob, what's the matter with you?"

"Back in 1996, demand for beef fell, and the price of cattle dropped," I said. "TCFA hired a marketing research company to investigate, and they concluded that this television host you just mentioned had been urging people to switch from beef to fish or chicken. Lots of women follow her TV program and quit buying beef. Cattle prices fell almost forty percent."

Chris gave me her look of disbelief. In the short time I'd known her, I'd come to recognize the wrinkled brow, the narrowing of eyes, and the firmness of lips. The "look" told me she doubted my facts.

"It started when a guest on her show commented on mad cow disease," I said. "He said it would make AIDS seem like the common cold.'"

"Really," Chris said. Her "look" softened from out-and-out disbelief to a hesitant maybe.

I continued. "Then your friend, the host, uttered those infamous words, 'I'll never eat another hamburger,' a phrase that was quoted on every front page in America."

"So, what happened?"

"So a group of West Texas cattlemen sued the company that produced the show. I'm surprised you don't remember this."

"In the 1990s I was stationed in the Washington, D.C. area," Chris said. "About that time I was sent to Kenya to investigate the bombing of the American Embassy in Nairobi. That assignment took me out of the country for almost a year."

The waitress brought our food. K-Bob's marketing philosophy equated quantity to quality, and as a result, the servings were huge.

Chris looked at the mountain of food, shook her head in disbelief, and said, "Welcome to cholesterol city."

"Might as well die happy." I sliced off a big bite of steak, dipped it in gravy, and stuffed it in my mouth. It was delicious.

While I chewed, she carried the conversation. "Next time we go to lunch together, how about letting me pick the restaurant?"

I shrugged my shoulders and, in spite of a mouthful of food, muttered a single word, "Sure."

"Have you ever eaten at The Lettuce Works?"

I swallowed my food and shook my head. "Never heard of it."

"They have great salads."

"What else?"

"Soup."

"That's all? Just soup and salad?"

"Very healthy."

"Probably recommended by Orchid."

"I thought we weren't supposed to mention her name?"

I felt my face flush. If I could see myself in a mirror, I'd bet I looked bright red. "Enjoy your steak and potatoes," I snapped.

The next few minutes passed silently, which was fine with me. I cleaned my plate. Chris ate less than half of hers, then carefully placed her silverware diagonally across her plate, a gesture to signal she had finished eating. She put her hands in her lap and looked at me.

"Dessert?" I asked.

"No, but I'll wait while you have yours."

"The peach cobbler here is wonderful."

"No, thanks."

"They serve it hot with a big scoop of ice cream."

"Sounds great," she said with a smile. "Go ahead."

"You're intimidating my appetite."

"Jim Bob, do you eat like this all the time?"

"Sure, don't you?"

"If I did, I'd weigh three hundred pounds." She shook her head. "How much do you weigh?"

"Around one-fifty. Hasn't changed much since high school."

"And how tall?"

"Five foot, seven inches." I smiled. "Hasn't changed since high school."

"Same as me." She chuckled. "How do you do it?"

"Do what?"

"Eat like a lumberjack and not gain weight."

"Maggie says it's my metabolism."

"Maggie?"

"My wife."

"Tell me about her."

"She's slender like you, but tiny. A wonderful mother. We'll celebrate our twenty-seventh next year."

"Tell me about your kids."

"Just one, Elizabeth. Twenty-five. She's a singer."

"A singer?" Her smile widened, and I could see her interest.

"Yeah. May I brag?"

"Go ahead. That's what parents are supposed to do—brag on their kids."

"Liz is in Dallas auditioning for the Metropolitan Opera."

"Wow."

"She made the finals."

"No kidding."

"If she wins tonight, she gets $10,000 and a trip to New York to sing with the Met orchestra in Lincoln Center."

"Why aren't you in Dallas, cheering her on?"

"Exactly what my wife wants to know."

"And your answer?"

I shook my head. "Whose side are you on?"

"Maggie's," she snorted. "And Liz's. I'm surprised you have to ask."

"I mentioned this yesterday morning to Ted," I said. "He chastised me for even thinking about going to Dallas."

Chris laughed.

"He said, 'Jim Bob, if you left town to go hear some opera singing, people would never forgive you.' He's probably right. You saw how Paul Edwards treated me for my slip with the TV reporter."

"Damn, what is this, the cattleman's fraternity?"

"No. It's people's lives. They and their businesses are at risk."

"But you and I agree," she said. "This will probably blow over, and things will return to normal."

"Eventually," I replied.

"Meanwhile—"

"They're counting on you and me to find out where this came from."

Chapter 18

Bushland, Texas

That night, home alone, I called Maggie's hotel room in Dallas and left a message. A little after midnight, my phone woke me.

"Hello," I answered, my voice groggy with sleep.

"Daddy. I won," Liz squealed.

"Oh, wow! Tell me about it," I roared, now wide-awake.

"One of ten in the United States."

"They picked ten, tonight?"

"No, silly. They picked me. I'm the winner of the Dallas Regional Auditions. But there are ten regions in the country."

"What about singing in New York?"

"Next month, on Thursday night, October 21st, all ten of us will appear in the national finals in Lincoln Center."

"Liz, that's wonderful. I'm so proud of you."

"They gave me the check."

"That's even more wonderful," I said. "Ten thousand?"

"No," she said. "They withheld taxes."

I laughed. "Welcome to the adult world."

"Daddy, this is *prize* money. How can they do that?"

"You can probably file to get it back at the end of the year."

"But this is a *prize*. I won it."

"The IRS would say you earned it."

"That's so unfair. They took almost $1,800."

"What're you going to do with the other $8,200?"

"Well, to start with, we're going to have a party." She warmed to the topic. "I'm going to take you and Mom and some others to the Amarillo Country Club for a steak dinner."

"Really?"

"Yep. How about Wednesday night next week?"

I had no idea what my commitments would be, but I said the only thing I could say to my daughter, "Sure."

"How's it going with the mad cows?"

"We're fight'n hard."

"But you can get away for my party?"

"Kiddo, I'm so proud of you, I wouldn't miss it for the world." I meant it with all my heart and soul. Then, foolishly, I walked out onto the proverbial limb and sawed it off. "And I'm going with you to New York for the big show on October 21st."

"I'll hold you to that," she said. "I think Mom wants to speak with you."

"Congratulations, Liz."

"Thanks, Daddy. Here's Mom."

I held the phone for about fifteen seconds. In the background I could hear happy people talking and a loud pop that might have been a champagne cork. Then Maggie came on the line.

"Isn't this wonderful?" she asked.

"Liz sounds thrilled."

"Everyone's sky high. Mother called the catering office, and they brought some finger food and six bottles of champagne."

"Six? Good grief, how many people?"

"I don't know. A room full."

"Sounds like quite a party."

"Wish you were here."

"Me, too," I said. And as the words left my lips, I thought about my family, about what a fool I was to have let a damn job come between me and the things I loved most.

"Everyone asks about you."

"I promise, I'll be there for the next round."

"New York?"

"Yes. But I have a request."

"You don't want to stay at Mother's?"

"Bingo."

"But—

"We could stay at the New York Hilton. It's not far from Lincoln Center."

"Mother would be hurt. I don't think we can do that."

"Suppose Liz had to stay at the hotel to be near the contest?"

"Well—"

"And we stayed at the same hotel because we wanted to be close to Liz?"

"Dr. James Robert Masterson, you are a devious man."

“Just trying to keep harmony in the family, ma’am.”

“You’ll have to be the one to break the news to Mother.”

“Of course. Let me speak to her.”

“Not now!”

“Why not?”

“I don’t want to be anywhere near by when you call her.”

“Okay, when’re you coming home?”

“Day after tomorrow. Liz wants to organize a dinner and invite her friends.”

“Yes, she told me.”

“You’ll have to be there.”

“Hey, I want to be included.”

“I’ve heard that before.”

“Maggie, please.”

“Honey, Mother’s waiting on me to lead a toast to Liz.”

“I love you.”

“And I love you, even when you’re not here.”

We said our goodbyes. I turned out the light and tried to go back to sleep. Ten minutes later I turned the light back on, went to the kitchen, and poured myself a double scotch on the rocks. I plopped down in front of the TV to sip my drink and watch late-night news on CNN.

Things couldn’t be better for my daughter. I thought about how lucky I was to have a beautiful girl who was going to sing at the Metropolitan Opera. Then, as I sipped and mellowed out, the news broadcast started on a piece about the 1980s mad cow epidemic in England.

I watched with interest until, near the end, CNN showed another rerun of my little speech in the Sagebrush feedlot—those infamous words that had come to haunt me, "You get it, cattle or humans, you will die."

Things couldn't be worse for me and my veterinary practice.

CHAPTER 19

Masterson and Associates Veterinary Services Inc.

I drove to the office for The Big Day—the day I expected the National Veterinary Services Laboratory to confirm that we had mad cow disease in Sagebrush, Texas. I called Ames, Iowa, to ask when they would make their announcement. Of the half-dozen people I knew by name—the vets, administrators, lab assistants, and others—no one would speak with me. I ended up with an assistant media officer, a woman who wouldn't give me her name.

"What time today will you release your test results?" I asked.

"What test results?" she replied.

"Your tests for BSE."

"I have no knowledge of any tests for mad cow disease."

"Hey, I'm the veterinarian who sent you the brain tissue from those six animals in Sagebrush, Texas."

"I'm sorry. NVSL currently has almost two hundred samples from all over the country involved in laboratory testing. I don't have a comprehensive listing."

We talked on for several minutes, long enough for me to realize that I'd hit a stonewall of feminine professional courtesy. This woman was good. I gave up and called Congressman Young.

"Stan, what's going on?" I asked.

"The NVSL is sending their samples to Great Britain," he replied.

"What on earth for?"

"Jim Bob, I don't have to tell you what a big deal this is. They can't afford to make a mistake in their diagnosis. It's only prudent to get the UK labs—the most experienced BSE experts in the world—to check their tests."

"Stan, this is nothing more than a stall tactic."

"If the government confirms we have BSE, the reaction will be devastating."

"What do you think we have now?"

"Suspicion."

"I don't suppose you've bothered to check on cattle prices in the past few days?"

"It's front-page news. Hard to miss."

"Down the limit every day this week."

"Yes, I know."

"And every day we postpone the inevitable only makes it worse."

"So you say."

"No, so says the market. Hell, talk to Paul Edwards or any member of the Texas Cattle Feeders Association."

“Jim Bob, I have a responsibility to the American public. As chairman of the House Agriculture Committee, the government is expecting me to lead congressional oversight of the country’s food supply.”

“That sounds like politics.”

“Well, next year is an election year.”

“And?”

“And there is always some public mistrust of the government—people who think the USDA will give in to special interests.”

“You think by announcing your test results you’d be giving in?”

“Look at it this way,” he said. “You’re on the side of the cattle industry. The media regard you as a special-interest person. In fact, they regard you as one of the leaders.”

“So?”

“So, you’re calling me, urging me to announce the fact that we have BSE.”

“I’m asking you to tell the truth.”

“Whatever. The point is, I’m not giving in to special interests.”

I couldn’t believe what this guy was saying. His stall tactics made me so mad I couldn’t think. For the next few moments I sat there gripping the phone, paralyzed by, what seemed to be, governmental bumbling on a grand scale.

“Jim Bob, you still there?” Stan asked.

“Yeah,” I replied. I bit my tongue, trying to control my anger.

“Trust me. You’ll not regret that we asked for a second opinion from the British.”

I wanted to unload, to explain why I thought it so unnecessary. And I could think of dozens of reasons for immediate government action. I wanted to yell at the top of my lungs. Stan apparently misread my pause as acquiescence.

"I have more information," he said.

"More good news?"

"I just got off the phone with Ray Underwood. The NVSL has ordered him to quarantine Sagebrush Cattle Feeders."

"What good will that do?"

"Give us time for testing."

"Testing? I've already FedExed samples to Ames."

"The government wants to take their own samples—do their own tests. They're sending a team of experts."

"Stan—"

"Jim Bob, it's already decided."

I hung up.

The phone rang. I didn't answer and, instead, went out to Ida Mae's desk in the reception area. With her phone to her ear, she punched a button, putting her caller on hold.

"It's Paul Edwards," she said. "He's been holding all the time you were talking to Congressman Young."

"Tell him I'll call him back in fifteen minutes."

She did. And then immediately, she frowned and held the phone away from her ear. Apparently he didn't like it. She replaced the phone and turned to me. "What's going on?"

I shook my head and walked out the front door to a beautiful fall day in the Texas Panhandle. Seventy degrees, a light breeze from the southwest, not a cloud in the sky. I climbed into my Chevy Suburban and headed west on I-40 toward the headquarters of the Texas Cattle Feeders Association. Using the truck's Onstar telephone, I called Ted Austin.

"I'm thinking about driving up to Sagebrush," I said. "Wanna go?"

"TCFA regards you as the enemy," he replied. "It's not prudent for me to be seen with you."

"Did you know the feds are about to quarantine Paul's feedlot?"

"When?"

"As we speak. And the NVSL is sending a team to take samples of his entire herd."

"Do they know how big his operation is?"

"Probably not."

"This is ridiculous."

"I'm on I-40. I'll be at your front door in five minutes."

He hung up, which I took to be an affirmative response to my invitation.

Minutes later I pulled up to his front door and found him waiting. As we headed north on US-287 toward Sagebrush, I briefed him on my long conversation with Stan. We agreed that the government's stalling tactics were, at best, counterproductive for the cattle industry. Together, we decided I should call Stan again, and this time, urge total, honest, open communication—a public announcement about our situation.

I punched the button. "Onstar ready," came the telephone's response.

I gave the number for Stan's direct line to the phone on his desk.

"Hello," he answered.

"This is Jim Bob."

"I'm glad you called. I have bad news."

"Go ahead. Ted Austin is here with me."

"The House Agriculture Committee just held an impromptu meeting."

"So, what's new?"

"This was an informal meeting here in my office. What we call a gut check to see what members are thinking."

"Yes, go ahead."

"No official action, just an off-the-record quickie to see which way the wind is blowing."

"I'm listening," and I was beginning to sense this politician's reluctance to tell me something he knew I didn't want to hear.

"You need to remember," he added, "that committee members from across the aisle are sometimes motivated by the fact that I'm from Texas and they're not."

"Stan, what's the bad news?"

"Eradication."

"Meaning?"

"It was suggested that we kill all the cows in Texas."

CHAPTER 20

Sagebrush, Texas

We pulled up to Paul Edwards' headquarters. I parked next to a white pickup with government plates and "U.S. Department of Agriculture" lettered on the door.

"Is that Ray Underwood's truck?" Ted asked.

"Probably," I replied. "But the feds' trucks all look the same."

"He's probably in there serving the quarantine notice."

"Probably."

"What'd you think? Are we going to tell him about Stan's bombshell?"

"Paul's going to be in an ugly mood," I said. Conversation lapsed into a few moments of silence that seemed like hours. Finally, I killed the engine and cracked open my door. "There's a limit to how much bad news a person can take at any one time. Let's play it by ear."

We entered the building and made our way back to the familiar corner office. The open door allowed us to hear angry words.

"Sorry you feel that way, Mr. Edwards, but with or without your cooperation, I have my orders." Ray Underwood's voice boomed with a commanding presence, a side to his personality I had not seen—or in this case, heard—before. "As your USDA Area Veterinary Inspector I'm telling you, Sagebrush Cattle Feeders is now under Federal Quarantine."

I stepped into the room. Ted followed. The hostility that engulfed me was so furious it felt like a West Texas tornado.

"Mind if we join you?" I asked.

"Why not?" Paul bristled with anger, and the veins at his temples bulged with a dangerous outline. "There's enough misery for everyone."

Ray plopped a large, thick, manila envelope on the desk. "This packet details the regulations and federal penalties. Feel free to call me if you have any questions." He turned and left. Silence followed. The sound of his footsteps echoed from the oak-floored hallway like a hammer. Immediately I thought of someone pounding nails into a coffin.

"Wow," Ted exclaimed. "Has Ray been training with the Gestapo?"

"Gawddamned bureaucrats," Paul growled. "They don't give a shit about us poor working stiffs."

I chuckled. It came over me spontaneously. I couldn't help it. The last thing I'd intended was to make light of the situation, but the thought of Paul Edwards, a billionaire cattleman, characterizing himself as poor, struck me as ludicrous. I struggled to wipe away the smile.

Paul glared.

"What's so funny?" Ted asked.

Their obvious disfavor helped me regain control. "This is serious business, and we're here to help."

"A little late for that," Paul said.

"In a situation like this, it's never too late," I countered.

Paul looked at me with distrust, like he thought I was either crazy or stupid. Probably both.

"What do the feds have planned?" I asked.

"Testing," Paul answered.

"Obviously, but what are the details?" I asked. "Which cattle? What kind of testing? Who's going to do it?"

"It sounded like he's going to test my entire herd."

"All 490,000 head?" Ted asked. "That'll take months."

"He said they're sending in a hundred testing teams, and that they'll start tomorrow."

"Maybe not months," I said. "Let's do the math." I pulled a pencil from my pocket and found a scrap of paper on his desk. We sat. Paul poured the coffee while I scribbled.

If the feds could find a hundred teams to take samples, if they used the Masterson blood test, and if they were exceptionally motivated—a lot of ifs, but theoretically possible—they might process fifty head per hour or five hundred cattle per day. A hundred teams testing five hundred steers and heifers would be fifty thousand animals per day. If they were good, really good, they might process the entire holdings of the country's largest cattle feeding company in ten days. Maybe.

After I explained this to Paul and Ted, I cautioned them about other considerations. First, the government would likely want random sampling of brain tissue. If they slaughtered one out of each thousand—and it seemed to me they shouldn't do less—that would be 490 head, or 50 per day to accomplish it in 10 days.

Second, if any cattle tested positive, they would have to be destroyed, and that could take enormous time. Without knowing the number, I couldn't see any way to estimate that possibility.

Paul sipped his coffee, and as we talked numbers he started to relax. The bulging veins at his temples had finally disappeared.

"You think we could finish this in ten days?" he asked.

I nodded. "However, this is the USDA—the bureaucrats. The politicians are thinking of a different approach."

"Which is—" Paul let the question linger.

For a moment, no one spoke. The quietness of the room garnered an ominous feeling to our conversation and what was coming next. Paul's eyes darted from Ted to me, and I could see fear in his face as though he already knew.

"Eradication." I said the word softly. So softly I wondered if Paul heard.

"Impossible." Paul erupted in a rage leaving no doubt he'd heard. "That would take weeks, maybe months."

Paul rose and paced the floor while he continued ranting. "At $1,000 per head, we're talking $490 million if they take down my herd. And where's it going to stop?"

Ted and I remained seated. "No telling," Ted answered. "Stan told us on the phone, while we were driving up here, that the House Ag Committee is thinking about killing all the cattle in Texas."

"That's just talk," I cautioned. "A knee-jerk reaction."

"Politicians and bureaucrats," Paul shouted. "The bane of the cattle business."

Clearly, we needed to change the tenor of the conversation. "Ted, how many cattle in Texas?"

"TCFA estimates about 35 million head," he answered.

Paul continued ranting. "At $1,000 per head, it would cost $35 billion to take down all the cattle in Texas. That's *billion* with a 'B.' How ridiculous is all this government wrangling going to get?"

The three of us looked at each other. We knew there was no answer to that question.

CHAPTER 21

Masterson and Associates Veterinary Services Inc.

Ida Mae keeps the books. And this sweet, grandmotherly, "little old lady" doesn't hesitate to remind me that we are in business to earn a profit. She watches our billable hours with the diligence of an IRS agent and, I think, appears to take a measure of delight in badgering me when she finds that we're in danger of failing to earn enough to pay the bills. When I came to work the next morning, she had the ledger out—waiting for me.

"You haven't billed a single hour in almost a week," she said. She shook her finger at me to emphasize my transgressions.

"Ida Mae, did I ever tell you your finger reminds me of someone?" I asked.

"Who's that?"

"My mother-in-law."

"Good." She smiled, a big toothy, ear-to-ear show of teeth. "I understand she's a top-notch motivator."

"Nag."

"But a good one?"

"World class." I smiled back as I thought about Katherine's nagging prowess. I honestly couldn't imagine anyone better.

"So who are you going to bill today?" When it comes to billable hours, Ida Mae has the tenacity of a pit bull.

I retreated to the coffee pot, poured myself a cup. "Let me think about it, okay?"

"Thinking doesn't pay the utility bills."

"Could we change the subject?"

"Fine." Ida Mae frowned. "The FBI called. She's coming to see you at eight thirty."

"Maybe we could figure out a way to bill Christine O'Shay." I sipped my coffee.

This time Ida Mae scowled. "That's not funny."

I watched as she made the silent retreat of a poor loser. Then I looked through the stack of pink slips from yesterday. None looked like prospects for billable hours. The threat of BSE had squelched the area's need for veterinary services. While I pondered this dilemma, my phone rang.

"It's your wife," Ida Mae called from her desk.

"Thanks." I pushed the button. "Good morning. Maggie."

"We'll be on Southwest #28, arriving at 5:05 p.m."

"Want me to pick you up?" I asked.

"No, I left my car at the airport. How about meeting us at Red Lobster for dinner?"

"Fish?"

"I guess you haven't heard. Everyone's switching from beef—according to this morning's headline in the *Dallas Morning News.*"

"It'll never happen in Amarillo."

"I don't want to talk about it." Maggie repeated the question. "Red Lobster, 5:30?"

"Traitor."

"This'll give us something to talk about."

"How's Liz?"

"Still on cloud nine."

"I've missed you."

Maggie wasn't impressed. "What about after dinner?"

"It's a date."

We signed off, leaving me with thoughts about how long it had been since I'd shared an intimate moment with my wife. A minute later Christine O'Shay walked into the room. She wore navy slacks with a white blouse and black leather jacket. Her subtle femininity projected a sexiness that overpowered all other aspects of her appearance. If she had on a bikini, she wouldn't look more exciting. My mind went blank.

"Don Norton called me," she said as she took the chair in front of my desk.

The fluid grace of her movements captured my attention. "Who?" As she leaned forward, I noticed how the collar of her blouse slid away from her neck.

"Donald Norton, the vet at Sagebrush Cattle Feeders," she said. "He may have some information about the woman who made the video."

My mind snapped back. "Paul's vet. What's he got?"

"He thinks some of the guys who work at the feedyard may have recognized her."

"Really?"

"It's a lead! I think we should drive up to Sagebrush and start interviewing."

"We?"

"You said we were in this *together.*"

"Well, yes."

"Well, I'm offering to drive."

"I'll have to be back to meet my wife and daughter for dinner at 5:30."

"Good for you. I'll make sure you're on time."

"Join us for a fish dinner?"

"I thought you were strictly beef?"

"Everyone's switching to fish."

She stopped and gave me a hard look. "I read this morning's headline in *USA Today*, but you're not serious?"

"I'm serious about you having dinner with me and my family. Maggie just happened to pick Red Lobster as the meeting place."

"I'd be delighted to meet your wife and your young opera star."

We drove to Sagebrush Cattle Feeders and found a beehive of activity. I counted at least a dozen white pickups with USDA markings. Two dozen other cars—some with Hertz, Avis, and other rental-car logos—completely filled the regular parking lot. Chris parked her black Crown Victoria, the FBI's version of an unmarked police cruiser, out on the driveway's shoulder among the other overflow vehicles. We walked almost a quarter mile to the feedlot's headquarters, only to be met by USDA security.

For a change, I was glad to be with the FBI.

The security folks called both the Lubbock regional office and the D.C. national headquarters to get bona fides for Christine O'Shay. Once certified, she vouched for me, and we both received clip-on passes to go into the premises. Getting through security took the rest of the morning.

We found Paul Edwards and Don Norton out in the pens, talking with a couple of men who wore white USDA hardhats and government ID badges. Apparently one was the quarantine team leader and the other was from the National Veterinary Services Lab—the guy responsible for testing. Each projected a commanding presence, an official persona that left no doubt about who was in charge.

Paul Edwards surprised me. He greeted me like a celebrity and, for a change, took great pains to introduce me to his guests.

"This is Dr. Masterson," he said.

"James R. Masterson?" the NVSL guy asked.

I opened my mouth to speak, but before I could get a word out, Paul interrupted, "Yes, *the* Masterson—as in Masterson test."

"A pleasure to meet you, sir."

"Yes, an honor."

The two guys in white hats shook my hand in a deferential manner. They treated me like a rock star, and I wouldn't have been surprised if they had asked for my autograph.

"Mind if I watch your testing?" I asked.

"Yes," one answered.

"No," said the other. "No, we don't mind if you watch."

Paul turned to Chris, "Why don't we leave him in the hands of the government while you and I go investigate the video camera woman?"

Paul and Chris left. Don Norton and the quarantine guy excused themselves. The NVSL testing chief and I started going from pen to pen. With each USDA team, he presented me as a luminary. Work stopped as everyone shook my hand and made ingratiating comments about my blood test. We repeated this pen after pen, perhaps fifty times. Gradually I got the picture. Testing was going to require more time than I had estimated. Much more. At my suggestion we set up an informal time-and-motion study and spent an hour watching two groups in two different pens. We did the math and came up with an estimate that it would take the government a month—maybe six weeks—to test the entire Sagebrush Cattle Feeders herd of 490,000 animals. And that was an optimistic estimate, based on driving these men hard, working sunup to sundown, seven days a week. I doubted they could do it.

Chris suddenly appeared. “We have a lead,” she said.

CHAPTER 22

Dumas, Texas

Chris and I hurried back to the parking area where we'd left her car. I looked at my watch. "It's four o'clock."

"You're to meet your wife and daughter at what time?" she asked.

"Five-thirty. We need to start back to Amarillo in about thirty minutes."

"Let's get with it."

We got into her car. She pulled a red strobe light from under her seat and placed it on the roof. Suddenly, I saw a new side to this attractive woman as we pulled out of the parking area at high speed—gravel flying, and siren wailing.

I pulled my seat belt and shoulder strap as tight as it would go while we drove the ten miles south to Dumas at speeds over 100 MPH—heading toward the Days Inn Motel. On the way Chris summarized her findings. Three workers had recognized the drawing. Of the three, a man in his late fifties, Hector Garcia, remembered the woman best partly because his wife Yolanda worked as a maid at Days Inn.

Hector said the woman first came to the Dumas area shortly after September 11, 2001, over three years ago. She came with a man, presumably her husband, and stayed at the Days Inn for several weeks. Hector and Yolanda had talked about the couple because of their strange behavior.

"What was strange?"

"The husband—boyfriend, whatever his status—got a job at Sagebrush Cattle Feeders driving a feed truck."

"What's so strange about that?"

"He wanted to feed the older animals, the ones in the cow/calf operation."

I reacted immediately because BSE is thought to attack only older cattle. "Go on," I said, holding onto the seat belt as Chris passed car after car.

"Two other things bothered Hector," she continued. "First, this guy seemed to have lots of money—too much for someone who'd taken a low-paying job driving a feedlot truck. And second, he only worked a couple of weeks."

"I'm surprised Hector and Yolanda remembered this couple. They stayed such a short time."

"But they came back."

"When?"

"The first time was about a year later."

"First time?"

"Yeah," Chris said. "Only, when they returned, the woman worked at the feedlot, and the guy hung out at the motel."

"A woman feed-truck driver?" I asked.

"Sagebrush Cattle Feeders is an equal-opportunity employer."

"What happened?"

"Same thing. She worked a couple of weeks and then left."

"Didn't anyone think this strange?"

"Yes. Yolanda did."

I thought about this for a moment. "The people at the feed yard didn't put the two together. But Yolanda knew them as a couple, a man and a woman living together at the motel."

"Yes, and she and Hector talked about it."

"Why didn't Hector say something to Paul Edwards or someone in management?"

"He did. He told the foreman who supervises the feed trucks."

"And—"

"And the woman and her boyfriend left before anyone investigated."

"But you said they came back more than once?"

"Yes. They showed up again, about ten days ago. That's when the woman took her photos."

I felt my gut wrench at the news. "They're still here?"

"Hector says they're staying at the motel." As she said the words, we slowed to pull into the motel parking lot. Chris killed the siren and the strobe. She hopped out and started toward the motel office.

I followed along to the registration desk, which was very busy. Apparently the feds, those working at Sagebrush Cattle Feeders, had taken every room. Others—walk-in customers looking for a room that night—were being directed to the nearest available accommodations, sixty miles south in Amarillo. They didn't like it, they didn't understand it, and, as we stood there, we heard one say he thought the motel was lying about not having rooms.

Chris interrupted the argument, showed her credentials, and asked to talk privately with the manager. We went into his nearby apartment and closed the door.

"We need to see Yolanda Garcia," Chris said.

"What about?" The manager reacted with apprehension. "If this is about drugs—"

"No, it has nothing to do with drugs," Chris reassured him. "We're conducting a routine investigation, and we think Yolanda may be able to help us."

Discussion continued for a few minutes and I could see his concern, his loyalty, and his attempt to protect Yolanda. Finally, with some reluctance, the manager took us to an upstairs hallway in a remote part of the motel where we found her making a bed. The manager introduced Chris, who again showed her badge.

"I met with Hector this afternoon," she said.

"I am U.S. citizen," Yolanda replied. She looked frightened and her hand shook as she reached into her pocket and brought out her citizenship card.

"Thank you," Chris said. "But this is not about immigration." She smiled, slowed her speech, and lowered her voice to a soothing, supportive timbre. "We've come to ask your help in locating some people who are staying here at the motel."

Yolanda shook her head. "I only clean. I do not know guests." A look of fear etched her face.

"Hector told me about a man and woman who have worked at the feedlot, who drove feed trucks. He says they have a room here."

Tears glistened in Yolanda's eyes, and she looked at the manager. "I only clean."

"Maybe I can help," the manager interrupted. "Do you have a name?"

"Unfortunately, I don't," Chris replied. "With some time, I can probably get the names, but I was hoping Yolanda might be able to help us."

The manager turned and conversed with Yolanda in Spanish. I understand a little of the language because of those in the cattle business some of us call "Gringo-Mexican," and could pick up a few words. However, I didn't need that ability to hear the name "Smith" used a number of times. The manager pulled out a cell phone and called the front office. In English he asked for the room of Mr. and Mrs. Yusuf Smith. His expression changed to a look of grim disappointment. Then he punched off his phone.

"Room 216, but they checked out this morning."

"Could we look at the room to be sure?" Chris asked.

"It's already been assigned to a USDA veterinarian who's working the feed yard investigation."

"Could we check your records on the Smiths? We need credit cards, where they came from, description of their car, license plates. Anything you might have that would give us a lead."

He tried. For the next hour, he and his employees did all Chris asked and more. But the bottom line was, we learned almost nothing. The Smiths paid in cash, used their cell phones rather than the motel's landlines, kept to themselves, and left no personal belongings. We got descriptions. Both looked Arabic—dark skin, black hair, black eyes. They were in their late twenties or early thirties. Both spoke a foreign language, thought to be Arabic or Farsi. And they had lots of cash. Lots!

Our time at the motel ran to an hour and a half. I kept looking at my watch, and Chris could see my anxiety. Finally, when it seemed we had pulled all the available information, we left. Again, she did the strobe, and we flew back to Amarillo at speeds in the triple-digit range. Arriving at the Red Lobster a little over an hour late, we found Maggie and Liz standing at the front counter, paying for their dinner.

I introduced Agent Christine O'Shay to my wife and daughter.

"We're late because of me," Chris said.

"No need to apologize," Maggie replied. "We're used to it."

"We've found a new lead," Chris continued, "and may have identified the people who know where the infection originated."

"Sounds important." Maggie looked Chris up and down.

"If we can find where the disease comes from, and if we can identify it before it spreads, we can contain it."

"No need to explain," Maggie said. "I understand perfectly."

I stood on the sidelines, watching and listening.

"We'll head on home and leave you two to have your dinner."

"Maggie," I said, "I'll go with you."

"You haven't had your dinner."

"That's okay."

"What about your guest?" She turned to Chris, but her look said it all.

Maggie hurried out the door and stalked toward the car.

For a moment, Liz just stood there, bewildered. "I'd better go," she said.

Immediately, I nodded. “I’ll check with you tomorrow.”

I ran to catch up with Liz. By the time we got to the car, Maggie had slid into the back. We watched as she threw the keys into the front seat. “Someone else drive.”

I looked at Liz. She shook her head, shrugged her shoulders, and went around to take the front passenger seat.

I drove.

Chapter 23

Our home in Bushland, Texas

Maggie sat on the side of the bed. "Who was that woman?"

"Like I said, she's the FBI agent who's been assigned to the case," I answered.

"And when I called and you weren't home, you were with her?"

"No."

"Where then?"

"The one night I wasn't home, I worked at the office."

"With her?"

"No, that was before the FBI sent her to work on the case."

"So you say."

"Maggie, what ever happened to trust?"

"I don't know. You tell me."

"It's still there, at least from my side."

"If its still there, why don't you show it?"

"If you give me a chance, I will."

"A chance?" Her voice rose an octave. "You had a chance to go with us to Dallas, to come late to Dallas, to return my calls from Dallas. You promised to have dinner with us tonight, to talk with your daughter, to act like you're interested. How many chances do you need?"

"Maggie, please, I can explain."

She didn't let me. "I wish you could have seen the pride the other fathers showed in their daughters and sons at the audition. Your daughter won, and you were the only parent who wasn't there." Maggie's voice broke, and she started to cry. "The *only* one."

"I know, and I'm trying to find a way to make it up to her."

"By running around with Miss Gorgeous?" Tears flowed. She reached for a box of Kleenex.

"I'm not running around." I put my arms around Maggie.

"Don't." She shrugged away my arms.

"Maggie, please."

She sniffed, wiped her eyes. "I'm tired. I'm upset. Let's talk about this in the morning."

"I think we should talk about it now," I said. I thought about advice years ago from my mother. She told me that when there's a misunderstanding, the best time to face it, to resolve it, was immediately. I tried. Maggie wouldn't let me.

"That's the trouble," she answered. "We always have to do things your way. On your schedule. When does my opinion count?"

"Okay," I said. "Tomorrow morning."

"I'd like you to sleep on the couch."

"Maggie, I love you. I want to be with you."

"See? There you go again. What I want doesn't matter."

I tried to think of how to approach her. What to say? I backed away. "Tell me what to do, and I'll do it."

She turned and went into the bathroom, sobbing. I picked up a pillow and a quilt and put them on the sofa in the den. Then I went into the kitchen where I found Liz standing at the counter with a plate of cookies and a glass of milk.

"Congratulations," I said. "How about a hug?"

We embraced, and we stood there, our arms locked around each other, for a long time. It was an emotional moment, a silent expression of our love in a troubled time. When we broke, I kissed her on the forehead, a traditional gesture that went back to when she was in elementary school.

"I'd like to hear about the winning performance," I said.

"It was just like all the others." She smiled. "You've heard me sing these same arias, dozens of times."

"Humor me." I gave her a tap on the nose. "Tell me the details."

"Well, they have a requirement of three selections in three different languages."

"And you chose—"

"'Chi il bel sogno,' from *La Bohéme*."

"Puccini, Italian," I said.

"'In dieser feierlichen Stunde,' from *Der Rosenkavalier*."

"Richard Strauss, German."

"'Ain't it a Pretty Night,' from *Susannah*."

"Carlisle Floyd, English."

Liz smiled, "My dad, the veterinarian opera buff."

"No, just a father who's so proud of his kid that his buttons are popping." I held out my arms and we engaged in another embrace. She squeezed me tighter than before.

"What about you and Mom?" she asked.

"Let's give it some time," I answered.

"I hope I'm not the cause of this."

"Absolutely not."

"Can I help? Act as peacemaker?"

"Kiddo, I think the way you could help most is to stay neutral. Stay out of it. Let your mother and me work this out."

"What about the woman you brought to the restaurant tonight?"

"What about her?"

"She certainly is pretty."

"So?"

"So, is there anything between you?"

"Yes. We work together."

"Dad. You know what I mean." She looked down at her shoes.

"Elizabeth Jane, I want you to look at me."

She did. And I held both her hands I looked squarely at her.

"As God is my witness, there is nothing more than a professional, working relationship between Christine O'Shay and me. We are working together on the mad cow outbreak. That's it. Period."

"Sorry, I had to ask." She held out her arms and hugged me again.

"What do I need to do to win your trust?" I asked.

She released me. "Nothing. And I apologize for asking."

"No need to apologize."

"In my defense, you have to admit she's drop-dead gorgeous."

"Liz, how about a word of advice from your old man?"

"I'd love it."

"Beauty's only on the surface. It's what's inside that's important."

"So, how do you rate Agent O'Shay?"
"On a scale of 10, she's a 5 or 6."
"And Mom?"
"A 10 plus, at least."

CHAPTER 24

At home in Bushland, Texas

In the middle of the night, someone woke me.

"I'd like you to come to bed with me," a voice whispered.

"Do I know you?" I smiled, egging her on.

"I can't sleep," Maggie said. "With you out here and me tossing and turning in there by myself."

She leaned over, kissed me on the lips, and pulled the quilt away. "You coming?"

I followed her into the bedroom, still fully clothed. The alarm clock with red numerals showed 1:05 a.m.

Maggie wadded up the quilt and threw it in the corner. She came to me, put her arms around my neck, and kissed me with great passion. "I missed you so much, thinking about how silly it was to be mad at you." She pressed herself against me.

I held her even closer.

She started unbuttoning my shirt. "Maybe I can make it up to you."

"I'll try to be agreeable, ma'am."

"Agreeable?"

"A little more than agreeable."

Together we pulled off my clothes and I fell into bed with her. We made warm and satisfying love—a sense of reunion. Then, with our arms around each other we talked late into the night.

The next morning, we made love again, and it was wonderful. "Making up after an argument is the best sex there is," I said.

She smiled, but I sensed she didn't quite agree.

"Almost makes me want to have another falling out."

She punched me in the stomach—hard. "Not me," she sniffed. Then, while I struggled to get my wind, she stomped off to the bathroom. I soon heard the shower.

Maggie fixed a big breakfast. Liz joined us.

"Dad, I want to have a dinner next week for local friends and teachers," Liz said. "A thank you for Amarillo people who helped me make it to the Met."

"I remember," I said. "Sounds great,"

"You pick the night," Liz said. "I want you there." She smiled at the implications. We both knew this was required attendance for me.

"Any night," I responded. "I wouldn't think of missing it."

"Tuesday night at the Amarillo Country Club?" Liz looked first at her mother then at me. We both nodded.

I ended up leaving the house an hour late. When I got to work, Ida Mae and Fred were in my office watching TV.

"It's hit the fan," Fred said.

"NVSL made their announcement?" I asked.

"Not exactly," Ida Mae responded. "It's a mess. I'll let Fred tell you." She went back to her desk to answer the phone.

I looked at the screen to see a CNN Special Report in progress. The divided screen showed Congressman Stanley Young in Washington and an NVSL spokeswoman in Ames, Iowa.

"What's happening?" I asked.

"Late last night a lab technician in Ames leaked the news," Fred said. "About thirty minutes ago, ten o'clock eastern time, the House Agriculture Committee confirmed it."

"They're saying we have BSE in Texas."

"Six confirmed cases in Sagebrush."

"What else?"

"They have live shots of the testing in progress at Paul's feed-yard."

"We expected that."

"The Chicago Board of Trade has suspended cattle trading until further notice."

"Good for them."

"Japan and several other countries have banned beef imports from the U.S."

"Fred, we knew all of this was going to happen," I said. "What's new?"

"Interviews."

"Interviews with whom?"

"Everybody," Fred retorted, irritation coloring his voice. "Government officials, people on the street, old, young—you name it. A TV camera crew talks to them."

"Specifics. Name some people they've interviewed," I said.

"Well . . . the beef packers . . . Swift, Excel, Tyson, and some others I've never heard of."

"What did they say?"

"Slaughter facilities in Texas are closed for now," Fred answered. "In other parts of the country, it seems to be business as usual."

As we talked, the screen changed to a group of congressmen assembled on the capitol steps. A title at the bottom of the screen identified them as members of the House Agriculture Committee. Fred and I stopped our conversation to listen.

As chairman and a representative from Texas, Congressman Young took the lead. His comments were cautiously supportive. Two others took a neutral, "let's wait and see" position. Then a firebrand from Virginia, a congressman known for his support of tobacco farmers, gave a "kill every cow in Texas" speech. This was followed by two others who favored eradication, "Like we did for hoof and mouth disease."

The reporter closed his interview saying, "It's too early to summarize government thinking." He concluded the report with a statement that the committee would meet formally on Thursday—two days away.

Next came a commercial.

I had my hand on the remote "mute" button when the opening caught my eye. It showed actor James Garner wearing a white Stetson, cooking a steak on an outdoor barbeque grill. "Beef, it's what's for dinner" in big letters flashed across the top of the screen. Then with an exaggerated Texas drawl, Garner extolled the safety record of the American beef industry. The thirty-second ad closed with guitars and a full-screen overlay, "Beef is safe."

The phone rang. Ida Mae said, "It's your FBI girlfriend." I winced and started to caution my secretary about the need to be careful about how we referred to Christine O'Shay. Instead, I said "Okay," and pushed the button.

"Where are you?" I asked.

"Sagebrush Cattle Feeders," Chris answered. "You okay?"

"Fine."

"How're things at home?"

"Fine."

"Anything I can do?"

"Not a thing."

Chris seemed nervous, confused, like she wanted to say more but didn't know how to phrase it.

"Any leads on the man and wife at Days Inn?" I asked.

"The FBI has a sketch artist who's working with people who remember seeing them. We'll have drawings by the end of the day."

"Where do we go from here?"

"These two came from somewhere. We'll use both drawings to start checking with airline and car-rental employees."

"Want me to help?"

"I have some good news," she said, avoiding my question. "The bureau has assigned three more agents to the case."

"A response to CNN?" I asked.

"We're like every other government agency. The more squeaking we hear, the more grease we throw at it."

"You ain't heard nothin' yet. This is just the first wave of the story."

"What do you predict?"

"Big. Very big. This'll be the lead story on all the evening news programs and front-page headlines in every major newspaper for the next week. Maybe longer."

"Really?"

"If you doubt me, look at Great Britain in 1986."

"I'll pass it on."

"How many agents on the case?"

"As of this morning, four."

"When you pass it on, I have a suggestion."

"Okay."

"Tell your boss you need thirty."

"I don't think we can shake loose that many."

"Chris, if they decide to take down 35 million cattle in Texas, you'll need 3,000 agents."

"No way. We didn't have that many working the World Trade Center at the peak of the investigation."

"Trust me," I said. "You'll need them."

Chapter 25

Masterson and Associates Veterinary Services Inc.

Throughout the day, the media frenzy built momentum as BSE news dominated television and radio. Local reporters, from both print and broadcast media, kept a steady vigil at our front door. CNN sent a team of reporters and technicians from Atlanta.

Ida Mae did a commendable job of controlling the reception area. When she wanted, she could turn on her drill-sergeant personality and order people around with a commanding presence. However, when Rolf Brewster, the popular CNN news commentator, walked up to her desk, she wavered and came back to see me.

"Do you want to speak with him?" she asked.

"Not really," I replied.

"He's nice, and he's come all the way from Atlanta to talk with you."

"Ida Mae, he's just like all the others. He wants to sensationalize BSE and make it sound like it's dangerous to eat American beef."

"Is it?"

"Of course not."

"Maybe it would help if you told him."

"He doesn't want to hear it," I said. "A safe hamburger is dull and boring. A dangerous one is exciting. He's trying to build this story."

"Whatever. He's standing out there at my desk."

Her concern caused me to think strategy for a moment. From the time we first tested blood samples six days ago, I knew this was coming. I should've planned for it, and I kicked myself for not having developed an organized response.

"How many people are out there?" I asked.

"Dozens. I can't count them all," Ida Mae answered.

"Let's set up a press conference." I looked at my watch and saw that it was almost noon. "Tell everyone we'll hold it on the front steps at one o'clock."

"What about Rolf Brewster?"

"Tell him first," I said. "Then go outside and tell all the rest."

She shook her head, obviously disappointed.

"Ida Mae, treat him carefully, like the celebrity he is."

She puffed up, offended. "Why would I treat him otherwise?"

"You and I both know you can be tough," I reminded her.

"But he's so nice."

"So you turn on the charm. Tell him I'm working hard to get ready for the press conference, and that you're trying to help your boss."

She didn't like it. She heaved a sigh of exasperation and left the room.

I went back to find Fred at the microscopes, cleaning the lenses. The lab looked spotless, ready for an inspection. “In less than an hour we’re having a press conference, and I need your help,” I said.

“Sure. What can I do?”

“Three things. First, go outside and count the number of people. Next, go to McDonald’s and get hamburgers for everyone, including Ida Mae, you, and me. Then, be back here by one o’clock, ready to pass them out.”

“You’re going to give everyone at the press conference a hamburger?” Fred asked.

“Yep. And I want you to stand with me on the steps and eat yours in front of the TV cameras.”

“Jim Bob, that sounds silly.”

“I know. But so is this whole thing about beef being dangerous. Somehow, we have to convince the American public that their hamburger meat is safe.” I gave him a $100 bill.

He left.

I sat at my desk and sketched out the points I wanted to make, then added a list of the questions I thought most likely to be asked, along with possible answers. Time flew.

Ida Mae came to the door. “Fred’s here with your order from McDonald’s.”

“I have a favor to ask,” I said.

“Fred said you want me to stand on the steps and eat a hamburger.”

“Would you, please?”

“I’m on a diet,” she said. “I’m not supposed to eat fast food.”

“For Rolf, would you make an exception? One small burger?”

“No,” she said, setting her jaw.

Ida Mae can be stubborn, and over the years I'd occasionally seen her dig in with a refusal. But just as I was ready to excuse her, she laughed.

"For you, I'll eat two," she said with a big smile.

Hook, line, and sinker. I smiled back, realizing she had fed me a line and I had swallowed it. "One's plenty." I grabbed my notes and, arm in arm, we walked out to the front steps to face the mob of television cameras, microphones, and reporters.

Fred passed out hamburgers. Then he came up on the steps and stood with Ida Mae and me. Together we made a show of enjoying our food. Not everyone ate but enough did to make it a party-like atmosphere. When reporters tried to ask me questions, I held up my sandwich, continued to chew my food, and mumbled, "In a minute."

It doesn't take long to eat a small hamburger, after which I took a napkin, wiped my face and signaled for quiet. Fred—bless him—had brought a big black plastic garbage bag and circled through the crowd for trash.

I made my points. Yes, we had found six cases of BSE. No, we didn't know where it came from. Yes, the disease was deadly, but in my opinion, not a significant danger to the American food supply. USDA safeguards would protect American beef. We had learned from the British. Personally, my family and I would continue to eat steak, hamburgers, and all the other beef dishes we loved.

Then came the questions.

They hammered me for thirty minutes. I'd anticipated most of what they asked, but one reporter, Brewster, threw me a curve.

"What do you think about the special guest Orchid's scheduled for today? Brewster asked.

"I don't know," I replied. "Who's the guest?"

“The nation’s mad cow expert.”

I laughed. “You might want to check his credentials.”

“He says mad cow will make AIDS look like the common cold.”

“Let me offer some facts.”

“Go ahead.” He held his mike in my face.

“From 1986 through 2003, during the worst outbreak of BSE in history, when 35 million cattle in Britain were slaughtered, do you know how many humans were diagnosed with the disease?”

“No.”

“One hundred and thirty,” I said. “Worldwide.”

“Says who?” he asked.

“The EEC, the British Government, and the United Nations World Health Organization, to name a few.”

“One hundred thirty had the disease. How many died?”

“Let me ask you about the acquired immune deficiency. During the same eighteen years, how many died of AIDS?”

“Millions?”

“No one knows for sure, but the National Institutes of Health, the NIH, estimates 18.4 million.”

“You didn’t answer my question,” Brewster continued.

“One hundred and thirty,” I said.

“So the disease is always fatal?”

I called a halt. These people didn’t want to hear BSE characterized as a minor threat. They wanted a story. A big, scary story. With the hamburger party, my presentation, and the question session, I had stood on the steps for almost an hour. I felt exhausted. So I smiled, waved, and went back to my desk where Ida Mae waited with a stack of pink phone-message slips.

Fred came in.

“Thanks for getting the hamburgers,” I said.

“Here’s your change.” He laid a small stack of bills on my desk. “I don’t think it did any good. They had their minds made up.”

“Did anyone refuse to eat a burger because they thought it would give them BSE?”

“No. People don’t connect the disease to something common like a McDonald’s hamburger.”

“But they will,” I said.

“Maybe.” He shrugged his shoulders, like he thought the idea far-fetched.

“And when that happens—we’re in bigger trouble.”

Chapter 26

Masterson and Associates Veterinary Services Inc.

At four o'clock we put a "closed" sign on the door. Then Ida Mae, Fred, and I gathered around the TV in my office to watch the Orchid show. Not my favorite thing, but this day a required activity.

After the opening Orchid introduced her first guest, the guy who started all the controversy, At first everything stayed light-hearted. They joked about the 1996 trial in Amarillo, about going into cattle country and winning the infamous lawsuit brought by Texas cattlemen. Orchid was generous, even somewhat magnanimous about her victory. He was not. I thought him egotistical and self-serving, and when Orchid asked him about his credentials as "the world's most highly acclaimed expert on mad cow disease," his exaggerated, self-absorbed answer was, at best, an amalgamated misrepresentation, and at the low end of the scale, a collection of bold-faced lies.

At least he didn't repeat his "BSE will make AIDS seem like the common cold" statement.

And Orchid didn't reiterate her "I've eaten my last hamburger" comment.

The 1996 lawsuit apparently had made them cautious.

On the other hand, their conversation about beef left no doubt about where they stood. And since the U.S. government now confirmed the six cases of BSE in Texas, "the expert" used that as proof he was right to have sounded the alarm in 1996. Beef was dangerous. Beef could kill.

Watching their attack made me sick. Nauseated.

"I'm going home," I said. "Would someone lock up?"

Fred said he would.

Surprisingly I found only three vehicles when I walked out to the parking lot—Fred's, Ida Mae's, and mine. The media had packed up and left. I climbed in my Suburban and headed west on I-40. On the way I called Ted Austin at the TCFA office.

"You watch Orchid?" I asked.

"No, but the staff did," he answered. "I couldn't stomach it."

"I'm five minutes away. You have time for a cup?"

"I'll make time."

We signed off, and when I walked into Ted's office, he had strong black coffee waiting for me along with a bottle of Jack Daniels.

"We've just spent all our money," he said.

"How much?" I asked.

"Three million. Every penny that TCFA has saved since we

were chartered in 1967."

"How do you spend that kind of money so quickly?"

"A Madison Avenue advertising agency." He sipped his coffee. "Those guys have a direct pipeline to the media."

"I thought it took a certain amount of time to prepare the ads."

Ted smiled. "When you and I had breakfast at IHOP last week, I could see this coming, so I called and told them to get ready."

"Ted, you sneaky sonovabitch."

"They've been working around the clock. Madison Avenue follows the money. They can smell it."

"So, what'd you get?"

"Twenty-five of the largest newspapers in the country—full-page ads in tomorrow's editions. Thirty-second spots on the evening news of the three major networks, plus some comparable spots on Fox and CNN. Hourly radio spots on network news for a week."

"Ted, I'm impressed."

"I would hope so. We're broke."

"You have help from others?"

"Some. But the NBA, the National Beef Association, sees this as a Texas problem. They're only spending $500,000."

"It helps."

He shook his head, and his whole persona radiated disagreement. "Jim Bob, we're fighting for our life."

"I know."

His body language escalated to hostility and his voice rose in frustration. "I'm not sure you do," he said. "Where do you think that $3 million came from?"

"From your members, obviously."

"From Paul Edwards and others like him."

"They'll continue to support you," I assured him.

"Let's look at Paul," Ted answered, shaking his head. "He's quarantined. Can't sell. It's costing him $250,000 a day to feed worthless cattle."

"Paul has deep pockets. He'll survive."

"We've all heard that he's a billionaire."

I nodded. "That's common knowledge."

"Let's say that half of that is invested in property—his feed yards, the buildings, the pens, trucks, equipment."

"And?"

"And if the cattle feeding business goes belly up, so does the money he has invested."

"So you're saying he's only a half-billionaire?"

"His herd is reported to be 490,000 animals."

I nodded and wondered where he was going with this.

"Probably would have averaged a thousand dollars a head last week," Ted continued, his face growing more grim with each point.

"That's $490 million, almost a half billion."

"Which leaves his net worth at $10 million."

"Hey, I could live comfortably on ten mil."

"But we figured he's spending $250,000 a day to feed his herd, right?"

I thought for a moment before answering. "In forty days he'll be broke?"

"You got it." With those three words, Ted drained his cup, a gesture of finality—end of the story.

"Wow, from billionaire to bankruptcy in just a little over a month."

"And that's the biggest and the best of the cattle feeders," Ted reminded me. He named a dozen names. Names I recognized. Cattlemen I did business with. "The little guys aren't going to last that long."

For the first time, the reality of our local situation hit me. If my customers—the area feed yards that hired me on a consulting basis—went broke, then I would have no income. I thought about my five-year-old veterinary facility. It was state-of-the-art and the pride of my professional career—but it carried a big mortgage. How long would it be before I had to apply for bankruptcy? Not long. Probably not much longer than Paul Edwards.

And my home? My prize herd of two dozen purebred Black Angus?

"This is crazy," I said. "These herds are disease free, safe to eat."

"You know it—I know it," Ted said. "Orchid and the American public don't."

As I sat there in Ted's office, sipping coffee, pondering the panic, the reality that we were pawns in a seemingly hopeless situation crept over me like a chill. I felt it ripple down my upper torso, and I physically shook.

"I can see two things that we need to work on," I said.

"Ears," Ted replied.

"We need to get the government involved."

"Quickly."

"And we've got to find out where Paul's cases came from."

Ted nodded.

Chapter 27

At home in Bushland, Texas

Maggie's a great cook. And that night, when I walked into the house, the aroma of her dinner preparations made me want to forget all my troubles. She served a magnificent meal of rump roast with carrots, potatoes, onions, and brown gravy. With homemade bread, butter, and honey, it was to kill for.

I opened a bottle of expensive merlot that we'd been saving, and we drank a toast to the future. Liz was pumped. Her prospects couldn't be better. Maggie gushed and talked about how much she looked forward to next month's trip to New York. I did my best to put on a happy face—not a word about the impending crises in the cattle business and how it might affect our family.

Liz added sparkle to our dinner conversation. She bubbled as she related her plans for next Tuesday's dinner at the country club. The guest list included three of her favorite teachers, a couple of fellow students who had been her best friends, our neighbors the Austins, the minister and his wife—a total of twelve.

We ended our meal with hot apple pie and ice cream. I felt stuffed. And I welcomed the end of a day when I could sit around the kitchen table and listen to the exchange of details about my family's lives, a personal time in the refuge of our home over a truly wonderful meal. The magic was broken when the phone rang.

I excused myself to answer it in another room.

The blonde at Channel 2 wanted to interview me again. I told her I didn't have any new information and would get back to her as soon as there was something to report. She didn't like my answer. I promised to call her at daybreak.

The phone rang again. Ray Underwood, the Area Veterinary Inspector, asked me to meet him at his office at eight-thirty a.m. I agreed. He wanted to talk with me about his plan to search for the source of the infection.

Then Congressman Young called and asked me to fly to Washington to testify before the House Agriculture Committee. I said no. Instead, I agreed to set up a video conference at Amarillo's Texas A&M Veterinary Lab to try and answer the committee's questions.

The calls kept coming. Chris O'Shay asked to meet at my office at noon. She wanted my help in making plans to bring in more FBI agents.

Ted Austin called with the latest developments at the TCFA. The association planned to hold an emergency meeting of their members on Saturday morning at the Amarillo Civic Center Auditorium, and he wanted me to speak. I said no. Too many cattlemen remembered my oft-quoted words about BSE—*you get it you will die*. Ted understood my reluctance.

I looked at my watch, surprised to find it was almost eleven o'clock. I unplugged the phone and headed for bed where I found Maggie, already asleep. Trying not to wake her, I slipped under the covers and attempted to relax. For the next hour or so, thoughts raced through my mind about beef, about disease, about what I could do.

The next morning I woke to the aroma of hot biscuits. I slipped on a robe and followed my nose into the kitchen to find Maggie with a potholder pulling the hot bread from its baking pan onto a serving platter. I sneaked up behind her to place my hands on her breasts and kiss her on the back of her neck. "I only married you because you're such a great cook." The biscuits looked and smelled wonderful.

"I thought you were going to sleep away the morning," she said, as she continued to transfer biscuits.

I glanced at the kitchen clock, amazed to see that it was already half-past seven. "Damn, I'm supposed to be at Ray Underwood's lab at 8:30."

I ran back to the bedroom, hurried through my morning ablutions, dressed, grabbed a handful of Maggie's biscuits, and drove five MPH over the speed limit, trying to make it on time to my meeting with Ray. I arrived at the A&M Lab only a few minutes late.

"Sorry," I said.

"You're fine," Ray answered. "We're all busy. I'm just glad I caught you."

"How's your investigation?"

"Before we get started, have you followed this morning's news?"

"No," I said. "Fill me in."

"Jim Bob, this is bigger than any of us thought. The media are distorting the story out of proportion."

"It feeds on itself."

"Yes, and it grows exponentially."

"So what're we going to do?" I asked.

"Fight like hell," he answered.

"I agree."

"And we've got to zero in on the source. I've been studying BSE epidemics, especially those of the last quarter century. In England, Ireland, Canada, Mongolia, and several countries in central Africa, the source was an infected animal—one imported from another country."

"That's what cattle feeders do," I replied. "We import young cattle to feed them—fatten 'em up for market."

"Jim Bob, in case you've forgotten, I know a little bit about the cattle feeding business."

"Sorry. I know you do."

"But you're right. Most of the animals in TCFA pens are trucked in from the area."

"It'll be a massive job to trace all these herds," I said. "Ted Austin has the numbers, but I think we're talking thirty-five million head."

"Has to be done."

I shook my head in disbelief—the gigantic task seemed impossible. "Ray, who's going to do this?"

"You, me, TCFA members, truckers, auctioneers, feed-company workers. We all have a stake in this."

"And you're going to organize this giant witch hunt?"

"Let's not call it a *witch* hunt."

"*Parent* hunt?"

Ray smiled weakly. "And, yes, the government is going to organize it," he said. "But we're asking you and everyone else to help us."

"Okay, I have a suggestion."

"Let's hear it."

"Start with the six infected cows at Sagebrush," I said. "Trace them to see where they came from."

"We have a team en route as we speak."

"To Paul's feed yard?"

"Yes. And we're setting up a field office to trace all 490,000 head. We're not leaving Sagebrush Cattle Feeders until we find out where every single animal came from."

"Wow." Ray's information stunned me. I had always thought of this gray-haired, soft-spoken government technocrat as a person who reacted—a scientist who waited for a problem to come to him. Now, he was leading the charge. I tried to tell him how impressed I was with his actions.

And I related to him Christine O'Shay's information about the couple that had worked in Paul's feed yard and stayed at the Days Inn Motel in Dumas. "The FBI is trying to follow up any leads."

Ray thought for a few moments. "Doesn't sound very promising. In all other BSE outbreaks throughout the world, the infection passed from animal to animal. If the fibbies want to chase this couple, I'll leave them to it. Meanwhile, my guys will concentrate on possible infection from imported cattle."

"What can I do?" I asked.

"Keep doing what you're doing," he said. "And share your information. When you find anything that looks suspicious, give me a call."

"And you'll do likewise?"

"Jim Bob, it'd be silly for me to hold anything back. Right now, you know everything I know."

"Let's keep it that way."

We shook hands, and as I drove away I felt closer to Ray Underwood than at any time in our professional relationship.

CHAPTER 28

The Texas A&M Agriculture Research Extension Center, Amarillo

I drove the short distance to the A&M building where the receptionist greeted me with a smile. "Dr. Masterson, I've been trying to reach you."

"Well, here I am." I used to think it desirable to be sought after—that celebrity status would be a plus, a mark of achievement. The last ten days had turned my outlook 180 degrees. At the moment I wished for a bit of anonymity.

"Washington's trying to set up a video conference with you and the house ag committee. Could you do it now?"

"That's why I'm here."

"We're on C-SPAN this morning," she said, looking at my jeans, open-collared shirt, and boots. "All the others are wearing coat and tie."

"I'll be glad to go home and change."

She looked at her watch, thought about it for a moment, and, with an expression of disapproval, said, "No, the hearing would probably be over by the time you returned."

Still frowning, she ushered me into a large room that looked like a television studio. Three technicians scurried around moving TV cameras, microphone booms, and lights. I took a chair in the middle of all their equipment while they set a row of four monitors in front of me. An officious-looking woman introduced herself as the director and gave me an earpiece. Almost immediately I could see myself on the first monitor. Seconds later, monitor number two showed images from the hearing in Washington, and Congressman Young's voice boomed into my ear.

"Jim Bob, can you hear me?"

"Yes, I can hear you fine," I answered. "How's it on your end?"

"Good." He turned, apparently scanning his room, and asked, "Everyone okay?"

On the third monitor I could now see a wide-angle view of the room and committee members nodding their heads.

"Thanks for joining us this morning on such short notice," Stan said.

"Glad to do it," I replied.

"The committee's looking at a number of options, and we'd like your advice about how we can best go about this."

"I'm here to offer anything I can do to help."

"First—"

Before Stan could get his question out he was interrupted.

A commanding voice cut through, and I had no idea where it

was coming from. "We're sure you agree that the nation's food supply must be protected, that *safe food* must be the committee's first priority. We'd like your assurance that you're not going to allow selfish, parochial interests to color your testimony."

I looked at the monitors. In the wide-angle shot, I could see a congressman in the second row talking and gesturing. Then the fourth monitor gave me a solo shot of him, and during his last few words, his phrase about "selfish, parochial interests," I could see a close-up of his face and read his nametag. "Congressman John Zahrenski, Virginia." I recognized him as one of the leaders in the tobacco lobby.

"Congressman Zahrenski," I answered, "I assure you that you have my complete support, and that I, too, agree the nation's food supply must be protected."

"Good," he replied. "We're mighty pleased to hear that you're not favoring Texas cattlemen at the expense of the interests of all Americans."

Then I said fourteen words that would make front-page news in every newspaper in the country. Words that would haunt me. At the time I said them, I knew it was poor strategy, but the temptation was too great. I couldn't resist. So I said, "Just as you wouldn't allow selfish parochial interests to favor tobacco farmers in Virginia."

An explosion erupted. My earpiece overloaded with static, and I had to remove it. I watched as Stan pounded his gavel. In the wide-angle monitor I could see many committee members laughing. The camera on congressman Zahrenski showed an angry, red-faced opponent. And I began to realize an important lesson in national politics—it's one thing to disagree, but something completely different to embarrass your rival on national television, even if it was only C-SPAN.

When I saw Stan stop hammering his gavel, I put my earpiece back in. Another congressman, VanderCook, from Michigan, was defending Zahrenski and berating me. I listened.

"We must end these cheap shots," the congressman said. "It's imperative that we quit bickering and concentrate on protecting the food supply. Obviously, anyone from Texas cannot have an unbiased point of view. I suggest we move on."

I watched as other committee members stumped for eradication. Twice, Stan referred to me as an "expert" and urged the committee to hear my testimony. A third time he referred to me as a witness from the scene. Every time he was shouted down.

My reckless comment about Zahrenski's actions supporting tobacco farmers had hit too close to home. I had "skunked" any chance I might have had to influence this committee. After an hour of sitting and watching, I pulled off my earpiece and left. It seemed to me that it would be only a matter of time until a public outcry became a governmental edict to eradicate Texas cattle.

Chapter 29

Masterson and Associates Veterinary Services

The BSE story grew. Day by day it built its domination of the news. Tuesday we had the NVSL leak. Wednesday, Orchid and her "expert" inflamed the buzz. Thursday, government reaction gave the national media another opportunity to expand the story. Friday morning, as I scanned the front page of the *Amarillo Globe-News*, I counted six different articles about mad cow disease—all relentlessly pessimistic.

I read every word of every story and tried to think of ways for the cattle industry to rebut the avalanche. My mind refused to function—as though my brain had turned off its creative-thinking switch—and declined to meet the challenge.

Out of desperation I went to the public library and spent the rest of the morning reading national newspapers, searching for some new, fresh approach to our problem. With painstaking thoroughness I went through the *New York Times,* the *Washington Post,* and *USA Today.* All had made "Texas Beef" their feature story. The landslide of negative information added to my feeling of helplessness. I felt caught in a mass of hysteria over which I had no control.

I looked at my watch to see it was almost time to meet Chris O'Shay for lunch. She'd picked a restaurant called The Lettuce Works. I had to look up the address in the phone book.

It never occurred to me that restaurants might have gender identification, but the minute I walked in the door I sensed this one had a feminine bias. Looking around the small dining room, all I saw were women. I joined Chris at a table in the corner.

"I think I'm the only male in this restaurant," I said.

"Speak in a falsetto voice and no one will notice," she answered.

A moment later, when the waitress brought glasses of water and menus, I pushed my voice, an octave higher and said, "Thank you."

The waitress looked at me askance. "You okay?" she asked.

Chris kicked me under the table.

"Ouch," I said, my voice slipping to its normal bass range.

The waitress rolled her eyes, but pulled out her pad and pencil to take our order.

Chris ordered a mesquite-grilled salmon salad. I looked for a hamburger or something hearty, preferably with beef. The nearest I could find was vegetable-beef soup. I took it.

"How're things at home?" Chris asked.

"Couldn't be better," I said.

"Sorry about the scene at Red Lobster."

"Not your fault."

"I promised you we wouldn't be late."

"Chris, we both know it was imperative to follow our leads," I said. "The fact that we were late was as much my fault as yours."

"Am I still regarded as *that* woman?" When she said the last two words, she smiled. She looked gorgeous.

"Things are fine." I tried to change the subject. "How're you coming with the couple at the motel?"

"Big mystery. Three times they came to Dumas without leaving a trace."

"Professionals?"

"Definitely. They went to great lengths to make sure nothing could be traced."

"You remember some of the people at the motel thought they might be Arabic? Could they be Islamic terrorists trying to attack our food supply?"

"My first thought."

"But?"

"But one very important fact rules it out."

"What?"

"Al Qaeda and other Islamic terrorist groups do not include women."

The waitress brought Chris' salad and my soup.

I stuck a spoon in my vegetable-beef and paused to think about Chris' comment. "Seems strange that these two keep coming to Dumas and messing around the only feed yard in Texas with documented BSE."

"Have you talked with Ray Underwood?" she asked.

"Yes, this morning."

"Ray's done impressive research on all worldwide BSE outbreaks of the last quarter century."

I took a big spoonful of soup and burned my tongue. Quickly, I swigged a mouthful of ice water. "He told me each one involved an infected animal imported from another country."

"Pretty hard to bring an animal to the motel or to sneak it into Sagebrush Cattle Feeders."

"But there are other ways," I said.

"Such as?" she asked.

"They could bring infected animal remains—blood or bone meal—and mix it into the feed."

"Jim Bob, that's a reach."

"But possible."

"What about the fact that one of the two suspects is female?" she asked.

"Maybe this is a more progressive branch of al Qaeda?" I meant it as a serious question. It came out as flippant. Somehow, when we talked about male-female things, it always came out wrong, even suggestive.

"You just don't give up, do you?"

"This infection had to come from somewhere."

"I think I'm with Ray Underwood," she said. "We need to trace where the animals came from."

I quit eating. "So, you're giving up on the couple?"

"We're not giving up," she answered, her tone shifting to a defensive voice. "I'm only supporting Ray's theory and giving it top priority."

"I think you're making a mistake."

"Hey, we're covering *all* the bases." Again she smiled the smile that reminded me I was sitting at a table with the most beautiful woman in the room. Not a come-on, but yet, somehow flirtatious.

"How many agents do you have working on this?" I asked.

"That's the good news. We now have a total of twenty-five."

"Where do these new people come from?"

"Mostly nearby regions—Dallas, Oklahoma City, Wichita, Albuquerque. A couple from the national headquarters in D.C."

"Did you ever circulate the drawings at the car rentals and airlines in nearby cities?"

Chris thought about it for a moment. "No, but that's not a bad idea." She pulled out her Blackberry and made a note.

"Anything I can do to help?"

"Not at the moment," she said. "And it looks like you were right about this being a big story."

"For what it's worth," I said, "it's going to get bigger."

"How's that possible?"

"One-third of all the beef in America comes from this area, from within a radius of 150 miles of Amarillo."

"Impressive." The way she said the word, without feeling, made me think she couldn't care less where the meat in her hamburger came from.

"More than that, the implications are disruptive for the country's food supply."

"I guess I don't follow," she said as she stifled a yawn.

"Did you know the beef packing plants in this area have shut down?" I asked.

"I can read," she replied in a huff.

"And our grocery stores and restaurants are now trucking in beef from other areas of the country."

"I hadn't thought about it, but they have to get their supplies from somewhere."

"What's happening to beef prices?"

"I guess they're going up."

"Through the roof," I said, an edge in my voice.

"Temporarily," she responded.

"Let's play a game of *what if.*"

"I hate games like that."

I hated them, too, but it didn't stop me from going after my point. "What if next week the price of hamburgers double?"

"People will eat fewer burgers."

"And—"

"I don't know. You tell me."

"McDonald's, Burger King, and Wendy's will start laying off employees. The price of pork and chicken will rise. Some restaurants, the local mom-and-pop steakhouses, will be forced to close."

"I thought we agreed this would be temporary," she countered.

"In Britain the beef panic lasted eighteen years."

CHAPTER 30

The Amarillo Civic Center Auditorium

White pickups filled the parking lot, and I walked toward the auditorium entrance with hundreds of people. At first, ten o'clock on Saturday morning had seemed like a poor time for the Texas Cattle Feeders Association to schedule a meeting, but I was wrong. It hadn't discouraged attendance.

Somewhere I'd read that the civic center seated 2,500. As the flow worked its way into the hall, I could see that it was going to be standing room only. This was a meeting called by the TCFA for their members, but once inside I rubbed shoulders with truckers, feed company workers, beef packers, auctioneers, veterinarians—people from every aspect of the cattle business. Obviously, we all felt threatened.

I mentally congratulated Ted Austin's organizational skills. He'd effectively publicized the meeting to every farm and ranch in the area. I recognized cattlemen from the Oklahoma Panhandle and from Eastern New Mexico, people I knew who'd driven in from 200 miles away.

The media had also grasped the importance of the meeting and turned out in force. Even on Saturday morning—what was normally regarded as cartoon time on the slowest news day of the week—I could see anchor personalities from all the local TV stations, as well as some nationally recognized reporters. Down front, seats were scarce, but I found one on the side, next to the wall in the third row, a perfect spot where I could look forward to the stage and look back at the crowd.

Exactly on time, the TCFA president—a rancher from Hereford—called the meeting to order. As he gave an overview of the agenda, I scrambled to write down the speakers and their topics.

Dr. Ray Underwood, Area Veterinary Inspector, quarantines.

Joe Jackson, owner, Amarillo Livestock Auction, cattle market.

Vincent Harris, President, First National Bank, cattle financing.

Richard Davis, Chief of Staff for Congressman Stanley Young, government subsidy.

Paul Edwards, Sagebrush, cattlemen reaction.

And finally, Ted Austin, Executive Director, TCFA, organizing to fight the problem.

It looked like a long agenda. Too long for this antsy crowd who'd come to hear Ted—which was the reason for the meeting.

The president introduced Ray Underwood. A few people clapped. Obviously, this audience regarded our AVI as the face of the enemy—one of the feds, the guys who were closing our cattle operations. Ray tried to paint a big picture. He stressed the need to clean up our industry, eradicate disease, and regain the trust of the world, proving that America's beef was safe. His speech lasted ten minutes. Too long. *Way* too long. Out of an estimated attendance of 2,500, I doubted that even 100 responded with any applause. I felt sorry for Ray. He should've stayed home.

Next came a short speech by the owner of the Amarillo Livestock Auction. His news was all bad. There was *no* market for TCFA beef. The ALA planned to remain closed until further notice. Nothing new. He merely confirmed what everyone already knew. No applause.

Bank President Vincent Harris tried to put a positive spin on his bad news. But the truth was, Texas cattle were worthless. You couldn't sell them, trade them, ship them, or give them away. And though he praised his wonderful customers, the hard, unpleasant reality was that anyone who had borrowed money to finance their cattle was going down. Though he didn't say it in so many words, every person in the auditorium got the message. The only hope for the cattle industry was government support. No applause.

Placing Richard Davis, chief of staff for the congressman from the Thirteenth District, on the agenda was a mistake. And the TCFA president made a bad situation worse when he introduced Daris. "Congressman Young sends his regrets. He's busy in Washington, so he has asked his right-hand man to give us a briefing on government support for BSE." No applause.

Davis tried hard to say that Stan was fighting for us, that government support for the beef industry would be forthcoming, and that our congressman should be in Washington rather than here at this meeting. It was a tough sell, and, as I looked around at those seated behind me, all I could see was a field of stony faces. When he finished his short speech and left the podium, the room was silent. News of the bubonic plague would've received a better response. Young should have come. Sending someone in his place was the worst thing he could have done.

When the president introduced the next speaker, he alluded to the hoof and mouth epidemic of the 1980s. "Those of you who were in the cattle business remember the dire predictions. Every newspaper in the country said we were all going broke. For a while, I thought they were right. But thanks to the leadership of a cattleman with a little feed yard in Sagebrush, we're still here. Let's give Paul Edwards a warm welcome."

They did.

The applause lasted a long time, probably three minutes or more. It seemed like hours. I looked around at those behind me and saw working people—men with weathered faces, a few women—all wearing work clothes and most with intense, worried expressions, yet clapping with enthusiastic, heartfelt respect. These folks liked Paul and wanted to hear what he had to say.

"Twenty years ago," Paul began the moment the room finally quieted, "I had cattle with hoof and mouth disease. The government quarantined my feed yard, and my banker told me he'd have to foreclose. Every lawyer in the panhandle advised me to take bankruptcy. This happened to all my neighbors and probably to many of you. But we survived. How? By sticking together. TCFA led the way. As a group we lobbied for government support, and we got it. Collectively, we used careful science, fought our way back, got rid of the disease, and regained our market. And we can do it again."

He paused for effect.

The audience erupted with applause, cheers, and yells. Paul knew how to work a crowd. He continued, and using the technique of an expert, he lowered his voice to a whisper. Like everyone else in the auditorium, I leaned forward to hear what he was going to say.

"We're lucky," he said, softly. "We have the best damn cattlemen's association in the country. With Ted's leadership, your board of directors and the TCFA staff have put together a plan of action to attack BSE."

As Paul spoke he grew louder. Building to a crescendo, he emphasized each phrase. "I'm behind them. I'm supporting them. I'm going to do exactly what they tell me. I hope you will, too."

Then he sat down.

The applause was magnificent. People leaped to their feet, and the room came alive with emotion. Part of it was hero worship. Part of it was a release of frustration. Part of it was group psychology. Whatever. The result endorsed the next speaker. TCFA's representative could suggest that everyone follow him over a cliff and, like a buffalo stampede, they would have leapt.

The president gave Ted Austin a brief introduction. Ted, wisely, presented short, incisive, simple instructions. He said, "Here's what I want you to do." Then he made his points:

First, stick together. In unity there is strength.

Second, lobby the government. Especially Congressman Stanley H. Young.

Third, follow the science. Do everything by the book.

Fourth, don't falsify records. Cheating destroys public confidence.

And finally, work to win media endorsement. This is a battle for public support. The media hold the key to public thinking.

With those five points, Ted closed the meeting and received a thunderous ovation, the longest and loudest of the morning. I looked at my watch to find that it was not yet eleven o'clock. We'd been there less than an hour, and my fears—that this would be a long, boring meeting, and that many would get tired and leave—now appeared groundless. I'd bet that not a single person had left.

The meeting over, I waited for people to hurry out. Instead, they milled around, visiting with each other, exchanging ideas about the future. I didn't know any of those seated near me, but they turned and introduced themselves, and asked me what I thought about BSE, about the meeting, and especially about the future.

Gradually space in the aisles cleared, and I made my way down to the stage where I stood to the side, waiting to talk with Ted. I wanted to congratulate him on a very successful meeting. So did lots of others. More than a hundred queued up to shake his hand.

I waited.

Thirty minutes passed.

Finally, when the last of his well-wishers turned to leave, I approached him with a smile.

"Congratulations," I said.

Before Ted could respond, the TCFA President intervened. He came between Ted and me and proceeded to dress me down. "You have some nerve coming to this meeting," he said, his voice gruff, his face filled with anger.

The rebuff startled me. I didn't know what to say or do.

"You started this," he continued.

Immediately, I could see where he was coming from. He remembered my ill-chosen words at the Sagebrush Feeders—my infamous "you get it you will die" comment that had been so widely quoted.

"Ted—" I started to apologize again, for the hundredth time.

The president cut me off. "You gave them the sound bite that inflamed public opinion."

"I . . . I regret—"

"You're lucky I didn't know you were here," he said, anger choking his voice. "I would've called on you for the asshole of the year award."

"What can I say?"

"Less said, the better, as far as TCFA is concerned." Red-faced and breathing hard, he stared at me, obviously expecting me to leave.

I turned to Ted with a pleading look, hoping he would intercede on my behalf. He only looked down at his shoes.

I walked outside to my Chevrolet. Alone.

CHAPTER 31

At home near Bushland

On Sunday morning I read the paper and watched the weekend talk shows. That was undoubtedly a mistake.

The *Amarillo Globe-News* gave massive coverage to Saturday's TCFA meeting at the Civic Center Auditorium. All negative.

Meet the Press featured two members of the House Agriculture Committee—Congressman John Zahrenski from Virginia and Congressman Stanley Young from Texas. The program started with an overview of the disease and ended with a discussion of government subsidy for the beef industry.

Following the show's tradition, NBC had supposedly selected two guests representing opposing points of view. Republican Young, regarded as an advocate for subsidizing the cattle industry, would debate Democrat Zahrenski, who made no secret of his antagonism. As I watched the comments fly back and forth, it became obvious that Zahrenski carried a chip on his shoulder the size of a redwood tree. I kept waiting for someone to blame me for inciting his searing criticism of beef producers. Thankfully, no one did.

The Virginia congressman followed a brilliant strategy. To my surprise he brought up his support of the tobacco growers in his state. He alluded to his responsibility as an elected representative of Virginia farmers, his obligation to support them and their livelihood, and he made it sound commendable for them to grow tobacco, just as Thomas Jefferson and other distinguished Americans had done for centuries. Before Young could use the tobacco lobby against him, Zahrenski had justified it, as well as his support for his constituents.

Then Zahrenski switched to beef and why any subsidy for cattlemen must be viewed differently. Unlike hardworking Virginia tobacco farmers who were doing a good job, Texas cattlemen were sloppy, careless cowboys who had allowed a known disease to invade the nation's food supply. And worst of all, these despicable people were now trying to mislead the public with massive advertising.

"Have you seen the ads about 'Beef, it's what's for dinner?' The ones endorsed by celebrities like James Garner?"

"Yes," admitted Young.

"The cattle industry should be telling us about safety," Zahrenski yelled. "Instead, they try to hide a deadly disease by having movie stars tell us how to barbeque a steak."

NBC's host nodded his head. Stan just sat there, at a loss for anything to say. I felt my stomach churn. The opposition was clobbering us, and I could sense public reaction slipping away from the television screen.

At the end, Zahrenski hammered three points. First, the happy-go-lucky, lackadaisical Texas cattlemen must be held accountable for their apathy—we wouldn't have this infection if cattle feeders took care of their business. Second, misleading advertising by cattle interests was proof America had a deadly problem—as one Texas veterinarian had said, "Cattle or humans, you get it you will die." And finally, the only way to protect America's beef was eradication. No matter the cost, every cow in Texas must—and he reiterated the word, *must*—be destroyed.

Young's rebuttal came across as weak, confused, and ineffective. I wondered if, had I been sitting in Stan's chair, I could have done any better. Maybe not, but the program closed with a decisive impression that, first and foremost, BSE was not something to treat lightly, and that eradication was the answer. The *only* solution.

In his closing remarks, Young tried to avert the program's dominant "kill every cow in Texas" message, by saying that he was taking the next plane to Amarillo for a fact-finding visit to Texas feed yards. In a feeble attempt to put his finger in the dike, to stop the flood of negative sentiment, he urged the country, the congress, and the ag committee to carefully consider other solutions than eradication.

I thought it pathetic—too little, too late.

That afternoon I moped around, feeling sorry for cattlemen and for myself. My best friend, Ted, had backed away from our relationship and now regarded me as the area's number one enemy. Even casual acquaintances like Paul Edwards turned and ran the other direction when I approached them. No friends, no customers, and no ideas about what to do. It seemed that my professional career had taken a nosedive into oblivion.

Maggie had her kitchen. She busied herself making bread and baking pies. The aroma filled the house and smelled wonderful.

Liz had her music. She sat at the piano and vocalized. Beautiful, crystal-clear, high notes reverberated through the house.

I brooded until the doorbell rang.

I went to the door to find Liz's accompanist.

"What's happening?" I asked.

"We're rehearsing for Tuesday evening," she replied.

Liz joined us. "I'm going to give you and everyone else a preview," she said.

"You're going to sing at the dinner?" I asked.

"Just three songs," she answered. "I thought you'd like to hear what I'm singing in New York."

"You bet."

So she and her accompanist went through arias by Puccini, Strauss, and Floyd while I, an audience of one, listened. Their rehearsal lasted about an hour. I checked the buttons on my shirt to make sure they hadn't popped.

During the last song the phone rang. Maggie answered, and a lengthy conversation ensued. She was still talking after the accompanist left. I listened and figured out the identity of the caller when I overheard Maggie use the word "Mother."

The rehearsal had helped my spirits. Maggie's news didn't.

"Mother overheard the singing," she said.

"So?"

"She wants to come to the dinner Tuesday evening to hear Liz."

"Fine."

"She's only going to stay with us one night."

"Fiiiiiiiiiiiiiiiine."

"Jim Bob, please."

"Just what I need—a little constructive criticism. Like, I haven't had enough of that lately."

Chapter 32

The International House of Pancakes, Amarillo

Monday morning I agreed to meet Christine O'Shay for breakfast. On the way into the restaurant I picked up two newspapers—the *Amarillo Globe-News* and the *Dallas Morning News*. The hostess led me to a nearby booth, and I settled in to scan the morning's news while waiting. As expected, the Texas beef panic dominated the front pages of both.

TCFA ADS BACKFIRE read the headline for the Amarillo paper. The story quoted a Gallup Poll, which reported that 90 percent of the public thought the cattle industry was trying to cover up the seriousness of the BSE threat. Again they quoted me—a noted veterinarian for whom the test was named—and my "you will die" words. The article gave extensive data confirming my statement that the disease was always fatal. Congressman John Zahrenski's photo appeared just below the headline, and his three points were listed and bulleted in bold print. His comments about eradication hit me—and I'm sure all the cattlemen in West Texas—with devastating force.

I switched to the Dallas paper with its headline about congressmen and eradication. The use of the plural caught my eye, and I read the details carefully. Zahrenski, as expected, led the way, and his comments paralleled those I'd just read in the Amarillo paper. Nothing new from the Virginia congressman. Young's position was the big surprise.

CONGRESSMEN SUPPORT ERADICATION

> In a surprising development, Texas Congressman Stanley Young joined with his colleagues on the House Agriculture Committee and stated that he, too, favored eradication to fight the dreaded disease. In an impromptu news conference at the Amarillo airport, Young stressed the need for government subsidy to help beleaguered cattlemen in his district. He announced his plan to introduce a bill that would offer a modest ten cents on the dollar reimbursement for all cattle that had to be put down.

I read it twice, the second time with a knot in my stomach. As far as I was concerned, the news could not have been worse. It bothered me so much I didn't notice when someone took the seat opposite me.

"Earth to Jim Bob. Are you there?" Chris asked.

I looked up to find her big, beautiful smile. "Sorry, I just read some startling news."

She sighed, "What is it now?"

I read the paragraph aloud, shook my head in disgust, and tossed the papers on the empty seat beside me.

"Any other *good* news this morning?" she asked.

I told her about the poll and the fact that people thought we were involved in a cover-up.

"We?" she asked. "I'm not covering up anything."

"None of us are. But if the American public thinks we are, then *we*—and that includes you and me—still have a problem."

"Maybe there's more to it," she said. "I sometimes have this feeling the cattlemen are not telling me everything."

"See?" I acknowledged. "You're part of the 90 percent."

"Not really. It's just that I have a nagging feeling we're dealing with this deadly, always-fatal disease, and there's something wrong because I'm still eating beef."

"What's wrong?"

"I don't know. What haven't you told me?"

The waitress took our orders. Toast and juice for Chris. Steak and eggs for me. Coffee for us both.

"You think I'm holding back information? On you?" I asked.

"No," she answered. "Of course not."

"In case you haven't noticed, I'm eating beef at every meal."

"I know."

"How can you think anyone is involved in a cover-up?"

"I don't know."

"What's it gonna take to convince you?"

She thought about it for a while. The waitress brought a carafe of coffee and two cups. I poured.

In silence, we sipped for a moment.

Chris spoke first. "I guess if we got rid of the disease—if all the cattle tested negative—that would make me feel safe," she said.

"A big order," I replied.

"Too big?"

"No, just too many unknowns."

"Such as?"

"How widespread *is* the infection?"

"Wouldn't testing tell us?"

I didn't answer. Instead I added what I believed to be our biggest problem, "And where the infection came from."

"Sounds like we're back to square one."

The waitress brought our food. A small, round plate for Chris' toast, a huge platter for my steak and scrambled eggs, and a small round plate with two biscuits, butter, and jelly. Chris didn't seem to notice.

"I have some good news—sort of," she said as she buttered her toast.

"I'll take it," I replied.

"We've found that Sagebrush Cattle Feeders has been importing calves from Mobile, Alabama. Records show they've bought a truck-load every spring—usually in April—from an importer in Europe."

"Oh, no."

"However, they've always been screened."

"What do you know about the tests?"

"Nothing, other than a report confirming the cattle were examined."

"Sounds like we should investigate."

"You volunteering?"

"Yes, but—"

We talked about how to check on the testing procedure. I guessed these would have been Masterson tests and would have been done by licensed veterinarians in Mobile, probably in the port facility. It should be relatively easy to find out who signed off on the testing. Chris offered to make calls to the FBI office in Mobile. Our conversation shifted to the headline stories in the morning papers.

"This is really bad news," I said.

"Jim Bob, it's not my problem," she snapped.

"In a way, it is," I countered.

"I'm in law enforcement," she said. "If cattlemen want to waste their money on advertising, they're not breaking the law."

"Just a few minutes ago you were accusing these same people of not telling you the truth about BSE."

"That was different."

"How?"

She poured us more coffee, apparently stalling. She took a few sips from her cup, definitely stalling.

I waited.

"Hell, I don't know," she said finally. "Maybe it's not any different."

"You think the cattlemen—the cattle industry, those who paid for the ads—are guilty of false advertising?"

"Maybe it's just poor judgment," she said.

"So?" I asked.

"So, it's not my problem."

"The cattlemen are going down the tube."

"How many times do I have to tell you, that's *not* my problem?"

"Part of the reason is that the American people—including

Agent Christine O'Shay—think cattlemen are lying about BSE, about the safety of American beef."

"*Not* my problem," she said for at least the fourth time.

"Do you agree that a part of the FBI's responsibility is to protect American citizens?" I asked.

"Of course," she answered.

"I'm a citizen."

She nodded.

"I'm going broke," I said. "I'm going to lose my business, my home, everything."

"Really?"

"What's the FBI going to do about it? What are *you* doing to protect me?"

CHAPTER 33

At home in Bushland, Texas

I sat in the living room, dressed in my Sunday suit, white shirt, and best red tie. My shoes were spit-polished to a mirror shine. The clock read 6:27 p.m., still plenty of time for a fifteen-minute drive to the Amarillo Country Club and our seven o'clock dinner. I waited for three women—Maggie, Liz, and my mother-in-law, Katherine Barrington Smith. While waiting, I reread the bad news in the morning paper.

The headline article, CONGRESSMAN YOUNG'S STAND CALLED A DISASTER, quoted the response of TCFA's executive director Ted Austin, several prominent area cattlemen, and a number of other local leaders in the cattle industry. Those listed in the article felt the news couldn't be worse. Stan's promise to work for a 10 percent subsidy for slaughtered cattle spelled doom for Texas ranchers and cattle feeders, and eventually for people like me. If the cattle feeders went broke, so would I. Even the best news on the page—Stan's proposal for a pathetic little governmental subsidy—was too little, too late.

On the positive side, it appeared I was no longer in first place for the area's "asshole of the year" award. The paper didn't state it in so many words, but it left no doubt that Stan had taken my place and risen to the top of everyone's A.O.T.Y list.

Maggie appeared, dressed in her finest. "How do I look?" she asked.

I put down my newspaper, stood, and circled her with a frown on my face, a posture I'd assumed many times when judging a prime heifer at the county 4-H livestock show. "People will look at you and say, 'that must be the mother of an opera star.' "

"I shouldn't have asked." Maggie gave me a playful tap in the stomach.

I looked at my watch to see that we had less than twenty minutes for the drive.

"You have Liz's corsage?" she asked.

I held up a white orchid. "Right here."

"Don't forget to mention her hair. She spent most of the afternoon at the stylist."

I nodded.

Liz waltzed in wearing a frilly, ankle-length gown. She looked stunning. I don't know anything about the coiffure of hair, but hers appeared magnificent. "Wow. Very elegant. And I love the hair." I held up the orchid and smiled.

"Oh, Daddy. You shouldn't have." She giggled like a child and stepped closer so I could pin it on.

"How's your grandmother doing?" I asked as I finished the job.

"She's in the bathroom," Liz replied.

I checked my watch again. Six forty-five. Unless we left now, we'd be late for our own party. I looked at Maggie and rolled my eyes.

Maggie gave me her *look.* In our twenty-seven years of marriage, I had learned the meaning of that special glare. In no uncertain terms, it said, "Don't say it."

I didn't, but I thought it.

As I sneaked another look at my watch, Katherine appeared—complaining, "Jim Bob, your house needs a guest bathroom."

I helped her with her coat, thinking we needed a nearby motel.

She rattled on. "How can you expect me to get ready for an important event like this when I have to share a bathroom with Liz?"

I helped Maggie and Liz with their coats.

"I can't believe you've lived out here in this cow pasture all these years in a house with only two bathrooms."

The four of us piled into Maggie's Buick LeSabre. Thankfully, that brought an end to my mother-in-law's harangue. She and Liz took the back seat. Maggie sat in front with me.

As we passed the mailbox and turned onto the blacktop, another problem arose—my cell phone rang. From the back seat, I received more advice, "Good lord, do we have to talk on the phone tonight?"

"Please," Maggie whispered. Her eye contact said it all. Nothing from work could possibly be more important than Liz's dinner. I pulled the phone from my pocket, turned it off, and in so doing noticed the call was from the FBI. Probably Chris O'Shay. I didn't give it a second thought.

"Thank you," Maggie said as she leaned over and lightly kissed me on the cheek.

"I want you to know, I don't even own a portable telephone," Katherine said. "They're an invasion into one's privacy."

I drove fast and, surprisingly, we arrived a minute before seven o'clock. Together the four of us made our way to a small, private dining room. The accompanist was there to greet us along with two of Liz's friends. They'd decorated the room with balloons, streamers, and a homemade banner that read, "Elizabeth Masterson, Amarillo's Diva." Their festive touch thrilled Liz and set the tone for the evening. I could see this was going to be a happy time for my daughter.

Gradually, the other guests arrived. Last to enter was Mary Sue Austin, Ted's wife. As expected, she came alone. Ted had called earlier to express his regrets. Under the circumstances, he thought it best to disassociate himself from my family and me. Maggie had discreetly called ahead and asked the country club to remove his place from the table.

Liz didn't seem to notice.

We seated ourselves at the table, all except Liz and her accompanist. They went over to the piano at the end of the room.

Liz explained that it was difficult to sing immediately after eating, so we listened while she sang her three arias. I couldn't have been prouder. Those gathered at the table clapped almost as long and as loudly as I. It was a wonderful moment.

The wine steward poured champagne.

We toasted Liz and her future at the Met.

Then Agent Christine O'Shay appeared at the doorway.

Maggie frowned.

"I'll just be a moment," I assured her.

Chris walked a short way down the hall, her face dark, hardened. “Stan Young’s been murdered,” she said. “Three bullets—he was found in his hotel room about an hour ago.”

Chapter 34

The Amarillo Golf and Country Club

"I know how important this dinner is for you and your family," Chris said. "But I really need you to go with me to the scene."

"Chris, I don't know anything about murder," I said. "What can I do?"

"Obviously this is related to Young's stand on beef subsidies."

"You think someone from the cattle industry killed him?"

"Could be," she said, "and if it is, it'll be someone you know. That's why you have to come with me."

"Can't this wait?" I asked.

"No. We need to go now, before any evidence is tampered with or lost."

Reluctantly, I went back to make my regrets to Maggie, to Liz, to all the others. I didn't give details, just a general statement that something had come up. Then I pulled Maggie out into the hallway for a moment.

"Stan Young's been murdered," I said, a quiver in my voice.

"Oh, no." Her eyes widened, and she shook her head, hands to her face.

"The FBI thinks it may be someone in the cattle industry who did it," I said softly, "and they want me to go to the hotel."

Shaking with emotion, a tear rolled down her cheek. She reached out with both arms to embrace me. I held her tightly.

"I'm so sorry, Maggie," I whispered in her ear.

She relaxed her grip. "I understand," she said. "You need to go."

I rode with Chris—flashing red strobe on the roof, siren wailing—to the Ambassador Hotel. In the hotel parking lot, we found a macabre scene. I counted six law-enforcement cars with flashing lights, an ambulance, and a number of vehicles representing the media, all broadcasting to the world that something terrible had happened. In the lobby a barricade manned by two uniformed policemen blocked access to the elevators.

Chris showed her FBI badge. "Where's the scene?"

"Sixth floor," one of the uniforms replied, then looked at me, a question on his face.

"He's with me," she said.

The cops stepped back to let us pass. We took the elevator to the sixth floor where we found enough law enforcement to quell a riot. Again Chris showed her credentials and vouched for me.

"Who's in charge?" she asked.

"Chief Neal," answered the uniform, pointing to the left. "He's in room 608."

As we walked down the hall, I asked, "Does the chief of police go personally to the scene of a murder?"

Chris shook her head. "Not in a city the size of Amarillo."

"Then why's he here?"

"Because this is a big case. He's worried." At the door she again flashed her badge to a uniformed officer. "I'd like to talk with the chief."

"Wait here," he said.

We watched as he stuck his head into the room and called to Chief of Police Gerald Neal, "The FBI wants to speak with you."

Neal came over, his face flushed with resentment. "We're going to handle this," he insisted. "It's our jurisdiction."

"Of course," Chris answered.

An uneasy silence followed. After a moment, Chris spoke again, "I'll leave now if you'd like," she said.

"No. No, you're welcome to stay." He paused for a moment. "I didn't know the Amarillo fibbies had a female agent."

"They don't."

"Maybe I need to see your credentials."

Chris again flipped out her badge. It identified her as Special Agent in Charge of the Lubbock FBI Regional Office.

"How'd you get here so fast?" Neal asked.

"The mad cow investigation," she replied. "I've been living in this hotel for the past ten days. We now have twenty-five agents working BSE, both here and in Dumas."

"You're in charge?"

Chris smiled. "The FBI *is* an equal-opportunity employer."

Neal returned a half-hearted smile, a guilty look. "Sorry, I didn't mean to question your position or your status."

"No offense taken." She put away her badge. "I'm used to it."

"And if you're offering, I'd welcome your help on this murder."

"That's why I'm here."

The chief looked at me. "Who's this?"

"Dr. Masterson, the area's leading vet," Chris said. "He knows everyone in the cattle business. I thought we could use his help."

Neal backed away and gestured. "Come in."

"Before we start, let's clear the air," Chris said. "You're in charge. We take orders from you. But we have to feel free to make suggestions."

"Of course."

She looked down at his shoes. "I suggest we call Lubbock and get our CSI team up here."

"Go for it."

"Be with you in a minute." She walked a short way down the hall, away from room 608, and started making calls on her cell phone. I stood by and listened as she gave orders for a helicopter to bring the FBI's regional CSI team immediately and for an Amarillo agent to meet them at Tradewind Airport.

We walked back to the entrance. "They'll be here within the hour," she said to the chief and to two additional APD officers who had now gathered around the doorway.

"Impressive," Neal said.

From her briefcase Chris pulled out two pairs of plastic booties. She handed a pair to me and said, "Pull these on over your shoes." She looked at the feet of the three APD officers. None had coverings for their footwear.

"Anyone else been walking around inside the room?" she asked.

"Everyone hear the question?" Neal asked.

The two Amarillo policemen acknowledged they had, one of them grudgingly. He was a heavy fellow wearing a tan suit, obviously insulted by the implications of not wearing booties. "Just the two of us and you," he answered.

Chris turned to Neal. "Will you take charge of the case personally?" she asked.

"No," the chief answered. "I've appointed Detective Wyatt Reed to lead our team. He heads Amarillo's homicide division."

"That's me," said the guy in the tan suit, the fellow who wore a grudge on his face and a chip on his shoulder.

"While the chief's here, should we go over our working agreement again?" Chris asked.

"Sure."

"Wyatt, you're in charge," she said. "The CSI team, all other FBI personnel, and *I* will take our orders from you."

Wyatt nodded. I thought I saw some of his scowl slip away.

"However, APD has agreed to allow us to make suggestions."

"Fair enough."

"Total, open communication," Chris said, pushing the point. "*No one holds back any details*."

"I agree. I'll be sure everyone cooperates."

"May we take a look at the body?" she asked.

Wyatt led the way and the five of us filed into the room to view the grisly, bloodstained corpse. Wyatt showed us his only clue, three spent, nine-millimeter shell casings, now enclosed in small plastic baggies. He handed them to Chris.

"Winchester Black Max," she noted. "These are new on the market."

"Only one store in Amarillo that sells them," Wyatt replied,

"Panhandle Gunslingers. I'll check with them tomorrow and see who's buying."

I thought about people from outside the area. If the Arabic man and woman—the couple who stayed at the Days Inn Motel in Dumas—became our leading suspects, they probably wouldn't have purchased their bullets in Amarillo. But no one asked me, so I didn't say anything.

Within the hour, and as predicted by Chris, the CSI team from Lubbock arrived and I witnessed a professional team do their sweep of the crime scene. The word "sweep" took on special meaning. Not only did the CSI team vacuum the room with their own cleaner, they asked the three APD officers, including Chief Neal, to remove their shoes and, using a separate machine, one of the CSI agents carefully went over every shoe with a suction nozzle. Then he emptied the debris into a small plastic bag and carefully labeled it.

As the evening wound down, the body was loaded on a gurney and wheeled from the room. Chief Neal asked us to gather around for a parting comment, again interjecting his status as the senior law-enforcement official. "Wyatt, Chris, before I go, I want to leave you with a couple of thoughts."

Chris nodded.

"Sure," Wyatt said.

"This case is as high profile as it gets. Any murder of a U.S. congressman attracts national attention. The media is already gathered outside, looking over your shoulder, waiting to pounce on your slightest mistake. I want you to give this your best effort, your total mental and physical energy. No turf battles. Just one goal—bring the person or persons responsible to justice."

"Yes, sir."

"You've got it."

"And it would be nice if you'd solve this case quickly," Neal said.

Chris arranged to meet with Wyatt the next morning, then she drove me home.

"Any clues?" I asked as we headed west on I-40 toward Bushland.

She shook her head as she drove, a worried look on her face. "The APD conducted interviews around the hotel. Nobody saw anything."

"Surely there's something."

"The hotel has no surveillance cameras. Right now we've got squat."

"You can trace the shell casings."

"But if the perps are from out of town, which is a distinct possibility, then checking with a local store is worthless."

"So you've got zero?"

"*We've* got zero. As I remember, someone keeps telling me we're in this together."

It was after midnight when I fell into bed.

CHAPTER 35

Masterson and Associates Veterinary Services

The next morning, headlines in the *Amarillo Globe-News* were the biggest and blackest I'd ever seen in a newspaper. But if I thought the news of Stanley H. Young's murder would take BSE out of the spotlight, I was wrong.

The paper jumped to the conclusion that Young's death was related to the cattle industry. Without one shred of concrete evidence, every reporter who authored a front-page article assumed some disgruntled rancher or feed yard owner had put three bullets in our congressman. Stan's tepid support for cattle problems loomed like a giant finger pointing at a cowboy vigilante.

As the morning progressed I watched television, listened to radio, scanned national newspapers. I found that the *Globe-News* was not alone. Virtually every news source—broadcast or print, local or national—made the same assumption.

So did local law enforcement. With the APD, Amarillo Police Department, leading the way, Chris and her FBI agents, and the Potter County sheriff's deputies, all zeroed in on the West Texas cattle industry as the first place to look for suspects. And they wanted me to name names, to point the finger at one of my friends or acquaintances.

Chris came to see me at my office at nine o'clock. I poured two cups of coffee while she started her interrogation, "Where were you last night from 5:30 to 7:30?" she asked.

"Am I a suspect?"

"Yes, along with everyone else in West Texas who has anything to do with cows."

"Chris, this is an insult."

"I know," she said, "but the sooner you answer the question, the sooner we can get on with our work." Her voice came at me like a laser, and I found a side to this beautiful woman I'd not seen before.

For the next few moments our eyes locked—mine belligerent, hers implacable. The silence threatened to sever our personal relationship. Then I caved.

"I got home last night about five thirty, showered, dressed, drove my family to the country club at seven. I'm not sure what time you picked me up, but I think it was about a quarter to eight."

"Your family can vouch for you?"

"Wife, daughter, and mother-in-law."

"I tried to call you at a quarter to seven," she said.

"And you should have heard my mother-in-law's reaction," I responded.

"Sounds like she'd make an airtight alibi."

"I'd like to see you or anyone else win an argument with her."

Chris smiled. "Sorry I had to ask."

"Are you gonna confront everyone like this?"

"Welcome to the real world of homicide," she said. "Would you ask Ida Mae and Fred to join us for a minute?"

"Chris!"

"It'll just take a minute."

"Leave me out of this."

She did.

Five minutes later she came back and took her seat. "They both have good alibis."

I poured her a fresh cup of hot coffee. "I'm not sure I should be a part of your murder investigation."

"You want the murderer to go free?"

"Of course not."

"Would you agree that the cattle industry will be helped when we find the person who killed Young and he, or she, is brought to justice?"

"Yes, but—"

"But, you don't want to help?"

"I don't want my friends and neighbors—my colleagues, the people I do business with—to think I'm accusing them."

"Jim Bob, you can't have it both ways."

"Why can't you leave me out of it?"

"Because I need your help. You know the people. I don't."

"Look, I'm in enough trouble already. Friends like Ted Austin and Paul Edwards will hardly speak to me."

"Tell me, what did you think of the way I left you out while I questioned Ida Mae and Fred?"

"Okay, I guess."

"Suppose I approach Ted and Paul in the same manner?"

I thought about it, sipped my coffee, and eased toward a decision.

"Okay. If you'll let me be a silent partner, if you interrogate others as you did Ida Mae and Fred, I'll do everything I can to help you."

"Thank you."

"You're welcome." I sat silently and nursed my cooling coffee while she rustled through her briefcase. "What's the next step?"

"We start with the people who have the most to lose."

Chris pulled out the membership list of the Texas Cattle Feeders Association. We spent the next two hours going over names, ranking their loss as high, middle, or low. Then we made lists of people in related fields—truckers, feed suppliers, vets, beef packers, even those less affected, such as bankers and commodity brokers.

When we finished and she prepared to leave, I felt discouraged.

"You have several thousand names," I told her. "I don't see how you can contact all these people."

"We start at the top, those with the most to lose, and work down," she said.

"You're taking agents off the BSE investigation?"

"No, we're doubling the force."

Her answer surprised me. I guess it showed.

"And besides, these two searches may be related," she added.

"How?"

"It's obvious. Both are focused on BSE."

"But not in the same way," I countered. "The motivations are separate and distinct. It has to be different people."

"What about earlier cases of BSE?" she asked. "When you've

worked epidemics in other places, I'll bet you had related murders."

"This is my first case," I said.

"Your first? How could that be?"

"We've never had a case of BSE in Texas. This is the first one."

"But you invented the test."

"Yes, in my lab—in the next room."

"You've been called the nation's leading expert in mad cow disease."

"I know the science."

She slumped back in her chair, her face a mask of disbelief. "But you've *never* participated in an actual outbreak?"

"Outbreaks have taken place in Europe, in Africa, Mongolia—always in locations a long way off," I explained. "And the disease turned rampant before anyone contacted me."

"Your first case?" She shook her head in disbelief.

"Which may explain my faux pas."

"What faux pas?"

"If I'd had experience in working epidemics, I'd never have made my little speech to the TV cameras in Sagebrush."

"You get it you will die?" she asked.

"I've learned a valuable lesson."

Chapter 36

The International House of Pancakes

Chris asked me to meet her for breakfast the next day. I arrived early, picked up copies of both the Amarillo and Dallas papers, and braced myself to read bad news. While I sat in a booth, the waitress brought a decanter of coffee, poured a cup, and I read on.

Two stories shared the headlines. NO CLUES IN CONGRESSMAN'S MURDER and MORE BSE CASES FOUND IN SAGEBRUSH. Both were featured in the *Amarillo Globe-News*. The Dallas paper printed similar headlines.

Chris joined me. We ordered. I poured her coffee.

"No clues?" I asked, quoting the papers.

"That's what we told the news media," she answered.

I leaned forward in anticipation. "You have something?"

"Maybe."

I recognized her answer for what it was—a tease. In the two short weeks I'd known this beautiful woman, I'd found her covert, seductive manner to be the one negative aspect of her personality. With a subtlety that defied masculine awareness, she used her physical attractiveness to taunt or provoke some poor guy into making a fool of himself. I'd seen her stand close, or smile, or do nothing but enter the room and look gorgeous. But she knew. Just as she now delighted in waiting for me to react to her hint about this clue. So I eased back in my seat, picked up my coffee, sipped, and waited.

We stared at one another.

I waited.

She smiled.

I sipped some more, eyes still locked and steady.

She blinked—dropped her gaze. "I have three possible clues that need investigating."

"Really?"

"First, the results of the vacuuming tells us that someone tracked in some dried mud on their shoes."

"Could it have been one of the APD guys?"

"No, their shoes were relatively clean, just dirt and dust."

"Could the mud have been residual, left from some previous occupant of the room?"

"We don't think so," Chris replied. "The hotel maid gave the room a thorough cleaning the morning before the congressman moved in. CSI examined the vacuum cleaner she used and found no mud particles. It had to be tracked in the evening Young was murdered."

"So, we have mud particles—"

"Which turned out to be high in organic matter."

Impatience caused my voice to rise, "Damn it Chris, spit it out."

"Bovine manure, plus straw, tiny bits of alfalfa, flecks of grain, and other particles found in cattle feed."

"Great. Now you've narrowed your search to someone in the cattle business."

"Hey, it's a clue—more than we had yesterday."

"You said you have three clues?"

"Second, we checked all the retail outlets that sell ammunition for a nine-millimeter handgun to see how many stock Winchester Black Max."

"And—"

"There's only one, Panhandle Gunslingers."

"Do they keep records?"

"Yup."

"And you're going to tell me that hundreds of farmers and ranchers have bought these bullets?" I asked.

"Nope," she answered.

"Thousands?"

"Three."

"Only three people in the Texas Panhandle have purchased Winchester Black Max, nine-millimeter ammo?"

"I have their names. Billy Joe Garrett works as a guard at PanTex. Terry Milligan owns a Bar-B-Q restaurant in Canyon. And Theodore Austin."

"Ted?"

"The executive director of TCFA, your friend and neighbor."

"I've known Ted for fifteen years," I said. "He'd be the *last* person I would suspect of murder. He and Stan were good friends."

"None of the three have alibis."

"Are you checking out the other two?"

"Absolutely, and I have a third clue."

"Don't keep me in suspense."

"I went back to the motel in Dumas," she said.

"You think the couple who worked at Sagebrush Feeders might be involved in Stan's murder?" I asked, placing my cup on the table.

"We're checking all possibilities."

"And?"

"The maid, Yolanda Garcia, had discovered an item that was left in the room when the couple stayed there the first time."

"Five years ago?"

"Yes. But she forgot about it until yesterday."

"So?"

"So, yesterday she took some new articles to the lost-and-found and remembered. It was still there."

"What was it?"

"A baseball cap."

The waitress brought our food—banana nut pancakes for me, an English muffin and juice for Chris.

I took big bites of my pancakes. She nibbled at her muffin. Neither of us spoke for the next several minutes. The tension at our table became almost unbearable. I desperately wanted to know what a baseball cap had to do with our BSE outbreak or with Stan's murder, or perhaps both. She knew that I wanted to know, and I could tell by her slow, deliberate actions that she was dying to tell me. Finally, after I consumed half my food, she caved.

"The cap featured a Texas A&M logo."

Her answer disappointed me. "An Aggie baseball cap?"

She nodded. "Yolanda remembers the woman wearing it around the motel while the guy went to work at the feed yard."

"Five years ago?" It didn't sound reasonable to me that a maid would recall such an insignificant detail.

"The reason Yolanda remembered was because of an argument. When the guy came back from the feed yard and found her wearing the cap, he went berserk."

"So, trouble in River City?"

"Yeah, over a baseball cap."

"And Yolanda thought it unusual?"

"Inexplicable. So much so that she described the incident to me five years later, when the cap showed up again."

"And what does the FBI make of this?" I asked.

"You're the Texas A&M graduate," Chris said. "What do you make of it?"

I shrugged. "Could be almost anything."

"You own any Aggie clothing?"

"Of course."

"And why is that?"

"If you have to ask, you're a lot less intelligent than any fibbie I've ever known."

She ignored my attempted putdown. "You have any contacts in College Station?"

The light dawned. "You want me to make a trip to campus?"

She smiled. "Take a few hundred copies of our drawing, show them around the ag school—"

"See if anyone can give you a name?"

She nodded. "The Bureau has given me a choice."

"A choice?"

“On trips like this I usually take another agent. We almost always work in pairs.”

“So?”

“For a visit to College Station, I’d rather take an Aggie. Someone who has some personal contacts on campus.”

The next morning we caught the first plane to College Station.

Chapter 37

Rio Airlines, Flying from DFW to College Station

Commercial air service into the twin towns of Bryan and College Station, never good, had grown worse with the decline of the airlines following 9/11. The only service available was provided by small propjets flown by Rio Airlines, painted bright yellow in a futile attempt by some marketing expert to jazz up the image of their puddle jumper airplanes. Students nicknamed Rio the "Big Canary."

Chris looked puzzled.

"You'll get it when you see the plane."

She did.

Chris thought it humorous until we boarded a Cessna 404—a noisy, twin-engine, turboprop with eight tiny seats—the only way to get from DFW to the university's airport, Easterwood Field. Mercifully, the flight was short.

My old Swedish buddy, Sven Ingemar met us at the little terminal building. I introduced Agent Christine O'Shay. As expected, he fell all over himself to comment on the attractiveness of my traveling companion.

Finally, in the car, he changed the subject. "I've been reading about you," he said.

"How's the weather?" I asked, in my semi-humorous attempt to steer the conversation away from me.

"Jim Bob, you're 100 percent accurate. Spongiform encephalopathy is always fatal."

"I've learned the hard way that there's a time and a place to present your facts to a television camera."

"Given a chance to do it over, you'd withhold the truth?"

I smiled at his reaction. "Sven, I think the concept is discretion."

"So, it's not what you say, but when you say it?"

"Something like that," I answered.

"Would you be interested in tickets to *the* game tomorrow afternoon?"

"Of course." I looked at Chris. She rolled her eyes. We hadn't discussed the possibility of attending an Aggie football game.

He handed me a small envelope. "Two on the fifty-yard line."

"Wow. What do I owe you for these?"

"Compliments of the dean," Sven said. "The College of Veterinary Medicine gets a dozen comps for each home game for distinguished alumni. We had a cancellation, and you lucked out."

"Give my regards to the dean."

"You can tell him yourself," Sven replied. "That's one of the appointments I've arranged for you." He handed me two copies of our contacts for the day.

I passed one to Chris. Together we scanned the typewritten page, a list of names and office numbers. He'd scheduled us on a fifteen-minute timetable to meet with professors, administrators, and campus service personnel. At the bottom of the page he suggested another twenty names of retired people, their addresses and phone numbers.

"Sven, this is terrific."

"One Aggie to another, we want to help."

"Yes, this is exactly what we were hoping for," Chris added.

"And I have a room for you at the Memorial Student Center, the MSC," he said.

"*A* room?" Chris emphasized the singular.

"Jim Bob's staying with me and my wife at our home," Sven explained. "I Hope that's okay? We have a lot of catching up to do."

Chris flashed her gorgeous smile, the one with a hidden double entendre. "Fine."

Sven dropped us at the MSC. I left my bag in his car and arranged to meet him at his office at five o'clock. Chris checked into her room. We grabbed a quick lunch at the MSC cafeteria and walked across campus to the ag building.

For the next four hours, we followed Sven's list of appointments. A routine developed and repeated itself in meeting after meeting. Most remembered me and greeted me with warm hospitality. Next, I introduced Chris. She showed her FBI credentials and produced the drawing of our suspect. The response was always the same, a shake of the head, an apology for failing memory, and an expression of regret for not being able to help. By the close of the afternoon, we had zero recognition. No leads.

We walked back to the Memorial Student Center.

"You're invited to join us for dinner at Sven's," I said.

"Thanks, but I plan to call the retirees and make appointments for tomorrow morning," she replied.

"Want me to help?"

"No. You need to go with your buddy. And thank him for his assistance."

"So far, his information hasn't helped us any."

"Not his fault," she said. "Meet you at eight a.m. at the circular drive in front of the MSC?"

I nodded. "Maybe we'll have better luck in the morning with the retired folks?"

"Or maybe our suspect didn't attend A&M?"

I didn't have a response to that.

She took the elevator.

I walked over to Sven's office. Together we drove to his house where he grilled steaks in his backyard, and we had a wonderful evening reminiscing about our student days in the A&M School of Veterinary Medicine.

The next morning Sven loaned me his car, and I drove to the MSC to find Chris waiting. She had set up appointments with most of the names on the list. She also had their locations marked on a map. FBI efficiency. I was impressed and told her so.

The first appointment was with a retired professor of agronomy. It had been twenty-seven years since I had taken a class with him, but he remembered me. Chris showed her drawing. He didn't recognize the face. Just like the day before, we got a shake of the head, an apology for failing memory, and an expression of regret for not being able to help.

Chris had scheduled our visits on a twenty-minute time frame. It pushed us, but we managed to go from house to house and stick pretty close to the expected time. Always, the retirees welcomed us and tried to help. However, after three hours of door-to-door contact and continual negative responses, I was ready to call it quits.

"How many more?" I asked.

"Only two," Chris replied.

"I'm beginning to get the picture that Ms. X owned an Aggie baseball cap but didn't attend this university."

"Wanna call it quits?"

I nodded. "We'll need a little time to get ready for the game." I looked at my watch and saw that it was almost noon.

"Of these last two names, one is on this street," she said.

"Shall we make it the last stop?"

"Sure. It's in the next block, 1208 University Drive. Dr. Margaret Azise, professor of animal nutrition."

"I remember her," I said. "I think she's from Pakistan. A tough, tough grader. Students used to enroll in her classes with fear and trepidation."

"It's the next house on the right," Chris pointed to a neat-looking white house with green shutters.

We rang the bell. A small, dark-skinned woman wearing a sari answered. "Come in," she said.

As was our routine, we followed her into the living room and took seats. "Thank you for agreeing to meet with us," Chris said. "Would you like to see my FBI credentials?"

"No, I remember Jim Bob. He's been on television so much, he's become our most infamous graduate."

"Would you like to hear my infamous words?" I smiled back.

She laughed. "I think we're all trying to do the same thing—help eradicate BSE."

"And to that end, we're trying to locate someone," Chris said as she pulled out another copy of the drawing.

"Bashiyra Fahatah," Dr. Azise said. "But she went by Barbara. Barbara was her Americanized name."

Chapter 38

1208 University Drive, College Station, Texas

I was stunned.

Chris, too, sat speechless.

After hours of searching and interviewing, the words came so effortlessly—Bashiyra Fahatah, but she went by Barbara—I didn't know how to respond.

A massive bookshelf spanned an entire wall at the east end of Dr. Margaret Azise's living room. She rose from her chair and walked to it while lecturing us about her collection.

"I saved all the yearbooks during my tenure here," she said as she gestured to multiple shelves of large, maroon volumes. "Thirty-six years and I have every one." She pulled three and brought them over to the coffee table in front of us.

We each took one.

"F-A-H-A-T-A-H," she spelled. "I suggest we start with the index in the back. Look for page numbers."

We did.

And we each located photos of Bashiyra Fahatah. Chris found one in the sophomores of the 1989 book, I in the juniors of 1990, and Dr. Azise in the seniors of 1991. We compared the photographs. "That's her," Chris said, her words bubbling with excitement.

"You doubted my memory?" Dr Azise asked, her voice a sharp reprimand.

Chris backtracked immediately. "Oh, no. I was complimenting you for identifying her."

Azise smiled—it was a smile I remembered from my college days. It still had its intimidating effect. "Too late," she said, with a grin that lit her face with sardonic irony. "But that's okay, Agent O'Shay. We found the person you were looking for."

Chris kept trying. "Dr. Azise, you have no idea how many people we've asked. You're the only one who remembered."

The elderly woman stood, reached over, and patted Chris on the arm. "If you'll join me around the kitchen table, I have tea and scones."

We followed her into a bright, cheery kitchen. The table and chairs were white, trimmed in yellow, and centered next to a huge picture window that looked out onto a beautiful backyard garden. Azise served us small, homemade biscuits and steaming hot tea from a silver, double-tiered teapot.

"You take cream or sugar?" she asked.

Chris and I declined, but our hostess heaped both into her cup.

I eased back in my chair and decided to let Chris take over the interview.

"What can you tell us about Barbara?" Chris asked.

"She had many of problems," replied Dr. Azise. "That's why I remember her so well."

"Grades?"

"Everything *except* grades. Barbara is highly intelligent."

"Can you give us some examples?"

"Barbara Fahatah was a conflicted young woman. In Texas we'd say, she had a burr under her saddle. From my Pakistani view, she was a women's libber from a country that railed against equal rights for women."

"Saudi Arabia?"

Dr. Azise nodded. "Certainly among the most repressive in the Muslim world, if not *the* most tyrannical and exploitive."

"So, she became Americanized?"

"That was the strangest part—she hated America."

"Why?"

"Her grandfather and her uncle were ahead of their time. In the post World War II era, they thought American oil companies were exploiting the country by taking Arabian oil."

Chris looked at me and shrugged her shoulders. "What does this have to do with Barbara's hate?"

"Members of her family—especially her grandfather and her uncle—led protests against Aramco, urging the country to expel all Americans and nationalize their wells, pipelines, and refineries."

"Fifty years ago?" I butted in.

"Yes," Azise replied, "and as a result, her grandfather and uncle were both killed."

"Who killed them?" I asked.

Azise raised her shoulders, held out her hands palms up in a gesture of uncertainty. "No one knows, but the important result for this young woman is that her relatives died in a protest against the infidels, the hated Americans."

I shook my head in disbelief. "You're telling us that this bright young woman—from one of the most conservative of Muslim countries—hates Americans who steal her country's natural resources, yet chooses to come to here to study agriculture?"

"Not exactly," the professor replied. "She was *sent* here by her family. Most likely her father and her brothers made the decision for her."

"So she arrived here in the 1980s, yelling and screaming, 'I hate America.'"

Dr. Azise nodded. "And she became a champion of women's rights."

"Crazy," Chris said.

"I would use the word conflicted," Dr. Azise countered. "But a memorable student."

"A protester—like an indoctrinated kid in Palestine who throws rocks," I added.

"No." The elderly professor smiled, shaking her head as though addressing a student with the wrong answer. "Bashiyra Fahatah wouldn't be satisfied with throwing rocks. She would want to pilot one of the planes that flew into the World Trade Towers."

"Al Qaeda would never use women in the front ranks of terrorism," I argued.

"Don't be too sure," Chris countered. "Today they're sending women suicide bombers on Russian planes and Israeli buses."

Margaret Azise nodded. "And the first female that breaks al

Qaeda's gender barrier will be Barbara or some feisty young women like her."

Outnumbered by feminine viewpoints, I could see it was time to change the direction of our conversation. "What else can you tell us about Bashiyra Fahatah—Barbara?" I asked.

"She was one of my best students, an expert in animal nutrition."

"Someone who could contaminate cattle feed to spread bovine spongiform encephalopathy?"

"Technically, for her, that would be no problem," Azise replied. "And with her anti-American views, she might relish the opportunity."

Chris and I glanced at one another.

"You have any idea where we could find Barbara?" I asked

"No, but the alumni office might have an address."

We finished our tea, thanked Dr. Azise for her help, and returned to the car. It took some doing, but we managed to roust the director of alumni relations and meet him at his computer. He found that Bashiyra Fahatah had returned to Saudi Arabia following graduation and had never been heard from since. A dead end.

We Xeroxed copies of Fahatah's photo and thanked the alumni director for his time. We watched as he hurried off to the stadium to join some 85,000 other Aggie fans.

My watch told me that the game had been underway for about fifteen minutes. I pulled out the two tickets from Sven.

"Shall we?" I asked.

"Jim Bob." She shook her head and stared at me with a look of exasperation.

"Opportunity is only a few hundred yards away."

"We've just been given our biggest and best clue for Stan's murder, not to mention the BSE epidemic," Chris answered. "How can you even think about football?"

"It's a struggle," I said, a huge smile breaking across my face.

A roar went up from the stadium that could be heard all over campus.

"You're serious?" Chris asked. "You want to take time out for a game?"

"Not just any game," I said. "This is Kyle Field. The twelfth-man tradition needs us."

Chris heaved a big sigh, gave me a look of disgust, and said, "I have no idea what the twelfth man has to do with anything, but, if it'll get you back on the case, I'll go with you to the stadium."

So we went.

And I explained how, on January 2, 1922, when an underdog Aggie team was playing Centre College, then the nation's top ranked team, the coach called for volunteers from the stands. E. King Gill, a former player, suited up and stood ready throughout the rest of the game, which A&M finally won 22-14."

Although Gill did not play, he had accepted the call to help the team and he came to be known as the Twelfth Man, because he stood ready for duty in the event the eleven men on the gridiron needed assistance. That spirit had grown vigorously throughout the years and developed so that the entire student body at A&M was now recognized as the Twelfth Man.

The story, the huge crowd, and the "thumbs-up" Aggie atmosphere soon softened Chris' resentment. She especially enjoyed the Aggie Band—300 players with an overpowering sound. And when they formed their signature "T" with a small "A&M," and played the school song, she clapped and cheered with as much enthusiasm as the most devoted fan.

I found myself thinking about how it felt to accompany such an attractive woman. When people passed us climbing up the stadium steps, they stared. Especially the guys. For the first time I felt—just a tiny little inkling—a bit of social interaction between us. It was almost like a date.

On a beautiful, October afternoon—in one of the most storied football stadiums in America—we relaxed, ate junk food, forgot about BSE, murder, and all of our troubles.

Best of all, Texas A&M won the game.

CHAPTER 39

Rio Airlines, Easterwood Field,
College Station, Texas

On Sunday we flew back to Amarillo—College Station to DFW on the "Big Canary," and DFW to Amarillo on American Airlines. Between flights, Chris talked constantly on her cell phone and energized the search for our suspect. Over and over I heard her caution her contacts, "Keep this confidential."

On Monday we met with Wyatt Reed and Ray Underwood. Wyatt reported no news on his three suspects in the murder of Stanley Young. Everyone agreed that Ted Austin seemed above suspicion. Both the fellow who worked at PanTex and the restaurant owner in Canyon had been heavily screened with absolutely no leads. APD had now returned to working the list of two thousand names from the local cattle industry. However, with our new information of Barbara—Bashiyra Fahatah—he reacted with excitement about the possible involvement of Arab terrorists.

Ray agreed to keep investigating the imported cattle from Mobile, to publicize them as the leading source of the BSE epidemic, and to withhold any information about Barbara or her boyfriend from the media. We now had two major investigations underway, and it seemed to each of us that they were somehow related.

Contaminated feed became a much more important possibility. This was my bailiwick, my area of expertise. I asked for and was given full access to all feed sources that might have been associated with the infected cattle or that might become involved in the future.

On Tuesday, Fred and I drove to Sagebrush with a good supply of plastic bags for gathering samples. After making our way through heavy security, we parked near the feed yard's storage building where we met Paul Edwards.

"How's it going?" I asked.

"Welcome to la-laland," he answered.

"Looks like the blood screening is in full operation."

"The feds have over a hundred of their agents involved in giving Masterson tests."

"Wow, that must be some kind of a record."

"A record in futility," he groused. "The only BSE they've found is in the older animals in my cow-calf operation."

"As expected?"

"I could have told them that," he spat out his words in disgust. "Saved 'em a hell of a lot of trouble."

"You have the numbers?"

He did.

Fred and I listened while Paul showed us his clipboard and the details of the federal quarantine. His cow-calf operation was small—only slightly more than 500 animals. His clipboard listed 276 cows, all grouped by age and test result, and a total of 238 calves, all born in the current year. I read the numbers.

Age 10 and older, 17 animals, all tested positive, all now slaughtered.

Age 9, 21 animals, all positive, all slaughtered.

Age 8, 29 animals, all positive, all slaughtered.

Age 7, 35 animals, all positive, all slaughtered.

Age 6, 34 animals, all positive, all slaughtered.

Age 5, 31 animals, all positive, all slaughtered.

Age 4, 39 animals, 21 positive, 18 negative, all that tested positive now slaughtered.

Age 3, 41 animals, all negative, none slaughtered.

Age 2, 29 animals, all negative, none slaughtered.

Totals: 276 animals, 188 slaughtered, 68 still in the herd.

All 238 calves tested, all negative, none slaughtered.

Fred and I studied the data for a few moments. Fred spoke first.

"Seems obvious," he said. "The older cows had BSE, and you've now eradicated the disease from your cow-calf operation."

Paul nodded.

"This is only 514 animals," I said. "What about the rest?"

"The 490,000 in my cattle feeding operation?" Paul smiled. "I assume you know the age of my feeder cattle?"

"All are less than 30 months?"

"Just like every other feed yard in Texas," he said. "When feeder cattle hit 1200 to 1300 pounds, usually 24 to 28 months of age, you're wasting money on feed. It's time to take them to the meat packers.

"Are the feds testing all of your feeder cattle?" Fred asked.

"Typical government bureaucracy," Paul's voice brimmed with anger, "All 490,000 head, all less than 30 months of age."

"How many have they tested?"

"As of yesterday, 235,000—almost half."

"How many are positive for BSE?"

Paul smiled—a knowing smile with a smirk. "Wanna guess?"

"Zero?" asked Fred.

"Of course," Paul spat out the words. "Even kindergarten kids should know BSE takes four to five years to develop."

"Paul, I believe that's a theory," I cautioned. "Not yet accepted as scientific fact."

"The British had their OTM rule, the "Over Thirty Months" policy that allowed younger animals to be imported and exported."

"You're right," I admitted. "And there's considerable evidence that BSE *is* slow to develop."

"Christ, what's it going to take?"

"More time. More documentation. Exactly what you're doing here at Sagebrush."

"Damn, this is crazy. I don't know why I ever got into the cattle business."

"Because you love it," I answered. "You love the process and all the things that go with it—the horses, the people, even the smell."

He laughed. "Jim Bob, I've never said I liked the smell."

"Let's change the subject. We're here to take samples of your feed."

"Be my guest," he answered.

Fred and I went into the feed storage and scooped up samples from every bin. Corn, soybean meal, alfalfa, cottonseed, oats, wheat, everything—we packaged it into Ziploc plastic bags and carefully labeled each. Then we spent hours going around to every feeding trough in the world's largest feed yard. By late afternoon we had small, representative amounts of everything that went into the stomachs of Paul's animals.

At the end of a long, tiring day, we climbed into my Chevy and headed south on U.S. 287. In early October the sun sets late in the Texas Panhandle, not until about eight thirty. Driving back to Amarillo, Fred and I watched the western sky turn from gold to burnt orange, then to pink. The low level of scattered clouds, the flat horizon, and the smell of cattle feed inside my Suburban, evoked a sense of peace as the last sliver of the sun fell from sight.

"Fred, we're going to need some help to process this," I said.

"I've called around," he replied.

"Who'd you ask?"

"The university, the A&M lab, the extension service, the AVI's staff."

"Sounds like every pressure cooker in the area."

"Everyone I could think of."

"What's the response?"

"They all said yes."

"They said they'd work us in?"

"No," Fred said. "Each lab told me they'd stop what they're doing—give top priority to testing our samples."

I nodded. "Anything associated with BSE goes to the front of the line. That's the panhandle spirit."

We pulled into the parking lot at my office to find Christine O'Shay standing by her black Crown Victoria. "I didn't expect a welcoming committee," I said.

"There's been a development in the murder case, and I wanted to give you a heads up," she said.

"Good news or bad?" I asked.

"Could be either, probably neither," she answered with a somber face.

"What kind of an answer is that?"

"Sorry, best I can do."

"So what's up?"

"Wyatt asked Judge Gleeson for search warrants for Theodore Austin's residence and office."

"And?"

"The judge said he'd have them ready tomorrow morning."

Chapter 40

Masterson and Associates Veterinary Services Inc.

Wednesday morning I had two major investigations worrying me.

Wyatt Reed and his trigger-happy task force were giving Ted's property a thorough search at both his home and his office. In a way I couldn't blame Wyatt—the media were breathing down his neck, constantly pressuring him for details. He and the APD needed to do something, to look like they were following up every lead, no matter how unlikely.

Fred took my Suburban and started delivering feed samples to the various cooperating laboratories. I expected it would take the entire morning to distribute the hundreds of small plastic bags we had collected in Sagebrush.

I made coffee and met with FBI Agent Christine O'Shay. It had been four days since we'd learned the identity of Bashiyra Fahatah, and nothing had surfaced. We passed over Ted and his problems and started in on Arab terrorism.

"I have bad news and good news," Chris said as I poured her a cup of coffee.

"The bad news is obvious," I replied. "We can't find her. So what's the good news?"

"The good news is that we've not had any leaks."

"No one knows we're looking for her?"

"Have you seen or heard anything reported in the media?"

"No." I sipped my coffee.

"And other than homicide task force personnel—those working the case—no one has talked about it."

"You sound like you expected a leak," I said.

"Hard to keep it confidential. Reporters would treat this as big news, a break in the case."

"Well, it is."

"Obviously, but the longer we can keep the public thinking BSE is caused by imported cattle—"

"Which it could be," I said.

"Let's be honest with each other—put all our innermost thoughts on the table."

"Okay," I said. "I'm voting for terrorists who brought contaminated animal protein, probably bone meal from infected cattle in England, and mixed it into the feed at Sagebrush."

"Me, too," she replied. "Now all we have to do is prove it."

"Which ain't gonna be easy," I said, using my Texas drawl to emphasize the point.

"But you're working on it?"

"Every lab in the area is processing samples."

"What've you found?"

"We only started this morning."

"How long before any word?"

"We might know something today."

"How long to finish the testing—to a final conclusion?"

"At least a week," I said. "We have a truckload of samples."

She sipped her coffee. "Wish there was some way to hurry it up."

"Meanwhile, what's happening on the murder?" I asked.

"At seven o'clock this morning Wyatt took all available officers, divided them into two groups, and charged off with his search warrants to Ted's office and home."

"Doesn't sound promising," I said.

"Let's put our thoughts on the table again," she said. "What do you *really* think?"

"Really—I don't see someone local murdering Stanley Young. I know these people, work with them, treat their animals. It's gotta be the Arabs."

"Okay. What motives can you give me for Bashiyra Fahatah, or her boyfriend, for killing our congressman from the 13th district?"

"Same as for bringing BSE to the area."

"Terrorism?"

"Do you remember the Tommy Thompson resignation, when he made his statement about protecting America's food supply?"

"Who could forget it?"

"As usual, we seem to be one step behind the terrorists."

"*If* . . . if BSE is being brought to us by terrorists."

"You ever get tired of 'what if' talk?"

"If I did, I'd have to quit this job."

We ended our morning coffee. Chris went to join the search in progress at Ted's office in the cattle feeders building. I went back to my lab to fire up the pressure cookers and do my part in our hunt for BSE infection.

At noon, Fred returned, and we doubled our efforts, each with our own microscope, searching for the pink-tinged, sponge-like tissue known as bovine spongiform encephalopathy. Tedious work. I was glad when Chris returned and interrupted us.

"Wyatt found a nine-millimeter Beretta with Winchester Black Max ammo."

"Where?" I asked.

"At Ted's house, in a drawer with his socks."

"Hell, we knew he bought the bullets. Surely you're not surprised that he had a handgun?"

"He was arraigned and posted $100,000 bail."

"Which means what?"

"We're sending the gun to the CSI lab in Lubbock for test firing. We'll have the results in the morning."

"Meanwhile, the media has a field day at the expense of Ted and his family."

"Hey. I don't make the rules."

"Seems so unfair. This poor guy will be convicted by public opinion before he has a chance to defend himself."

"He didn't have to buy the handgun *or* the bullets."

I tried to think of a rebuttal, words to defend my friend and neighbor. None came to mind.

"Coffee in the morning?" she asked.

"Sure."

"I'll stop by." She started out the door, then turned and gave me a smile. "Cheer up. Maybe tomorrow will be a better day."

After she left, Fred and I worked at the scopes until we were both bleary-eyed. The sun was setting when we closed the lab and headed for home.

Driving west on I-40, I punched the button for my satellite phone.

"Onstar ready," answered the phone.

"Home," I said instructing it to dial the pre-programmed number.

"Hello," Maggie answered.

"I'm on the way," I said. "What's for supper?"

"Have you heard about the Austins?"

"Yes, Ted was arraigned, posted bail."

"I've baked a casserole to take over to their house. Liz and I were hoping you'd go with us."

"Might not be the best thing. Let's talk when I get there."

Ten minutes later I pulled up to the back entrance of our house—what we call the kitchen door. Maggie and Liz came out carrying food.

"I called the house as soon as I heard the news on the radio," Maggie said. "Mary Sue's not handling this very well. It would help to have you go with us."

"Ted's really pissed at me right now. He blames me for inciting the media with my statement about BSE."

"Please?" Maggie urged.

"How about tomorrow? The tests will prove it wasn't Ted's gun that was used in the killing. He'll be cleared, and things will be returning to normal."

"Jim Bob, *tonight* is when the Austins need support from friends and neighbors."

As I'd done hundreds of times, I drove a mile north on the black-top to the Austin's mailbox and turned in. Since the day, fifteen years ago,when we'd purchased these two sections of grassland, divided the property into two small ranches and built our homes—our common interest in ranching gave us a friendship that brought us close together in times of adversity. However, this evening, as our neighbor faced an outlandish attack on his reputation, I felt uneasy going with my wife and daughter. I was uncertain he would see my presence as a show of support.

The three of us got out of the car and started toward the house. As we approached the door I heard a gunshot. A big "pow-WHOP," the distinctive sound of a high-powered rifle when its bullet hits living flesh. We stopped, unsure where the sound had come from. I looked at Maggie and started to ask if she'd heard what I did. Before I could get the words out, we heard a woman's scream—a loud, shrill, high-pitched wail of terror.

I ran ahead. Not bothering to knock, I tore open the door and ran into the kitchen. I heard sobs coming from the bedroom area.

There I found what was left of Ted Austin. The top of his head was blown off, blood spattered the entire bathroom, a rifle lay on the floor, and Mary Sue was holding his lifeless body.

CHAPTER 41

The home of Ted and Mary Sue Austin

My first reaction was revulsion. I felt my stomach churn and the initial urge to throw up. Then I heard footsteps coming down the hallway.

"Maggie, brace yourself."

A second later Maggie appeared at the door of the bathroom. The color drained from her face, and I thought she might faint. "Oh, God," she answered. "Oh, my God."

"Mary Sue needs your help." It was the best thing I could have said. Maggie rallied and immediately came to her friend.

"Let's try to get her out of here," I said. Together we half-carried her, first to the bedroom, then down the hall to a second bathroom. Maggie found a washcloth and tried to wipe the worst of the blood spatter from Mary Sue.

"Can you handle this?" I asked.

"I . . . I think so," Maggie replied.

Liz came to the door. She grimaced at the sight of all the blood, struggling to keep her composure. "What can I do?" she managed to ask.

"Clothes," Maggie said. "Look in her closet and see if you can find a robe."

Liz and I left the bathroom.

In the hallway, I deliberately stood between my daughter and the awful scene. I put my hands on her shoulders and looked squarely at her, much as I had done when she was a little girl.

"Liz, stay out of that bathroom. Get the robe, then help your mother find another room where you can take Mrs. Austin."

She nodded.

I stepped aside to let her pass, then went outside to my Suburban, turned on the satellite phone, and punched the button with the red cross.

Within seconds a strong, soothing voice addressed me, "Onstar emergency. How may I help you, Mr. Masterson?"

"There's been a death by gunshot. We need police and an ambulance."

"I show your location approximately three and a half miles north of Bushland, Texas. Is that correct?"

"Yes, it's the home of Ted Austin. Inform the authorities we have an apparent suicide."

Next I called Chris. She said she'd get Wyatt Reed.

For the next few minutes, I sat there—shaky, trying not to cry, willing my stomach to settle down. I took deep breaths and summoned the control to go back into the house. I stepped out of my Suburban as the first Potter County deputy drove up, red and blue lights flashing. Then I went to the uniformed officer to give an overview of our situation. We'd hardly finished our conversation when two more cruisers arrived.

Quickly the drive filled with police vehicles. Most left their strobes flashing, giving the ranch land an eerie feeling. Amid all the arrivals, I heard a familiar voice.

"What can you tell me?" Chris asked.

"Maggie, Liz, and I were bringing food," I said. "We had just gotten out of the car—I was standing about where you are—when we heard a shot."

"A pistol?"

"No. I've seen the rifle. Looked like a 30-06. Judging from the mess, I think he put it in his mouth and pulled the trigger."

Chris made a face. Shook her head.

"Ted's been under a lot of pressure," I said. "The TCFA advertising campaign backfired. He'd spent all their money, and still the cattle business continued to crash. Everything he tried was failing."

"No support from the government," she added. "Stan Young's weak efforts—his proposal for a 10 percent subsidy—was all that more than Ted could take?"

"To Ted, the cattle business was everything," I said. "He put his heart and soul into it."

Chris looked toward the house. "I'd better get in there."

"It's the bathroom off the master bedroom." As the words left my lips, the sight of that horrible scene came back, and I lost it. My stomach churned, and I threw up on the grass. Chris handed me a Kleenex.

I expected her to leave, to go into the house to inspect the crime scene. Instead, she lingered. Finally, she broke the silence. "Death is never easy, but especially when it's someone you know—"

I nodded again. "I think I'm okay now."

We stood silently for another moment—an awkward time. Then, Wyatt Reed walked up.

"What've we got?" he asked.

"Ted Austin took a deer rifle, put it in his mouth, and pulled the trigger," I said.

"Damn."

Chris started walking toward the house. Wyatt followed. I was glad I didn't have to go.

Next came an ambulance, a big box-like vehicle with enough lights to fill a stadium. A team of EMTs rolled out a gurney and carried it up the steps and into the house.

The media came in droves, creating a traffic jam. The sheriff's deputies took jurisdiction and started requiring cars to park out on the blacktop. It was a quarter-mile hike from the road to the house, a distance the TV people—with their cameras, microphones, and lights—complained about.

Maggie came out and suggested we take Mary Sue to our house to spend the night. I agreed and started working to free up our Suburban so we could back it out to the road. Two deputies helped juggle cars.

Maggie and our daughter had to practically carry Mary Sue. Her face was red, puffy, and distorted. I wouldn't have recognized her. We loaded her into the rear seat, and I backed all the way out the long drive.

The Austins had two grown children—one in Chicago, the other in Atlanta. Liz got the numbers from Mary Sue, called, and broke the news. Both Austin children said they'd catch the first plane to Amarillo. I felt really proud of Liz and the way she handled a tough situation. Her choice of words, her answers to their questions, and her quiet, always supportive tone of voice, were perfect for our friends in their time of need.

Maggie called our family doctor, and he came to give Mary Sue a sedative.

Wyatt and Chris came. Official business. Since Maggie and I had been the first on the scene, they wanted our statements. The four of us sat down around the kitchen table.

Wyatt took the lead. "With your permission, I'm going to record this." He set a small cassette recorder on the table.

"Fine," I answered

Maggie nodded.

Chris, who sat next to Maggie, remained silent. I couldn't help but remember the last time the two of them were together, at the restaurant, when Chris and I showed up an hour late. Tonight was a completely different setting.

"In your own words, I'd like each of you to tell me what happened tonight at the Austin's home.

We gave it, quickly and factually. First me, then Maggie.

"Did you see anyone other than Mr. and Mrs. Austin?" he asked.

"No," I said.

Maggie shook her head.

"In your opinion, could someone else have entered the home and shot Ted Austin?"

"No way," I answered. "I was there in seconds."

Maggie again shook her head.

"This is a difficult question, but I have to ask." He paused.

I knew what he was going to say. It made me mad, but I bit my tongue and prepared to give a civil response.

"Do you think Mrs. Austin shot her husband?"

"No," I said. "Absolutely not."

Maggie continued to shake her head.

"Do you have anything to add? Anything you think we should know about the death of Ted Austin?"

I felt as worn and weary as Maggie. We both shook our heads.

"As part of our investigation," Wyatt continued, "we'll need to have an interview like this with Mrs. Austin. Would it be possible to do it now?"

Maggie exploded, "Most certainly not," a scathing edge to her voice. "This poor woman has just suffered through the worst trauma of her life. You saw that horrific scene. How would you feel if you'd just found your spouse with their brains scattered all over the room?"

"She's right," Chris said, her first words of the evening. "This is no time to speak with Mary Sue Austin."

"Anyway, she's asleep," I said. "Our doctor came and gave her a shot. She's out of it until tomorrow morning."

Wyatt made his apologies and agreed to speak with her later. He and Chris left.

No one else came, the phone stopped ringing, and a terrible day came to an end. I fell asleep with my arms around my wife, thankful for the comfort and security of our home.

Chapter 42

Masterson and Associates Veterinary Services Inc.

The next morning Chris came by for coffee.

"I've been wrong before," I said as I filled her cup. "But never like this."

"About who murdered Young?" Chris asked.

I nodded. "I would've bet the farm it wasn't someone local."

She sipped her coffee.

"And of all the locals," I continued, "Ted would've been at the bottom of my list of suspects."

"Don't berate yourself too much. We all missed it. Even Wyatt."

"At least Wyatt arraigned him when he found the gun."

"Yeah, but for the wrong reasons," she said. "He was thinking that we'd test-fire the gun, compare the slugs, and declare Ted innocent."

"And—"

"We scoped the bullets." She seemed to be reading my mind. Ted's gun killed Stan Young."

Conversation died. For the next few minutes we each sat silently with our thoughts. After a bit, I stood, picked up the coffee pot, and gestured to Chris. "More?"

"Yes, please."

I filled her cup and mine, then returned to my seat.

"What're your thoughts about our other problem?" she asked.

"After being so wrong about naming a murder suspect, I'm surprised you'd ask."

"Hey, you wanna hear about some of my mistakes?"

"FBI makes mistakes?"

She smiled.

I gave my opinion. "I guess I'm still thinking a couple of Arab terrorists brought contaminated bone meal and mixed it with the feed at Sagebrush."

"Me, too," she said.

"But there's one thing that really puzzles me about such a theory," I continued.

"What's that?"

"If radical Islamists are going to attack our food supply, do you think they'd pick just one beef producer?"

Chris started to speak, then picked up her cup and downed the remaining coffee.

"We've not found BSE in any other feed yard," I continued.

"That *is* strange," she agreed, setting her cup down.

"Makes you want to take another look at those cattle Paul's been trucking in from Mobile."

"Do you know of any other feed yard that hauled in cattle imported from outside the country?"

I shook my head. "TCFA checked. Ted contacted their members—which includes the feed yards with 10,000 or more head, in other words, all the major cattle feeders—and found that Paul Edwards was the only one."

"Another dead end."

"I have a suggestion," I said.

"Okay."

"Let's go talk with Ray Underwood."

She agreed. I called him. Chris drove us to his office in her FBI cruiser.

We found the office of the Area Veterinary Inspector a beehive of activity. Dozens of white, government pickups filled the parking lot, and we had to drive around the block to find a spot where we could leave Chris' car. Inside the small building, space was at a premium. Imported, temporary workers from all over the country competed for workspace at card tables and folding chairs. Extra phones were everywhere and constantly ringing.

Ray now shared his office with two other inspectors.

He came to the door and greeted us with a grin. "Welcome to the world of crisis management."

"You must really feel important, all these people calling you," Chris said.

"This is the complaint department," he said. "People only call here when they have something to bitch about."

"Better yet," I piped in, "ask the government to pay you for every taxpayer you make happy."

"Then I'd really be in trouble," he answered. "With the mess we're in, it's impossible to give a positive answer to anyone."

"I take it you have no good news for us?" I asked.

He didn't answer. Instead, he gestured to chairs around a small table in the corner of his office and offered coffee.

We sat.

He poured.

"I don't want to get your hopes up, but—"

"You have news from Mobile?" I asked.

"No, Washington."

"In the FBI business, news from Washington is usually bad," Chris said.

"Same here," Ray continued. "However, the world of politics sometimes surprises even hardened, cynical old bureaucrats like me."

Chris nodded. "Over the years, the FBI has encountered a few. But political surprises from Washington are *always* bad news."

"This could be an exception," Ray countered. He gave us a little half-smile—one that said I might know something you don't. "What if John Zahrenski, a Democrat, took temporary leadership of the House Agriculture Committee, and wanted to exchange favors with the Republicans in Congress?"

Chris made a face, one I'd come to recognize as her expression of intense rejection. "Here we go again, playing the *what if* game."

Ray kept going. "What could he propose that would win favor with Republicans in cattle country?"

"Cattle subsidies would be at the top of my list," I answered.

"Maybe you've noticed there's been a scaling back of the number of cattle that would have to be put down."

"What's the new number?"

"Right now, at Sagebrush Cattle Feeders, the number is 188 cattle slaughtered." Ray smiled. This time a big toothy grin filled his face and indicated his delight at the equivocation. "Slightly less than the number Zahrenski was presenting to the committee a few days ago."

"Which was—"

"In the neighborhood of 35 million . . . if they followed his recommendation . . . if they eradicated every cow in Texas."

We all laughed.

Ray continued, "So Zahrenski has made a magnanimous suggestion to the ag committee."

"So what did he suggest?"

"He proposed a 90 percent subsidy."

"I don't believe it," I said.

"And I don't understand," Chris said with a puzzled look on her face. "Somebody please explain."

"If the ag committee passes it," Ray continued, "and if it's passed into law by the House and the Senate—*two big ifs*—then the government would pay ranchers and cattle feeders 90 percent of the market value of every animal slaughtered under the eradication program."

"Wow," I said. "The hoof and mouth subsidy was only 80 percent."

"What're the chances of this being passed?" Chris asked.

"Right now, my boss, and his boss—the Secretary of Agriculture—say they have the votes. It won't cost much, and both the Democrats and the Republicans see it as a political win-win issue."

CHAPTER 43

The International House of Pancakes, Amarillo

The next day, Saturday morning, I agreed to meet Paul Edwards for breakfast and then go with him to Ted Austin's funeral. We'd both been asked to serve as pallbearers. I arrived early at the restaurant, picked up my usual two newspapers, and took a booth to scan the morning news while waiting.

It came as no surprise that someone had leaked Zahrenski's plan for beef subsidies. Both Amarillo and Dallas papers chose it as their headline story. The "unconfirmed sources" sounded a lot like Ray Underwood—a 90 percent subsidy was on the table and the votes seemed assured of passage. I read it slowly and carefully.

"What do you think?" a familiar voice asked. Paul stood there in his funeral suit, black with a very light pin stripe, and a striped gray-black tie. I'd never seen him in a dark suit before and almost didn't recognize him.

"Makes me want to believe in Santa Claus," I replied.

He smiled and scooted into the seat across from me.

The waitress came and took our orders.

We exchanged pleasantries for a few minutes before Paul returned the conversation to politics.

"This is pretty much the way the subsidy for hoof and mouth developed," he said. "At first, nobody thought it had a chance. Then overnight, all the politicians discovered they would gain some votes if they jumped on the bandwagon."

"Crazy way to run a government," I said.

"It's the first rule in politics."

"Enlighten me," I replied. "What's the first rule?"

"Find the votes to get reelected."

"So, if you're a political statesman in the world's greatest democracy, you don't go after the issues that are needed by the people. You lock onto the ones that'll get you votes."

"Sounds like you're smart enough to run for congress."

"Yuch," I shook my head. "What a terrible job."

"The politicians are looking for someone to take Stanley Young's place."

"Who'd want it?"

"Me."

"Really?"

The waitress brought our breakfasts—steak and eggs for Paul, the usual banana-nut pancakes for me.

Between bites, Paul wanted to continue talking politics. "I've made a few calls," he said. "The powers that be have told me I can have it if I want it."

I smiled. "Wow, Congressman Paul Edwards, I knew him when—"

"When I was a cowboy about to go broke?"

"That was just a threat."

"So, you think we're out of the woods?"

"No. I think that even if congress passes the subsidy at 90 percent, we still have a major problem."

Paul's face clouded. "Go on."

"We've got to find out where the mad cow infection came from," I said. "There's no way to stop it until we find out how it got started."

"You working on it?"

"Damn right. As hard as I can."

"What've you found?"

"Pretty much nothing."

"I thought you had the name of the woman who taped the video at my place."

"Yes," I said, as I drizzled more syrup on my pancakes. "Her name's Barbara Fahatah."

"What else have you got?"

"Like I said, pretty much nothing."

"Why not put out an APB and ask every law enforcement agency in the country to look for her?"

"We did."

"I haven't seen or heard anything about it in the media."

"We've tried to do it surreptitiously, in the hope that if this woman and her colleagues don't know we have her name, we'll have a better chance of finding her."

"So, do you have any leads?"

"Zip."

"Maybe it's time to go public."

"That's the next step."

"Jim Bob, I want to help," he said. "I know cattlemen all over the country. Let me use my contacts."

"Be my guest," I answered.

I looked at my watch and saw that it was time to make our way to the funeral.

We finished up, paid the tab, and left.

The services were held at First Baptist, Amarillo's largest church and one of the biggest in Texas. Even that huge sanctuary couldn't hold the crowd. Obviously, Ted was not remembered as the person who killed an unpopular congressman, but rather, as the champion of the cattle industry. He, more than anyone, had turned this part of the world into a haven for bovines. In less than a half century, the Texas Panhandle had become the source of more than one-third of America's fed-beef. Ted Austin had been the cattleman's cheerleader.

We forgave him his minor faults—like killing people who didn't support our cows.

Paul, I, and six other men carried the coffin. On a beautiful October morning, we saw that Ted was ceremoniously lowered into the ground and then, as thousands of others did, we went our separate ways.

Sunday was a day of rest. I watched the Cowboys beat the Redskins. Maggie filled the house with the aroma of apple cobbler and a Tex-Mex casserole. Liz practiced and sounded better than ever. That evening we had our dinner on the back porch and watched my small herd of Black Angus grazing on the lush grass. We talked quietly about the Austin family and what we should do to help Mary Sue.

Monday started in my lab. Fred and I hit the microscopes with renewed effort to find the elusive disease.

"What're we going to do if we find it?" he asked.

"Trace it," I answered. "Find out where it came from."

"Suppose we don't find it?" Fred asked.

"Then we'll know to look elsewhere."

"So where would we look next?"

"Ray Underwood thinks the disease came from cattle imported through the Port of Mobile."

"Why not test those cattle?" Fred asked. "Seems like that would be a whole lot easier than what we're doing."

"They already did," I answered. "Or at least the government says they were screened using Masterson blood tests. All cattle imported from other countries are evaluated. It's the law."

"Any chance someone missed it?"

"Always a chance, but, no, there's no evidence that anyone messed up."

Fred heaved a discouraged sigh and went back to the pressure cooker for another sample. I empathized. He wasn't the only one who was getting tired of looking at feed samples under a microscope.

Ida Mae stepped into the lab. "Ray Underwood's on line one. Says he has good news."

I went to the phone. "What's up?"

"How're you coming on testing feed?"

"We need a couple more days to finish scoping all samples."

"Found anything?"

"Nope. As expected, Paul's feed is squeaky clean."

"Unless you find infected feed, I have orders to open the packing plants."

"Wow, what happened?"

"We're not finding BSE in any animals under four years of age."

"Hell, I could've told you that weeks ago."

"And the only infection found anywhere in the country has been in Paul's cow-calf operation."

"You know those animals were all tested and the infected ones put down."

"Yes. And with one possible exception, I believe we've eradicated BSE in the Texas Panhandle."

"What exception?"

"Feed."

I thought about his one-word answer. "The only possible feed that could be contaminated is what we're now testing."

"Golly, gee whiz, Jim Bob, it didn't take you long to figure that out."

"You mean when we finish scoping these samples sometime tomorrow—if there's no residue of BSE—we're back in business?"

"That's the plan," he said. "Give me a call the minute you know something. We have a lot of people waiting."

"Ray, this is really good news."

He chuckled. "You have any cattle you want to sell?"

CHAPTER 44

Masterson and Associates Veterinary Services, Inc.

Tuesday morning it rained, and in the Texas Panhandle, any day it rains is regarded as a beautiful day. The cold front that triggered the rain also brought lower temperatures. That morning, listening to Talk Radio 710 while driving to work, the newscaster predicted a high in the fifties and a slow, soaking rain throughout the day. It made me want to get to my microscope and hunt for BSE so that we could end this nightmare.

Even though I arrived thirty minutes early, mine was the third car in the parking lot. Fred and Ida Mae were hard at work, and the smell of fresh coffee gave the office a welcome, cozy feel. I poured myself a cup and settled in to call the other labs and give them the good news from Ray Underwood. Like hounds on a hunt who can smell the prey, everyone responded with an enthusiastic attitude. So much so, I felt compelled to stress the need to take it easy, to complete our screening with the same slow, methodical work we had been using for the past week. We were too close to let something slip by in a rush to finish screening today.

I had barely finished my contacts with the labs when the meat packers began calling. Apparently word had gotten out that the feds were going to allow the beef industry to return to normal production. First Swift, then Excel, followed by Tyson and other slaughter houses I'd never heard of, all wanted to know the same thing: "What time today would we have our results?" If they were going back to work tomorrow, they wanted time to notify employees.

Joe Jackson at the Amarillo Livestock Auction called. He wanted as much advance warning as possible to get word out to ranchers and truckers so they'd know when they could start bringing animals to the sale barn.

Good news travels fast, and by midmorning we had individual feed yard owners calling by the dozens. They'd heard that Ray Underwood would announce his decision *only* after we'd given the go ahead on safe feed.

Poor Ida Mae. She came to me with a plea to unplug the phones. I said okay. We could use my cell phone for necessary calls. She immediately contacted the other labs and gave them my cell number so that they could report to me when they'd finished their screening.

Excitement charged the air, and the morning whizzed by.

Shortly before noon, Chris dropped in. She wanted to talk and knew I couldn't take time to go somewhere for lunch, so she brought sandwiches. In the middle of a frantic day, I took fifteen minutes to eat with her and visit about going public with our search for Barbara Fahatah, et al.

"I think it's time," she said.

"Paul Edwards made an interesting comment Saturday morning," I replied as I took a bite of a McDonald's Big Mac.

Chris crossed her legs—a beautifully curved limb, displayed well above the knee. If we'd been sitting at a table, I wouldn't have noticed, but perched on lab stools at the counter by the microscopes, it came across as a very sexy moment. I couldn't help myself. I stared.

Chris went on, apparently oblivious to my reaction. "So what was Paul's comment?" she asked.

"Over the years, he's made a lot of personal contacts with cattle feeders in other parts of the country," I replied

"So?"

"So he offered to contact them personally and ask their help in trying to locate our two suspects."

"You're suggesting we do this instead of going public?" She frowned, and I could tell her immediate reaction was negative.

"How about a two-step process?" I replied. "Have Paul contact his friends, wait a week or ten days, then go public?"

Conversation lapsed as she thought about the implications. "How will he reach these cattle feeders?" she asked.

"We talked about that. He said he is already set up to send faxes and e-mails."

"He communicates with these other cattlemen on a regular basis?"

"Not regularly, just on special occasions," I answered. "And since this is really special, he offered to follow-up with phone calls to those he knows best."

"I don't know," she said, shaking her head. "Sounds like awfully small numbers. How many are we talking?"

"Almost a thousand on his list," I said.

"A thousand?" She seemed surprised.

"And there's an exponential effect."

"What do you mean?"

"He'll ask each of his friends to contact their friends."

"Oh." She appeared to be thinking about the multiplying result.

"So, if his thousand friends each contact a hundred of their friends—"

I could see wheels turning in her head as the numbers grew.

She smiled. "This could be promising."

"Cattlemen stick together," I said. "It's like a giant fraternity."

She nodded. "Especially when they're being threatened with BSE."

"So what do you think?"

"Okay, when do we start?"

"When can you get copies of the A&M photos of Barbara and her male friend to Paul?"

"He already has the police drawings."

"Shall we call now and give him the word?"

"You bet," she said.

Using Chris' cell phone, I did. Paul said he'd get his staff on it right away.

Chris left.

Fred and I finished our screening.

The other labs called, one by one. By three o'clock we had a complete report. No BSE residue had been found in any of the samples from Sagebrush Cattle Feeders. We had a clean sweep.

I contacted Ray Underwood and gave him the good news. In the background a cheer went up from the workers in his office as he made the announcement.

We were feeling good. Damn good. At the end of a two-week roller coaster ride, where I'd seen an impossible outbreak of a catastrophic disease lead to murder and suicide—and the potential devastation of our cattle industry—it felt wonderful to have some good news for a change. I looked at my watch and saw that it was almost 4:30 p.m. I called Fred and Ida Mae to the front and put my keys in the door.

"We're celebrating," I said, "and closing early. Let's go home."

In thirty seconds they were packed, out the front door, and into the light drizzle.

Walking the short distance to my car, I was thinking about opening some Champagne with dinner to celebrate our good news when Chris' black Crown Victoria came speeding into the parking lot. As her car drew near, she slowed just enough to keep from splashing me, stopped, and rolled down her window.

"What's up?" I asked.

"Get in," she ordered.

I did.

"They've found BSE in a dairy in Middleton, Wisconsin," she said.

CHAPTER 45

At home in Bushland, Texas

That night I drove home feeling like a whipped dog. One step forward, two steps back.

Maggie tried to comfort me. "What's going to happen now?" she asked, after giving me a long hug.

"I don't know." I had no idea which way the roller coaster was taking me. My life felt out of control.

"Almost time for the national news," she said. "Do we dare tune in?"

I flipped on ABC, Channel 7. BSE was their lead story.

Middleton, Wisconsin, a small town of 15,000 located just west of Madison, was shown on a map of the state. Next came scenes from the town and then shots of the Hinders Family Dairy. As dairies go, this one was relatively small, only about 500 cows. They had video of a "downer," a cow that stumbled and fell, the first sign of bovine spongiform encephalopathy.

Then came Amarillo.

I dreaded what might come next. Maggie took my hand.

As expected, they again showed fifteen seconds of me in the Sagebrush feed yard with my infamous "You get it you will die" statement.

The phone rang. I was grateful to have a reason to leave the room.

The caller ID read USDA and a ten-digit number that started with area code 608. I had no idea where the call was coming from.

"Hello," I said.

"Dr. Masterson?"

"Yes."

"Excuse me, sir, but are you the James Masterson who developed the test for BSE?"

"That'd be me."

"Let me introduce myself. I'm Henry Bozeman, the AVI for central Wisconsin. I'm calling you from Madison with bad news."

"BSE at the Hinders Dairy in Middleton?"

"Yes, how did you know?"

"It's the lead story on tonight's national news. We just watched it on Channel 7 here in Amarillo."

"I'm not surprised," he said. "It's taken over the media and created panic everywhere."

"What can I do to help you?"

"We're new to BSE testing and unsure of our results. I have discretionary funds for emergencies like this, and I'm calling to see if we could hire you as a consultant. Could you come to Madison for a few days, and if so, what would be your fee?"

Without a moment's hesitation I gave him an immediate answer. "Yes, I can come. No fee. Just pay my expenses."

"Hey, we wouldn't think of imposing on you. How about three days at $1,000 a day plus expenses?"

"Sure," I responded, a bit taken aback.

"Could you come tomorrow?" He sounded desperate.

"Probably, but I'll need to check on flight schedules and call you back."

"Dr. Masterson, we really appreciate this."

"I'll do what I can," I said. "By the way, could you give me the details of how you first learned you had a downer at Middleton?"

"I'm not sure of the exact sequence of events, but as best I can piece it together, I think it started when a woman brought a home video to one of the Madison TV stations last Saturday."

I felt my heart stop. "Really?" I clinched the phone with a white-knuckle grip.

"The TV station didn't know what to do with the tape," he continued, "and its been laying on someone's desk for two days."

"What . . . what happened next?" I had a hard time getting the words out. I grabbed a chair and sat down.

"The station ran it on their local news Monday night, last night."

"What happened after it ran?"

"All hell broke loose."

"Panic?"

"Unbelievable panic," he said. "The national media has swarmed Middleton. It's a small town, and they can't handle it."

"You have any information about the woman who brought the

tape to the local station?"

"Not much."

"Name, address?"

"We have a name, but I've not seen an address. I think she was a tourist. The Wisconsin Dells is a big vacation area, and it's near here."

"Give me her name, please."

"Just a minute," he said. He left the phone, and I could hear papers shuffling.

"Barbara Smith," he said. "Staying at the Days Inn Motel in Middleton. She says her home is Rushville, Nebraska."

"You have a description?"

"Well, I saw her in a video that was released by the local station."

"You have her on video?" I felt my voice rise into a falsetto squeak.

"Is that important?" he asked.

A surge of adrenaline caused me to tremble, and I almost dropped the phone. I counted to three, tried to relax, and then forced myself to speak in a slow, steady tone. "Would you call the station manager and ask him to hold onto the tape, please? And yes, it's very important."

"Well, sure. I'll make the call as soon as we hang up."

"I'll arrange to catch the first plane tomorrow. I'll call to give you my schedule. The FBI here in Texas may want to send someone with me."

"Really, from Texas?" He sounded surprised.

We ended our conversation with my promise to contact him with travel plans.

I called Chris—got her on her cell phone.

After relating the story about Middleton, Wisconsin, she immediately agreed to go with me. And a surprise, she said she'd arrange the transportation.

An hour later she called.

"The Bureau is providing a Lear Jet to fly us to Madison."

"What Bureau?"

"The Federal *Bureau* of Investigation," she said.

In all the time we'd worked together, I'd never heard her refer to the FBI as *the* Bureau.

"They'll pick us up at the Amarillo airport," she said. "Meet me at the general aviation gate in the morning at 7:00 a.m. Don't bother with breakfast. We'll eat on the plane."

"Wow."

"I've called the FBI regional office in Madison," she continued. "They'll meet our plane. And by the way, they've made contact with the local station about the TV tape."

"Double wow."

"Cross your fingers," she said. "This may be our break."

CHAPTER 46

Rick Husband International Airport, Amarillo, Texas

I'd never ridden in a Lear Jet before. This one was small, very sleek, and painted white except for a tiny American flag on the tail.

Chris had arranged for two additional agents from the Dallas office to accompany us. She introduced them as Gus and Manuel. The four of us filled the cabin, sitting two by two, facing each other in large comfortable chairs—in airplane jargon, what's called club seating. And when the pilot applied full power for takeoff, the force pushed me back into the seat, an angle of climb unlike anything I'd ever experienced. It felt like we were going straight up.

Just a little bit scary.

Soon we leveled off at 31,000 feet, and the pilot announced it was time for breakfast. An Amarillo caterer had loaded food on the plane for the four of us and the two pilots. Gus, apparently an old hand on trips like this, took over and distributed a gourmet meal—cheese omelet with ham, orange juice, toasted English muffin, and steaming hot coffee. Flying north at near the speed of sound, we watched a spectacular sunrise as few people get to see it.

Life in the fast lane took on new meaning for me. I loved it.

After breakfast, the four of us got down to business as we discussed our plans for the day. Chris took charge and made assignments.

She started with me. I was to go with Henry Bozeman, the central Wisconsin AVI, to the Hinders Dairy in Middleton and examine their cattle. They wanted me to review their testing techniques and then, depending on how things looked, we'd take blood samples and return to Bozeman's lab in Madison to process a series of Masterson BSE tests.

Gus' job was to team up with local agents and circulate drawings of our suspects. More than anything, Chris wanted him to interview local workers at cattle operations—dairies, feed yards, and cow-calf places—to see if anyone recognized our police artist drawings or had any information about Bashiyra Fahatah.

Chris and Manuel would go as a team to the TV station, talk with employees, and ask if they could help us develop any leads. The videotape was our highest priority. Chris wanted to duplicate a thousand copies and distribute them nationwide.

At the end of the day, probably around eight o'clock, we'd meet for dinner, exchange information, and develop our strategies for the next day.

The hour-and-a-half flight terminated in Madison where we deplaned into crisp cool weather. I liked Henry Bozeman immediately, and he seemed really glad to see me. We jumped into his white, USDA pickup and started west.

"Dr. Masterson, I've never met a famous scientist before," he said. "I'm not sure I know how to act."

I chuckled. "You want me to call you Dr. Bozeman?"

"Hank," he said. "No one calls me by my last name."

"At home everyone calls me Jim Bob. I wish you would, too."

"Jim Bob?"

"Yup."

"Somehow that doesn't seem proper for a person who invented the BSE test."

"Dr. Bozeman, you gonna give me a hard time over this?"

"No, sir. I'm so grateful you're here to help us. I'll call you anything you want to keep you happy."

"Thank you, Hank."

"You're welcome, uh . . . Jim Bob."

Hank turned out to be an excellent veterinarian. I went over all his BSE procedures and found them flawless. Also, the Hinders family ran a top-notch dairy operation. They kept meticulously detailed records on every animal with color-coded ear tags and computer summaries of milk production. If I wanted the date of birth, the genealogy, or the health-history of a particular cow, they had it. Immediately.

I found that dealing with both a highly skilled AVI and a state-of-the-art dairy operation made it easy for me to implement a BSE eradication plan. We took the blood samples, loaded them into Hank's pickup, and returned to his lab in Madison to run the tests. We worked hard and by early evening had the results.

Exactly as I recommended, Hank ruled that all animals "over thirty months,"—what we called the OTM herd—be put down.

Government subsidy would likely reimburse the Hinders family based on 90 percent of the market value of each. Then he ordered that all the rest be taken to a feed yard and finished to 1200 pounds before sale to a packer. The Hinders would lose their dairy herd, but they'd be reimbursed and in good shape financially to start over.

We called the Hinders, and Hank gave his ruling—a happy ending to a busy day.

Hank agreed to drop me off at the hotel. I invited him to join us for dinner, which he did. At government expense, we had T-bone steaks with all the trimmings.

The others listened to Hank and me as we reported on the Hinders Dairy. Our good news was well received. I praised Hank's impressive work, and he received a fair share of ribbing by the FBI.

Gus' report was one of frustration and disappointment. He'd spent the day with two Madison fibbies, contacting local dairies, feed yards, and cow-calf operations. They visited almost fifty sites, talked with hundreds of workers, and failed to find anyone who recognized the drawings of either Bashiyra Fahatah or her male companion.

Chris asked Manuel, the FBI agent from Dallas who'd worked the TV station with her, to give his take on the day.

"Channel 9 gave us their tape, and we've sent a copy by wire to the national lab in Washington," he said. "I have a preliminary report with the promise of more to come tomorrow." He passed out Xerox copies.

Bashiyra Fahatah, called Barbara by many, was born in Riyadh, Saudi Arabia, February 11, 1971. The Fahatahs are wealthy and known to be friends of Osama bin Laden and other opponents of the ruling House of Faud. While not listed by the government as "dissidents," the Fahatahs had some difficulty obtaining a visa for Bashiyra to attend an American University. She entered Texas A&M in September 1991 and received a Bachelor of Science in Agriculture degree in 1995. Records show she returned to Saudi Arabia immediately after graduation.

While no official information exists of her whereabouts over the past decade, the Bureau suspects she has been in America for eight to ten years and probably has established contacts with members of al Qaeda. Fahatah is well known for her anti-American attitudes and is considered the most likely female to break into the all-male tradition of Saudi extremists.

A more detailed search to follow.

I thought about the report and the vast resources it represented. It must be wonderful to work for a government entity that, twenty-four hours a day, seven days a week could provide such detailed research. At that moment, the FBI impressed me more than ever, and I was glad to be working with them—rather than against them.

"Jim Bob, did you take feed samples at the Hinders Dairy and check on whether the source of BSE contamination is the same as Sagebrush?" Chris asked.

"Sorry," I replied.

"He was busy checking animals with me," Hank said.

"I understand, but now that we've established the level of the infection, it's time to concentrate on where it came from," she said.

"I agree," I replied. "We'll start on it first thing in the morning."

Chris' cell phone rang. She excused herself and left the table.

"I should have taken steps to check the feed," I said.

"No, you were doing exactly what I asked," Hank replied. "One step at a time. Today we checked the animals—tomorrow we'll examine the feed."

"And you accomplished more than I did," Gus interjected.

Chris returned. She looked tired, discouraged.

"Bad news?" Manuel asked.

"The worst," she replied. "They discovered another outbreak of BSE."

"Where?" I asked.

"Rushville, Nebraska."

Chapter 47

Dane County Regional Airport, Madison, Wisconsin

The next morning I awoke early and went down to the motel's coffee shop to wait for Chris and a ride to the airport. I picked up a couple of newspapers to see the reaction to BSE in Wisconsin and Nebraska. It was worse than I expected.

Much worse.

Both the *Chicago Tribune* and the *Wisconsin State Journal* gave it big black headlines. "Epidemic" was the buzzword of the day, and for the first time, the media emphasized a BSE connection to fast food outlets like McDonald's and Burger King. The front-page stories read like an obituary for beef—the death of the American hamburger.

I called Maggie to see how things were at home.

"Where are you?" she asked.

"In Madison, Wisconsin, getting ready to go to the airport."

"Oh, good. You're flying home?"

"No. To Rushville, Nebraska."

"Rushville. Where there's a new BSE outbreak?" she asked. Her voice dropped, reflecting disappointment.

"Yes," I said. "How'd you know?"

"Everyone in the country knows. It's all over the news."

"Give me some details."

"The beef packers were supposed to open yesterday morning," she said, "but when the news about Wisconsin came, they just trucked the cattle back to the feed yards."

"They never processed any beef?"

"No. And last night, when news about another outbreak in Nebraska hit, the local media made it sound like an onslaught of Black Death."

"The FBI plane is taking us to Nebraska. We're leaving in a few minutes."

"Honey, did you remember that Liz is supposed to be in New York five days before her performance at Lincoln Center?"

"Yes." But the truth was, I had lost track of dates. I pulled out my pocket calendar. "Her performance is Thursday, the twenty-first?"

"And when she won the regional auditions, you asked me to purchase three tickets to New York on Sunday, October 17th."

"I guess I'd forgotten the exact dates of those tickets."

"That's three days from now."

"Okay, I'll be there to go with you." I noted the calendar.

She didn't say anything for a moment.

"I know how important this is for Liz. I'll be there."

"I want to believe you," she said, her words carrying coolness in her voice.

"Maggie, they're loading to go to the airport. I'll call you as soon as we have a scheduled flight back to Amarillo."

"I love you,"

Her words tugged at my heart.

"And I love you, too," I answered.

An FBI car took us to the airport where I recognized the plane and the pilots. It was the same, sleek Lear Jet and the same two pilots we'd flown with yesterday morning. Today, only two passengers, Chris and I, were headed west to the latest BSE outbreak. After we leveled off at 32,000 feet, she handed out the breakfasts.

"What information do you have?" I asked.

"Not much. "The Omaha office is sending two agents to meet us at the airport."

In contrast with yesterday's bright sunrise, today's weather produced thick clouds, which cast a dark, somber outlook on the task that awaited us in a small town in western Nebraska. Conversation died. We ate in silence, and I wondered how much more BSE the country could handle.

When we finished our breakfasts, I helped Chris clean up. The copilot gave us an expected time of arrival of about thirty minutes. The sound of the engines slowed, and I could feel the nose of the plane drop.

"These bastards are always a step ahead of us," Chris said, her voice bitter, and her beautiful face now a scowl. "They're running around the country with this deadly disease, and we have no idea where they're going to be next."

"What can you tell me about Rushville, Nebraska?" I asked.

"Population 906. A small farming community in the middle of nowhere. Nearest airport is Chadron, twenty miles west."

"I know Chadron State University," I said. "They have an ag school."

"Jim Bob, then why the questions?" She turned her anger on me. "You probably know more about this part of the country than I do."

Obviously she was in no mood for conversation about western Nebraska. I decided to let it rest. In a few minutes we heard the whirring sound of the landing gear as we broke out of the clouds. Seconds later we touched down, and I could feel the plane braking hard. The pilot turned around on the runway and taxied back to a small prefab, a steel building with a handmade sign that said, "Welcome to Chadron." As airports go, this was the smallest I'd ever seen.

We deplaned to find a three-person reception committee. Dr. Thurmond Seawright, the AVI for northwest Nebraska, was waiting for me, and two FBI agents named Chuck and Ray were there to greet Chris. We shook hands and made plans to drive to Diamond Cattle Feeders, a feed yard about thirty miles east. Chris rode with the fibbies in their dark blue Crown Victoria. I went with Thurmond, who, as expected, had a regulation white pickup with USDA lettering on the door.

Thurmond was a big fellow, probably 300 pounds or more. But jolly. And BSE didn't worry him a bit—just another day with a sick cow that needed treatment.

"What can you tell me about the situation at Diamond?" I asked.

"It's a small feed yard," he replied. "Only 10,000 head."

I chuckled. In most areas of the country, a cattle operation with 10,000 animals would be considered huge. Out here, in the vastness of the Nebraska prairie, folks called it small. "Have you inspected their operation?"

"Not really," he answered. "I drove out yesterday when I got the call. They showed me one cow that went down."

"You took samples for testing?"

"No," he said and cracked a big smile. "I called the NVSL, and they sent you."

"So you really don't know if you have BSE?"

"They *think* they do."

I was amazed at how casual he was. Apparently, he had no idea what the implications were for the country's food supply.

"Tell me about your lab in Chadron."

"It's a pretty good little facility. We're able to service our area and respond to most of the problems. If something new comes up that we can't handle, we send it to Ames."

"You have slicing machines for preparing samples and the microscopes for making a diagnosis?"

"Probably."

I smiled at his answer. Either he had the equipment, or he didn't. I decided to gather blood samples and then go to his lab to see for myself. No point in hassling him.

Diamond Cattle Feeders was located out in the middle of one of the most sparsely populated areas of the country. They headquartered in what is known as a "double-wide"—two trailer houses put together to form a temporary building, twenty-four feet wide by fifty or so feet long. We learned that Diamond was owned by some medical doctors in Chadron. These MDs had little or no knowledge of the cattle business and hired a manager who in turn selected a crew of about two dozen cowboys to run the feed yard. Apparently, high turnover was a problem. The manager was new, as were most of the other workers.

For the first few minutes I listened as Chris and her FBI cohorts questioned the manager and a couple of his employees. Using her laptop computer, she showed a DVD copy of the Bashiyra Fahatah videotape from Madison. As I expected, these new people had never seen her. Another dead end. Thurmond and I went outside to the pens to start taking blood samples.

Midway through the morning, Chris and the fibbies left to make similar inquiries at neighboring feed yards. She stopped briefly to tell me her plans. We agreed to meet for dinner at the Pizza Hut in Chadron.

Thurmond and I finished taking blood from the downer animals by noon. Then we gathered samples of feed. Thankfully, this "small" feed yard required much less time than Paul Edwards' huge operation. By mid afternoon we had both feed samples and blood samples, were back in Thurmond's white pickup, and headed west to his AVI lab in Chadron.

Thurmond had the necessary equipment. He let me process the blood samples. As expected, I confirmed that we had two dozen animals that tested positive for BSE. We agreed to run the tests on feed in the morning. He dropped me off at the Pizza Hut where I found Chris and her FBI cohorts, all in a foul mood.

"How'd it go?" she asked with a concerned look.

"Twenty-four cases confirmed," I replied.

"Any clue about where it came from?"

"We have feed samples to run tests in the morning. I'll probably have results by noon."

Business was light and a college-age waitress came to take our order—one pepperoni and one vegetarian-lovers supreme. As we waited a group of familiar looking people came in and took the big corner table.

While I was trying to place them, the waitress went over with menus.

"Rolf Brewster," the waitress exclaimed. "What are you doing in Chadron?"

CHAPTER 48

Betty's Café, Chadron, Nebraska

The influx of people hit northwest Nebraska like a flood of locusts. I first noticed it the next morning when we had to wait in line for breakfast. Chadron—the "big" city of the area, population 5,406—didn't have that many restaurants to absorb the hundreds of newspaper reporters, television crews, government workers, and people like me.

So Thurmond and I waited.

That made us late getting to Diamond Cattle Feeders where the crowd developed into a full-blown circus. We parked our USDA pickup a quarter-mile from the feed yard. My 300-pound companion complained about the walk.

"Jim Bob, where do all these people come from?" Thurmond

asked.

"Who knows?" I answered, and as we walked past a NBC television truck from KUSA, Channel 6, Denver, I pointed it out. "Thurmond, you'll need to be very careful what you say."

He stopped walking, breathing heavily. "I wasn't planning to say anything."

I stood with him, waiting for him to catch his breath. "See all these TV trucks?" We could see others parked along the road with logos from CBS, CNN, Fox, and ABC.

"Yeah, reminds me of when Dick Cheney came to Cheyenne."

"They're going to be after you for a statement."

"Why me?"

"Because you're the local AVI. You're 'the feds,' the authority figure."

"So, what?" he asked.

"I have a suggestion," I replied.

"Okay, let's have it."

"When they ask you about BSE, I think you should defer to your boss or to the National Veterinary Services Lab."

"Why would I want to do that?"

"Suppose a reporter from CNN asks, 'How many people are going to die from this disease?' What're you gonna say?"

The light dawned. He nodded his head.

"If you say, 'Everyone who eats tainted beef,' you're in trouble. It may be true but, just the fact that you gave them a quote, will add to the panic."

"But if I say, 'You'll have to contact the NVSL in Ames,' it gets me off the hook."

"The media is looking for bad news. They're desperate for you to help them make dire, disastrous predictions about America's food supply."

"Gotcha." He smiled.

I smiled.

"Then let's go meet the press," he said.

We resumed our walk, and as we drew closer to the feed yard's headquarters, reporters swarmed us. I recognized Rolf Brewster.

"Dr. Masterson," came his brief acknowledgment.

"Good morning, Mr. Brewster," I replied. "How've you been?"

He ignored my greeting and stuck his microphone in my face. I noticed a cameraman move into position. "The fact that the country's leading BSE expert is here in Rushville tells us we now have a true epidemic."

"I wouldn't know," I said.

"But you are here to verify the tests?"

"No, Dr. Thurmond Seawright asked for my help. I'm here to assist him."

"Dr. Seawright is the Area Veterinary Inspector?"

"Yes." I stepped back. "This is Dr. Seawright." I nodded to Thurmond.

Brewster and his cameraman immediately zeroed in on Thurmond. "Dr. Seawright, how serious is this outbreak?"

My big friend flashed a robust smile, one that filled his pudgy, round face. I could tell he enjoyed his new position as the center of attention. "I'll be glad to tell you everything I know," he said.

Finally, the media had a newsmaker. Immediately other cameras gathered around, and Thurmond had three mikes within inches of his lips.

"Would you tell us your name and your position, please?" someone asked.

"Sure," he said, stating his name, then added, "I'm 'the feds,' the Area Veterinary Inspector."

"We'd like you to summarize the status of BSE in western Nebraska."

"And I'd like to help you, but for a question like that you'll have to ask the NVSL, the National Veterinary Services Laboratory, in Ames, Iowa."

Immediately, I sensed their disappointment. This wasn't news. They'd traveled a long way for a local, on-the-scene statement. Instead, they got a country bumpkin who deferred to a national office known for withholding information.

Brewster tried again. "Dr. Seawright, what can you tell us about your situation here at Diamond Cattle Feeders?"

"I can tell you that they called me about a 'downer.' A cow that stumbled and fell."

"And you've tested that animal for BSE?"

"Yes, and sent the samples to Ames."

"And you're confirming the disease in this feed yard?"

"No, I'm confirming that I sent the samples to Iowa. You'll have to contact the NVSL about the disease."

Brewster shifted his mike to me. "Dr. Masterson, you're the expert. Tell us the results of your test."

"Sorry, I'm working for Dr. Seawright. He's asked me to refer all questions to him."

"Why are you so reluctant to admit the obvious?"

"Look, I'm just trying to help."

"This situation must be worse than anyone thought. Is that what you're hiding?"

"Hiding what?" I smiled. "That we've been testing every cow with a bad cough?" I started walking toward the headquarters building. "Ask Thurmond. He's in charge."

Thurmond smiled, waved, and followed me.

Inside, Thurmond and I conferred with the feed yard owners and their manager. These poor guys didn't know what hit them. I related our experiences in Madison and Amarillo, and the good news about two possible outcomes—a government subsidy for older animals and the OTM rule for younger ones. The owners, who now feared the worst, reacted with relief to these new possibilities—an alternate to complete financial ruin. I emphasized the need to contact their congressman and senators, to help build support for a government subsidy in a time of crisis.

About that time Chris walked up. I introduced her. Our conversation shifted to the question of how the infection might have originated.

"Do you import calves into your feed yard?" I asked.

"Of course," the manager replied.

"Where from?"

"Mostly from western Nebraska, some from surrounding states."

"Any from outside this area?"

"Occasionally. Depends on where we get the best price."

"From Mobile, Alabama?"

"Not since I've been manager."

"How about four or five years ago?"

The manager looked to the owners. One of them shrugged and said, "Maybe. Why is that important?"

"We're trying to locate the source of BSE in America," Chris interjected. "It would help us if we could publicize any cattle imported from the Port of Mobile. It might even help us catch the people who are bringing this terrible disease into our country."

"We want to help," the manager said.

"It's possible that some of our calves came from Mobile," one of the owners suggested.

The others nodded.

I turned to the feed yard manager. "Here's what I want you to do." Then I outlined a procedure much like what we went through in Amarillo three weeks earlier: hold a press conference, give the reporters a chance to ask questions, answer as many as possible, and try to give them something they can print or broadcast. Finally, I asked him to help us with the Mobile story. "Don't lie," I said, "but if you get a chance, help them make an inference."

He did.

First he went out on the front steps and announced that he would have a news conference at twelve o'clock, noon. Then, at the appointed hour, he read a short statement confirming that Diamond Cattle Feeders had twelve cases of confirmed bovine spongiform encephalopathy. He gave reassurance that the disease had been contained and posed no threat to the nation's food supply. When questioned about the source, he truthfully stated that he didn't know how his feed yard could have been infected.

"However," he said, "several years ago a truckload of calves had been brought from Mobile, Alabama, and authorities were checking to see if those animals could have been imported from Europe."

The media gobbled up the news.

They had their story.

Pressure eased. We finished our investigation, somewhat disappointed that we had no confirmation about the participation of Bashiyra Fahatah or her male companion. But we had good leads and strong possibilities. We decided to call it a day and head back to the motel in Chadron. When we arrived I found a note to call Paul Edwards.

"Howdy, Paul, what's up?" I asked.

"I have a friend, Heinrich Schmidt, who owns the Ellis County Cattle Feeders in Ellis, Kansas," Paul said.

"Where's that?"

"About fifteen miles west of Hays."

"So what's up?"

"Heinrich called me today. He recognized both the drawings and said they were former employees at his feed yard."

Chapter 49

The Days Inn Motel, Chadron, Nebraska

That night Chris called the Ellis County Feed Yard in Ellis, Kansas, and spoke with Heinrich Schmidt, the owner. She set up a visit for ten o'clock the next morning. Then she made all the usual arrangements.

So on a beautiful Saturday morning as the sun rose over the flatness of western Kansas, we flew into Hays, the nearest airfield, fourteen miles east of Ellis. And for the third time in four days, we met FBI agents and the local AVI. There, we followed our familiar routine—Chris rode with the fibbies, and I climbed into another standard-issue, white USDA pickup. When we arrived at the feed yard, we found an overall sameness to our task—the smell of the workplace, the pens of bovine animals, and the goodness of the people.

But with one huge difference.

This time we were ahead of the disease. These people had no sense of the impending bovine spongiform encephalopathy, its symptoms, or its disastrous repercussions. Nor did they have the slightest clue that the disease might have come into their feed yard.

Still, they were frightened by our presence.

It became immediately clear that our first objective should be reassurance. After the introductions, Chris turned to me.

"We have bad news and good news," I said.

Heinrich looked German. A large red-faced cattleman, he wore jeans, a sheepskin coat, and boots just like mine. He chuckled and said, "Let's hear the bad news first."

"There's a good chance middle-eastern terrorists mixed BSE into your feed and infected your cattle," I answered.

With German stoicism, Heinrich didn't blink or react in any way. "And the good news?"

"If you are infected, like those we've found in Texas, Wisconsin, and Nebraska, we can help you." I gave him a worst-case scenario for his feed yard, and then compared it to Paul Edwards' situation and how I thought the endgame would play out—for Paul and for him.

"If I have BSE, we'll have to start over?"

"Yes, I'm afraid so."

"But the good news is, we'll have the financial resources to do it."

"Assuming the government's plan for a 90 percent subsidy comes through."

For a moment Heinrich hesitated, as though thinking over his options. "When I talked with Paul, he recommended you."

The big German's comment surprised me. It was the first clue

I'd had since the crisis began about how Paul Edwards regarded me. "Maybe he's hard-up for veterinarians to recommend," I commented with a smile.

"Paul assured me I could trust you."

I laughed. "He's got his back against the wall. He has to trust someone."

"Same as me." This time Heinrich didn't laugh, didn't smile.

"Mr. Schmidt," Chris interrupted. "If you suspect that you have BSE, the sooner you know, the better you can deal with it."

The AVI spoke up, "She's right, Heinrich. And you'll want an expert to run the tests."

Heinrich Schmidt looked at me with a frown. "I guess I'm lucky to have *the* Masterson here to conduct his test in Ellis."

Again, the AVI gave me his endorsement. "Doesn't get any more expert than that."

"I disagree," I said. "Anyone who knows what they're doing can draw blood samples and look at slides under a microscope. But, if you want me to do it, I'll be glad to."

"*We* want you," the AVI said. He spoke the words like a command.

A meditative quietness settled over our little group. Reality was about to hit the town of Ellis, Kansas, population 1,873. For a moment I thought about the crush of notoriety that loomed over the horizon—dozens of jets at the airport, streams of journalists filling the country roads, hundreds of people crowding the restaurants and motels.

Heinrich broke the silence. "Okay, let's get it over with."

We took blood samples.

And we took samples of all the feed.

Meanwhile, Chris and her FBI pals showed their video to small groups of employees. Then they left to continue their search at other area feed yards, and at motels and restaurants in Ellis and Hays.

At the end of a long, tedious day, the AVI dropped me at the Holiday Inn in Hays.

Chris was in her room when I called. We agreed to meet for dinner, just the two of us.

"How'd it go?" she asked.

"About half of his cow-calf operation tested positive," I said. "Almost all the animals who are four years or older."

"What about the younger cattle?" she asked.

"Negative."

"You tested them all?"

I smiled. "He has 30,000 head in his feed yard."

"So?"

"I tested one animal in each pen—just a sample of the ones that have fewer than eight incisors."

"Eight front teeth?" she asked.

"Yup."

"What does that have to do with it?"

"You don't know much about checking the age of cattle do you?"

"Darlin'," she gently put her hand on my wrist, "I didn't know you cared so much about my bovine experience."

Her touch startled me and I froze. Our eyes met, and for a fleeting moment, a sexual tension vibrated between us.

Then she smiled and lifted her hand. "You checked all the cows with eight front teeth?"

"At age two, bovines have only four incisors," I replied. "By age three most have eight. All are on the lower jaw."

"Lower?" she asked. "What about their upper teeth?"

"Sweety, bovines don't have upper incisors," I replied, my voice edged with sarcasm. "They have a large, heavy gum—called a dental pad—along the front of their upper jaw."

She played along with a coy, contrite smile and a fluttering of her eyelashes. "Jim Bob, why are we talking about cows' teeth?"

"You recall that we have considerable evidence supporting the theory that BSE only affects older cattle?"

"Yes," she said.

"How did you plan to identify the older cattle?"

She squirmed, uncomfortably. FBI agents don't like to be made aware of their ignorance.

I let her squirm.

Finally, she spoke, "Well, I'd planned to find me a cowboy who could tell."

"Shucks, ma'am, you have me. And the way ah'm gonna do it is to look at their teeth."

"Which you did today?"

"Yes, because, if we're going to follow the OTM rule—that cattle over thirty months are the only ones old enough to develop BSE—then those are the only ones I'll need to test."

"Damn, you're smart," she teased and smiled at me.

I smiled back and thought about how our different backgrounds made us a good team. Then I changed the subject.

"What'd you find about Bashiyra Fahatah and company?" I asked.

"We have some good news," she said. "Some very good news."

"Lay it on me. I'm ready."

"They flew into Hays and rented their car here."

"That's the good news?" I asked, the disappointment obvious in my voice.

"You have to have a drivers license to rent a car."

"Sure, I knew that." I said, not wanting to admit I'd forgotten the requirement.

"And I have more good news," she added.

"I can't wait."

"Hertz Car Rental in Hays, Kansas, always makes a photocopy of each renter's drivers license."

"Gee whiz. Imagine that."

She held out a sheet of paper with a Xerox of a Texas driver's license. I read the name Yusuf Jabbar and recognized the photo. "Bingo," I shouted.

"Even terrorists get sloppy," she said. "So we're checking the address in Houston." She held out a second sheet of paper with another Texas drivers license.

I read the name Bashiyra Fahatah, recognized her photo, and noted that she gave the same Houston address. "Double bingo!"

"We've called Houston. Agents there have set up surveillance."

"Damn, you're smart," I said.

"Ah larned it from mah cowboy pardner," she replied.

Together we had a good laugh—one of the best since we'd been working together. She went to her room, and I went to mine where I found a red blinking light on my phone. Following the instructions, I played the message from my wife.

"Where are you? Why haven't you called? We're supposed to catch American Airlines to New York tomorrow morning at 10:15."

The words hit me like a dagger in my heart. I knew Sunday was the day. I'd intended to call, put it off, and then forgot. I dialed the number.

CHAPTER 50

Saturday evening, The Holiday Inn, Hays, Kansas

"Thanks for calling," I said. "How'd you find me?"

Maggie ignored my question. "Are you going with us?"

"I *will not miss* Liz's performance next Thursday night," I said. "I promise, I'll be there."

"So, you're not going with us tomorrow morning?"

"I wish I could. You know I'd rather be on that plane—flying with you and Liz to New York—than anywhere else in the world."

"No, I *don't* know. Why haven't you called?"

"We've had a break in the BSE epidemic. We think we've identified the terrorists who are behind it." I winced when the word *terrorists* slipped out.

"Terrorists? Our TV news says the infection came from imported European cattle."

"That's the FBI's cover story. This is all in strict confidence, you understand, but if the Arabs don't know we're looking for them, we think we'll have a better chance of catching them."

She hesitated. I could hear her breathing. "Why is it so hard for me to believe you?" she whispered.

"This will be over soon," I said. "Then you'll see everything for what it really is."

"We . . . we need you." She said the words so softly I could barely hear her.

"And I need you. Please, tell Liz I'm coming. Reassure her. I *will* be there."

Maggie didn't say anything.

I struggled to think of something else to say, something reassuring. Then I heard a "click."

"Maggie? Maggie, are you there?"

She didn't answer.

I thought about calling back, but I didn't know what else to say. I peeled off my clothes and fell into bed, hoping tomorrow would be a better day.

On Sunday morning Chris and I made plans over breakfast. I would go with the AVI to test the feed samples. She would organize two surveillance operations—one in Houston, the other at the Ellis County feed yard.

Chris' focus would be on locating our two suspects. My job was to prove that BSE was being brought into the American cattle industry via contaminated feed. At first I thought I had the easier of the two assignments. But as the day wore on and we processed batch after batch of the samples we'd taken from Heinrich Schmidt's feed yard, it became apparent that we had no evidence. If the source of the disease had been feed, it was a small amount, it had been introduced years ago, and all signs of it had now dissipated. We were back to square one.

Sunday night, Chris and I again met for dinner at the Holiday Inn Restaurant.

"How'd it go?" I asked.

"We're hot on the trail," Chris replied.

"So where are Bashiyra Fahatah and Yusuf Jabbar?"

"I can tell you two places where they are not—at their apartment in Houston, or at any of the motels in Ellis County, Kansas."

"So, what's the plan?" I asked.

"We're assigning half our agents to Houston, the other half here."

"What about Wisconsin, Nebraska, and Amarillo?"

"Just the locals."

I shook my head, doubting this strategy. "How many agents are assigned to Sagebrush Cattle Feeders?"

"Two, plus me."

"You're going back to Amarillo?"

"Let's talk about it. I can be ready tomorrow evening. How about you?"

"I think that'll work," I said.

She pulled out her cell phone and made two calls. I listened to her side of the conversations as she made arrangements for the FBI's jet. It surprised me how much authority Chris carried. She didn't ask—she ordered. Apparently, the plane would pick us up at the Hays Municipal Airport tomorrow afternoon at five o'clock.

"We'll check out in the morning," she said, "and take our luggage with us. I'll meet you at the airport sometime between 4:30 and 5:00," she directed.

"Sounds good."

The next morning, she left with her FBI colleagues.

I went with the AVI to the Ellis County Feed Yard. We drove the fourteen miles west to meet with Heinrich Schmidt in his office.

"I'm ready to start eradication," Heinrich said the moment we were all seated.

"First, we need to talk," I said. "The FBI has a plan to end BSE in America, but the government will need help from both of you."

"What can I do?" Heinrich asked.

"Just name it," the AVI added.

"We're almost sure the BSE in your animals came from contaminated animal protein, probably bone meal from infected cattle in England. We think it was mixed into the feed by Bashiyra Fahatah and Yusuf Jabbar when they worked here."

The AVI nodded, a pensive look crossing his features. "Sounds plausible."

"There's no other logical explanation," Heinrich said.

"It appears we have two good chances to catch them," I continued. "We've found an apartment in Houston where they've been living. The FBI has agents watching it around the clock." I paused to catch my breath and frame my thoughts.

Heinrich helped me. "The other of your two chances is here?"

"Yes," I answered. "In Texas, Wisconsin, and Nebraska, they returned, they called TV stations, and they helped publicize the downer cattle."

"So far, I've not had any downers," Heinrich said.

"Yes, but my tests show that the disease is rampant in your older animals," I answered. "It's only a matter of time."

The AVI entered the conversation. "You think the terrorists will return here to make sure the infection is highly publicized?"

"It's their pattern."

I waited.

Heinrich looked at his AVI. Heinrich turned back to me and sighed.

"You want us to sit here, continue to feed infected animals, and pretend everything's normal?"

I nodded. "That's about it."

"How long?"

"No one knows for sure," I answered. "Probably not long. I predict only a matter of weeks—maybe only days."

Heinrich again looked at his AVI.

"Sure," the AVI said. "We've got to do everything we can to catch these bastards."

I went over the plans. I told them that the FBI would have twelve agents watching the area, working around the clock. They took phone numbers—those of the local FBI, Chris O'Shay's, and mine.

We held a meeting with Heinrich's employees and stressed the need for secrecy.

By mid afternoon, we shook hands and said our goodbyes. The AVI dropped me at the Hays airport. At five o'clock, Chris and I boarded the FBI's Lear Jet and headed back to Amarillo.

Chapter 51

Monday evening, at home in Bushland, Texas

That night I called Maggie and told her I was coming. I promised to finish my BSE obligations in the morning and take an afternoon plane to New York. She suggested we have dinner at The Tavern on the Green in Central Park. That night sleep came easily. I was going to be with my family, and, best of all, for the next few days I'd be getting away from the raging controversy over safe beef.

Tuesday morning I picked up two newspapers and a McDonald's breakfast to take to the office. Sitting at my desk, the Sausage McMuffin tasted wonderful and brightened my spirits. The headlines in the *Amarillo Globe-News* and *USA Today* had the exact opposite effect. Both the local and national news portrayed the public's reaction as "panic." Beef could be dangerous. And for the first time, America connected a deadly disease—and the possibility of death—to fast food hamburgers.

USA Today pictured a Burger King in Chicago with "closed" signs. The *Amarillo Globe-News* showed a photograph of the McDonald's restaurant, where I'd bought my breakfast, and indicated that it would serve pork items like my Sausage McMuffin throughout the day. Grocery stores reported that beef sales had fallen to practically zero. Mad cow in Texas, Wisconsin, and Nebraska was enough to scare everyone.

I called American Airlines and booked a flight to LaGuardia, leaving Amarillo at 2:15 PM. It felt good to be getting away.

Paul Edwards phoned. He had a lunch meeting with, of all people, Congressman John Zahrenski. Paul wanted me to go with him.

There didn't seem to be any graceful way to decline. Reluctantly, I agreed and shortly before noon left the office to arrive at the restaurant early.

The Big Texas Steakhouse was on the way to the airport. I had my suitcase in my Chevy and planned to go straight from lunch to catch my plane. Sitting alone at a table near the front window, I watched a white Ford pickup pull into the restaurant's parking lot just as I had done three weeks earlier when I'd sat at this same table, waiting to meet with Ted Austin and Stan Young. It seemed incredible that they were both now deceased.

I looked across the tables toward the lobby, saw Paul's big white Stetson, stood, and motioned him over. A short, gray-haired man wearing a navy blue blazer accompanied Paul toward my table.

"Jim Bob, this is John Zahrenski, Congressman from Virginia."

"I feel like we've met," he said, extending his hand.

I shook it. "Pleased to meet you," I said.

We sat.

"What brings you to Texas?" I asked

"I'll let Paul explain," Zahrenski replied.

"Let's order. Then we can talk business," Paul suggested.

The waitress came with menus and took our orders for iced tea.

"Is it safe to order a steak?" Zahrenski asked. He chuckled as he said it. Neither Paul nor I smiled. Beef jokes in West Texas weren't funny anymore.

We studied the menu until the waitress returned with our tea.

"Ready to order?" she asked.

"What are you having?" Zahrenski asked.

"T-bone, baked potato, Caesar salad for me," Paul replied. "I'd like my steak rare."

"Same for me," I added.

"Make it three," Zahrenski said. "I'll take my steak medium."

The waitress left. Paul began the conversation, "John came at my invitation," he informed me, nodding toward Zahrenski. "He's agreed to help us with our subsidy bill."

Zahrenski frowned. "I said I *might* try to help. Things have changed these past five days, since the outbreaks in Wisconsin and Nebraska."

"In what way?" I asked.

"Last week, right after Stan Young's death, there was an upturn in both public opinion and congressional support," Zahrenski said. "We had the votes in committee—and, I think in both the House and the Senate—to pass a 90 percent subsidy."

"And now?" Paul asked.

The congressman wiggled his hand in a waffling motion, "I'm not so sure," he replied.

"Jim Bob has some news about terrorism," Paul said.

"I, too, have heard rumors," Zahrenski added.

I nodded. "That's all we have—rumors."

"I've heard that the FBI identified two Saudis who worked at my feed yard," Paul said, his voice insistent. "You have their names?"

Both men looked at me, waiting. I drank my iced tea, taking a moment to choose my words carefully. "Yes," I said. "Bashiyra Fahatah and Yusuf Jabbar."

"Well?" Paul asked.

"The FBI is trying as hard as they can to find them," I answered.

"This would make a decisive difference," Zahrenski said. "If Congress knew this mad cow epidemic was a terrorist plot, we could pass the subsidy in a nanosecond."

Paul leaned forward in his chair. "Let's announce the names," he said. "We know they worked in my feed yard. They've been recognized in the others. And what about Ellis County?"

"Ellis County?" Zahrenski asked. "Where's that?"

"Hays, Kansas," Paul replied. "I have a friend who hired them to work in his feed yard."

"There's another outbreak?"

"Unfortunately, yes," Paul answered.

"BSE in Kansas?" Zahrenski's voice boomed. "You're hiding confirmed cases in another location?"

"Congressman, please," Paul whispered. "Keep your voice down. I promised Jim Bob and his FBI friends I wouldn't say a word about what I know."

The waitress brought our steaks.

Zahrenski fumed, his red face telegraphing his anger.

"Would anyone like steak sauce?" she asked.

No one spoke. I shook my head. She left.

Zahrenski exploded. "This is exactly the kind of duplicity that caused me to block your subsidy back in September," he yelled.

People seated two tables away looked up. They stared at us.

I waited.

"How can you expect support from the United States Congress if you lie and withhold facts?" Zahrenski's voice filled the restaurant. Even the staff stopped and looked our way.

I waited.

"Jim Bob has a very good reason," Paul said.

"There can be no reason to withhold important facts like this," Zahrenski continued. "Either you're totally open and honest with us, or we can never support your request for a subsidy."

I sat there, hands in my lap, waiting for his anger to ease.

"Jim Bob, speak up," Paul urged.

"I've had it with you Texas cowboys." Zahrenski threw his napkin on his food, rose, and stomped away from the table, heading toward the door.

Paul stood, panic in his face. "Damn, now look what you've done."

I rose and grabbed his arm. "Wait."

Paul shook loose. "We had a chance for a subsidy. That's why I asked you to join us for lunch." He turned to go after Zahrenski.

"I'm going with you," I said.

"He's probably gone."

"But he rode with you?"

"Yeah."

"He must be outside, waiting for you to unlock your pickup."

Paul blinked. Obviously he hadn't thought that far ahead. "Okay, you can come with me—if you'll apologize."

"He's mad, but he's not going anywhere," I replied. "Give him a minute to cool off." I sat.

"If we find he's left—" Paul sank into his chair.

"Trust me, he'll be there." I motioned the waitress for the check, and finished my iced tea while she processed my credit card. Paul fidgeted, but waited. I checked my watch to see how much time was left before I had to catch my plane.

"Let's walk slowly," I said. "We can talk on the way."

"Jim Bob, if you've killed our chance for a subsidy—"

"Trust me." Sure enough, we found Zahrenski waiting by Paul's pickup.

I started with an apology. Then I explained how we planned to set a trap in Ellis County, Kansas.

Zahrenski listened. And as he listened, he reluctantly agreed to support our plan to catch the terrorists.

Paul didn't like it. He was paying a quarter million a day to feed worthless cattle. He wanted, *needed*, an immediate government subsidy. My plea to wait—to use this as an opportunity to catch the people who had infected his cattle—fell on deaf ears.

Then a surprising thing began to happen.

Gradually, Zahrenski started switching sides.

I couldn't convince Paul, but the congressman could. On a warm October afternoon we stood in the parking lot, and I listened as they argued. Finally, Paul agreed to give our Kansas trap a chance. In convincing him, Zahrenski had convinced himself. Both men now understood how crucial it was to hide our circumstances from the media.

I looked at my watch and saw that I had only thirty minutes to catch my plane.

I needed to cinch the agreement, so I promised to keep them apprised of our progress and assured them that either the FBI or I, personally, would contact them each day. And we put a two-week deadline on our plan. If we hadn't caught our terrorists by then, we'd meet to renegotiate.

I looked at my watch—1:57.

With apparent disappointment and more than a little resentment, Paul turned to drive Zahrenski back to his hotel.

I burned rubber as I tore out of the parking lot. Driving thirty MPH over the speed limit, I managed to make it to the airport-parking garage without getting a ticket. I grabbed my carryon bag and ran to the big windows at the head of the security line—where I watched my plane pull away from the gate.

Chapter 52

Masterson and Associates Veterinary Services Inc.

I drove back to the office and called American Airlines. For one hundred dollars, they changed my flight to the exact same time the next day.

Then I tried to call Maggie. She didn't answer, so I left a message. Sometimes, an answering machine was a blessing.

Next I called Chris. "You have time for a cup of coffee?" I asked.

She answered with a question. "Where are you?"

"In my office. How about meeting at Starbucks on Georgia Street?"

"You're supposed to be on your way to New York."

"Missed my plane. I've rebooked for tomorrow."

"What happened?"

"It's a long story. I'll tell you over coffee."

She didn't answer for a moment. "It's almost four o'clock. Why not meet someplace for dinner?"

"Sure," I said. Just the talk of food caused my stomach to growl. "I missed lunch. Where you wanna meet?"

"Lettuce Works?"

"Uh . . . is that negotiable?"

She chuckled. "Just testing."

"How about a steak at the Outback?" I asked.

"Steak? They're still serving beef?"

"God, I hope so. Five o'clock?"

"Would six be okay?" she asked. "I'd like to stop by the hotel and change clothes."

"Six at Outback," I said. "See you there."

I turned on my computer and found ninety-seven e-mails that had accumulated since my trip north to Wisconsin and Nebraska. I made a fresh pot of coffee and settled in.

Fred and Ida Mae left at the usual closing time.

It took until a quarter to six to finish the last of the e-mails. I shut down, locked up, and drove west to the restaurant to find very few cars in the parking lot. Chris—wearing jeans, sweatshirt, and sneakers—was waiting inside. The hostess at the front desk greeted me with an effusive welcome.

"Business that bad?" I asked.

She smiled. "We also serve chicken."

Chris stood, and the hostess led us to a nearby booth. On the way I looked around and found only one other couple on the no smoking side of the restaurant. A waitress came and took our drink orders—margarita for Chris, Foster's beer for me. We studied the menus.

"Business at a steak house is worse than I thought," I said.

"It's only six o'clock," Chris answered.

"The Outback is one of Amarillo's most popular steak restaurants. Every time I've come, this place has always had a waiting line."

"Welcome to the world of reality."

The waitress brought the drinks to our booth, pulled out her pad, and in typical Outback fashion, sat on the edge of my seat to take our orders.

"I'd like the small filet, medium, Caesar salad, and the mixed vegetables," Chris said.

"Same for me except I'd like the large filet. Rare," I added.

"Most people are ordering the chicken or the pork chop," the waitress replied.

"That's fine for most people," I said. "We want beef."

"I'll have to go see if we have any." The waitress left.

"A steak house without any steaks?" I asked.

"We can always leave and go to the Lettuce Works." Chris smiled—the coy, teasing expression I'd come to recognize in the three weeks we'd been working together.

I tried to give it back. "Darlin' I'd just as soon wait to see if they can find us some beef."

She kicked me under the table, her sneaker striking a glancing blow on my shin. "That's not funny."

The waitress returned. "We have some filets that are frozen. Will that be okay?"

"Sure," Chris said.

I nodded.

We paused for a moment. Even in casual clothes, Chris looked terrific.

"How're things?" I asked.

"Houston reports nothing. No one's come or gone."

"Ellis County, Kansas?"

"I talked with Heinrich Schultz this afternoon."

"What did he have to say?"

"Nothing happening at the feed yard."

"Any downers?"

"Not yet." She took a sip of her margarita. "Aren't you proud of me? I've learned the lingo."

"So has the American public. Everyone in the media uses that term consistently without explanation."

The waitress brought our salads.

My cell phone rang. It was Paul Edwards.

"I have a meeting tomorrow morning with the TCFA board of directors," he said. "I'd like you to go with me."

"Paul, I missed my plane to New York today because of a meeting with you. I've re-booked for tomorrow."

"What time?" he asked.

"The same, 2:15."

"This meeting's at ten o'clock. You'd have plenty of time to make your plane."

"That's what you said yesterday."

"What time will you need to leave?"

"They want me to check-in at least ninety minutes before departure. I'll need thirty minutes for driving to the airport. A little time to grab some lunch would be nice."

"If we're still going at noon, you just get up and leave."

He had me. I stalled, trying to think of some excuse not to go.

"Jim Bob, I agreed to go along with you and Zahrenski. This is costing me a quarter mil a day. The least you can do is help me with the TCFA board."

What could I say? "Okay."

"TCFA board room, ten o'clock?"

"I'll be there." I punched off.

"May I ask?" Chris said.

"Paul wants me to go with him to a TCFA board meeting so they can vent their anger at me over the delay in beef subsidies."

"Lots of luck."

"I'm not looking forward to it."

My cell phone rang again. I looked at the caller ID. It was the New York Hilton.

"Hello," I said.

"I got your message," Maggie said.

"I've already booked my flight, same time tomorrow."

"I know. That's what you said in your recording."

"Dinner tomorrow evening?"

"That's the plan. I've called The Tavern on the Green and changed our reservations."

"I'm looking forward to it," I said.

"Tomorrow's Wednesday," she answered slowly, her voice icy.

"I know."

"Liz is singing Thursday night."

"I know that, too."

"Where are you?"

"At The Outback."

"Having a steak dinner?"

"Of course."

"With Chris O'Shay?"

I hesitated, a fraction of a second. “Yes.”

Then came a silence. A long terrible quietness while I struggled for something to say. “Maggie, I—”

I heard a click, and the finality of it made my stomach knot.

“Maggie, you still there?” I asked. I knew she wasn’t.

No response. Then a dial tone.

“Trouble in River City?” Chris asked.

I tucked my cell phone in my pocket and took a swig of Foster’s. “Nothing I can’t handle,” I said, but I wasn’t so sure.

“Look, I don’t want to make things difficult for you at home. Just tell me what you think I should do.”

The waitress brought our salads, and I was grateful for the interruption. I didn’t have an answer.

Chapter 53

At home, Bushland, Texas

The next morning I went outside to check on my herd of Black Angus. I hiked the quarter mile trail to the windmill, saw that it was pumping water just fine, and found the big, round water trough full to running over. After counting cattle—twenty-five, all present and accounted for—I walked among them, checking to see that they looked healthy. These big, black, gentle animals had known me from their birth and grown accustomed to my visits. Somehow, I think they sensed the pride I felt in their growth and development.

Back at the house I cleaned up, repacked my suitcase, and drove to the TCFA building for my ten o'clock meeting.

Paul welcomed me and offered coffee. The members of the board of directors, eight cattlemen that I knew and worked with as a consulting veterinarian, greeted me with a noticeable lack of cordiality. We seated ourselves around the large conference table, and the TCFA president—a rancher from Hereford named Rod Hennessey—called the meeting to order. I couldn't help but remember our confrontation at the auditorium two weeks earlier, and his comment about giving me the "asshole of the year" award. The scowl on his face, and his refusal to shake hands, confirmed that his attitude toward me had not softened.

"I may have some good news," Hennessey said to start the meeting.

"God, I hope so," the rancher seated across from me replied.

"Let's hear it," someone demanded.

Several others responded with similar comments. Then the room quieted.

"I've arranged for us to speak with Congressman John Zahrenski at eleven o'clock," Hennessey said. He gestured to a speakerphone in the center of the table. "We'll put it on the squawk box so we can all hear what he has to say."

Paul, seated in the chair on my right, turned to me, a look of alarm in his eyes. He leaned over, his mouth close to my ear. "First I've heard of this," he whispered.

"The *Globe-News* reported he was in Amarillo yesterday," the rancher across from me said. "Why didn't we have this meeting while he was here so we could talk with him personally?"

"How come?" someone asked.

"Yeah," another replied.

Several others grumbled.

Hennessey held up a hand to quiet the group. "I didn't find out about it until he'd already left, but Paul and Jim Bob did. They had lunch with him."

Everyone in the room stared at us.

"I'll let Jim Bob explain," Paul answered.

My first reaction was anger. The son of a bitch was throwing me to the wolves. But my second thought—an almost instantaneous reflex—was one of understanding. Paul wanted the board to do something he couldn't: he wanted them to change my mind about immediate financial support from the government. I fell back on my own advice—when in doubt, stick to the truth.

I sat up straight and in a confident voice told the group, "We talked to him about his support for a 90 percent subsidy."

Hennessey waited, obviously expecting me to continue.

"The three of us decided it would be best to give it a couple of weeks."

The room exploded with anger.

"Why?"

"We need it now."

"I'm looking at bankruptcy."

"Doesn't that S-O-B know we're about to go under?"

Everyone had something to yell and shout—words to vent frustration.

Again Hennessey gestured for quiet. When he could be heard, he looked directly at me and, with hatred in his eyes, asked, "Jim Bob, why won't you come down out of the clouds and do something to help us?"

The room grew quiet—a stillness that heightened the emotion. I could hear air moving from the heating vents as I thought about how best to answer. Three options raced through my brain. I could give up on our plan to conceal the names of suspected terrorists and join these men in their demand for immediate government subsidy. Or I could explain the plan to everyone in the room, hope that they would support it, and would maintain the secrecy needed to allow it to run its course for the next couple of weeks, maybe longer. Or, least pleasant of the alternatives, I could suck it up, urge these leaders of the cattle industry to risk financial ruin based solely on my judgment, and in so doing, probably receive their enduring enmity.

I chose the latter.

"We're close to finding out where this disease is coming from," I said. "Yesterday, Zahrenski and I convinced Paul that this was the best course of action. We decided to give it at least two weeks before asking Congress for a subsidy. In fairness to him, let me say that this is costing Paul a quarter million a day. He didn't want to do it."

The quietness grew heavier. I could now sense an uncertainty about Paul. Hennessey turned to face his fellow cattleman.

"Paul, in a few minutes we're going to lobby Zahrenski for the subsidy," Hennessey said. "Are you with us?"

Everyone looked at Paul Edwards, including me. He hesitated for a brief moment before he nodded his head. It was a small gesture, and he stared down at the table to avoid looking at me as he gave it.

Hennessey sat in prolonged silence—an emotional pause that increased the schism separating my opinion from that of everyone else in the room.

"I guess it's time for me to leave," I said as I rose from my chair.

"Goddamned right," Hennessey said, "and—"

"Let him go," Paul interrupted.

I left. As a symbolic gesture, I firmly closed the door. It *was* time for me to go, to get on a plane, and to give Texas cattle country to the cattlemen. Musicians like my daughter had a word for it, the Italian for finish, or the end—*finé*. A sense of relief washed over me as I drove to Rick Husband International Airport.

What a difference from yesterday's frantic dash. Today I drove well under the speed limit to the airport parking garage. Then I walked at a leisurely pace to the American Airlines counter, thought about checking my bag but decided to carry it on, and stopped at the airport coffee shop for a turkey and Swiss sandwich. After passing through security I looked at my watch to see that it was only 1:20, at least thirty minutes until boarding time for my 2:15 departure.

I gazed out the wall of windows to watch our plane arrive. In no time at all, passengers began deplaning through the gate and out into the concourse.

Then my cell phone rang. The caller ID showed Sagebrush Cattle Feeders. I thought about not answering.

But I did.

"Hello."

Paul's words came in a loud, frantic, excited jumble. "They're at the motel. Right there!"

"Paul, slow down," I said. "I can't understand you."

"They're there damnit." Again a panicky rush.

"Paul, count to three, then say it again, slower, and don't yell."

I could hear his big, heavy breaths, more like snorts. A few seconds went by, and then he spoke slower and in a more normal tone of voice.

"Yolanda, the maid . . . at the Days Inn . . . in Dumas . . . called," he said.

"Yes, I understand."

"She said Bashiyra Fahatah and Yusuf Jabbar just checked into the motel."

"In Dumas?"

"Yes, and they drove a big truck—a huge U-Haul."

"They're there now?"

"Yolanda said they paid cash for one night."

"You've called the FBI?" I asked.

"I don't have Chris' number," Paul said. "That's why I called you."

"Okay, I'll call her. And Paul, I suggest you let the FBI handle this. It could turn nasty."

"Will someone contact me and tell me what's going on?" he asked. "I don't want them to get away."

"I'll call you, I promise." I punched the off button.

As I dialed Chris, I realized, without thinking, I'd made a decision to defer my flight to New York. I paused, heaved a big sigh, forgot where I was in the ten-digit number, punched the off button, and started over. This time I got it right. Chris answered.

"Jim Bob?" she said. "You're supposed to be on your way to join your family."

"I'm at the gate," I said. "The plane is here, ready to board."

"And you're calling me?"

"Paul Edwards says Bashiyra Fahatah and Yusuf Jabbar just checked into the Days Inn Motel in Dumas."

CHAPTER 54

Rick Husband International Airport, Amarillo

I stood by the curb with my bag, just outside the baggage area, the spot where Chris said she'd pick me up. While I waited, I used my cell phone to rebook my flight for the next morning.

I had two choices. A flight that left Amarillo at 5:45 a.m. arriving in New York at 1:30, or a 10:15 departure that arrived at 5:20, the absolute latest that would allow me to make Liz's eight o'clock performance at Lincoln Center. I chose the latter and called Maggie's hotel room at the New York Hilton.

No answer, so again, I left a message. I told her I'd meet her at the hall and asked that she leave my ticket at the "will call" window.

Then I looked at my watch and made a solemn vow. Nine o'clock the next morning, sixteen and a half hours from that moment, was the latest I could be back at the airport to catch my plane. No matter what happened in the next few hours, whether or not we proved a terrorist plot and caught the bastards, I was going to be on that plane and join my family.

Chris pulled up to the curb, red strobe flashing. I threw my bag in the back seat, buckled myself in the front, and braced myself for a fast trip to Dumas. She peppered me with questions as we tore out of the airport. Chris wanted to talk about terrorists.

I refused.

"Before we go any farther, let's have an agreement," I insisted.

"About what?" she asked. Her indifference told me she was already reading my mind.

"You have to promise me that, no matter what happens, you'll get me back to this airport by nine o'clock tomorrow morning."

"Jim Bob, we can talk about that later."

"Then stop the car. Let me out. I'll hitch a ride back to the airport."

"We can't stop." She still didn't believe I was serious.

"Damn it, I'm not going unless I have your word." I had to stand my ground. If I missed that flight tomorrow, it could mean my marriage.

She looked at me and shook her head. "Okay, I promise."

"I'm going to hold you to this," I vowed.

She swerved around several cars and spoke to me once more in her professional voice, "Now can we make some plans about what we're going to do when we confront these Arabs?"

"Just so we agree on my priorities." I wanted to apologize, but she had to know how important this was to me.

We made the turn onto Loop 335. She barely slowed as we

screeched around the tight corner and bluffed an eighteen-wheeler. Then she floored the accelerator and sped north at speeds in the three-digit range.

"Now, tell me everything you know about the terrorists," she said. Her fingers gripped the wheel tightly, and she leaned forward like a racecar driver.

I recounted my phone conversation with Paul Edwards.

"So all we have is Yolanda Garcia's ID?"

"Yes."

She eased back into her seat. I looked at the speedometer and saw it drop to ninety. "This doesn't feel right," she said. "They should be in Houston or at the Ellis feed yard."

"I guess we're about to find out," I replied.

Chris' doubts and my conditions put a damper on our conversation. We rode in silence for the next half-hour, the initial expectations of the U-Haul's discovery now fading. As we arrived in Dumas, Chris turned off the strobe and pulled into the parking lot at K-Bob's Restaurant. I counted six other law enforcement vehicles clustered in the lot. We parked away from the restaurant, got out of the car, and joined a group of about a dozen officers who were standing in the street. Two more police cruisers pulled up.

In her usual perfectionist style, Chris took command and asked for a briefing from the Dumas policeman in charge. He told us the U-Haul truck was now gone and that Yolanda was in the office, waiting with the motel manager. Gus and Manuel, the FBI agents from Dallas, had radios with a special frequency they distributed—one for each vehicle.

Chris asked all of us to wait while she checked the motel. Gus went with her. I climbed into an FBI cruiser with Manuel. We sat and waited.

"You're worried about her," Manuel said, after Chris and Gus had disappeared.

"A little," I admitted.

"Don't. She can take care of herself. She's been doing a terrific job for the past three years—since her husband was killed."

Suddenly, Chris' commanding professional demeanor made sense. All business. I thought the part I occasionally saw—the funny side, the touch of a kidder—must be a small sample of the other part she buried when her husband died.

"How'd he die?" I wasn't sure I wanted to know.

"In Iraq," Manuel answered. "He was a major in the Army Reserve. I think she's more like her old self with you than I've seen her in a long time."

Manuel's words caused me to worry about my relationship with Chris. I turned it over and over in my mind. An hour went by before she returned.

Again, we circled up for a briefing. I stood next to her, offering silent support, and admiring her for staying in this line of work.

"It's definitely Bashiyra Fahatah and Yusuf Jabbar," she said. "Positive ID from three people—Yolanda Garcia, the hotel manager, and the desk clerk."

"Where are they now?" asked a familiar voice. I recognized Wyatt Reed, Amarillo PD.

"We don't know," Chris replied. "They checked in, changed into khaki-colored uniforms, got in their U-Haul, and drove away. They left clothes, personal belongings, and suitcases in their motel room."

"Any clues about where they've gone?"

"None."

"What's the plan?" Wyatt asked.

"I suggest we stake out the motel and wait," Chris replied. "All their stuff is in room 221, upstairs, near the corner."

I sensed that no one liked the news. Several shuffled their feet. I heard a sigh and saw exchanged glances of disappointment. They wanted action, but Chris planned to play this one by the book.

"Anyone have something to suggest?" Chris asked.

No one did.

"Gus will be in charge of making assignments," she said. "We'll work in squads of four, two hours on, two hours off. Stay close, keep your radios on."

Gus took over. Half of the vehicles left, two officers in each. I looked at my watch to see that it was now 6:15 p.m.

"You hungry?" she asked.

"Starving," I answered, as we headed toward the restaurant.

"How about I buy you dinner? Celebrate our last meal together before we catch the bad guys?"

I nodded agreement. "And I take off for New York."

She stepped close, slipping her hand around my arm.

Chapter 55

K-Bob's parking lot, Dumas, Texas

By eight o'clock, nothing had happened.

Ten o'clock came. Still no sign of the U-Haul.

Time lingered in a torpor until, a little after midnight, Chris suggested we drive by the Days Inn to check on things. First we circled the block, and then she found a good spot just a short distance north with a full view of the motel parking lot.

We parked. Chris seemed unable to sit still—constantly thumping her fingers against the steering wheel, making calls on the car radio or the small hand-held radio with the special frequency we were using for the stakeout. Finally, the Dumas police dispatcher assured her he would call when something broke. And he emphasized that she needn't keep contacting him.

I lasted a while, and then dozed off.

Cold, shivering, I awoke to find Chris in conversation on the car radio. I looked at my watch—3:30 AM.

"Anything?" I asked when she clicked off.

"Nope," she replied. "Absolutely nothing."

"Obviously they've gone somewhere," I said.

She turned, and gave me a look of utter frustration. "Okay, cowboy, tell the rest of us. Where could that be?"

I shrugged and said the first thing that came to mind, "Sagebrush Cattle Feeders?"

"Gus thought of that," she replied. "We have two cruisers there, waiting."

I shook my head, trying to think of possibilities. "Maybe one of the other feed yards?"

She exhaled an audible rush of air—a sigh of exasperation. "We've contacted TCFA. That call was their president, Rod Hennessey. He's arranging for a dozen of their staff to come into the office as we speak." Chris looked at her watch. "By four o'clock they'll be making calls to all the feed yards within a hundred miles to see if anyone has seen our U-Haul."

She didn't ask me for any more suggestions. I could tell her feelings were raw. Anything I might say would only provoke an argument.

We sat in silence for a while. I shivered, but didn't comment about the cold. No sense in antagonizing her.

Finally, Chris broke our uncomfortable silence, "How about a cup of coffee?"

"Sure," I said.

She called the Dumas dispatcher for directions to an all-night convenience store where I paid for two cups of the worst coffee I've ever tasted. At least it was hot. The car's warm air felt good as we drove back to our observation spot. She turned off the motor.

We sat and finished our coffee. The cold returned.

I rubbed my hands together and looked at my watch—4:30. Two more hours until time to leave to catch my plane. I sneezed.

"You cold?" she asked.

"A little."

"Me too. I can't even feel my feet."

"Wish we could run the engine and turn on the heater."

"You know that'd be a dead giveaway if the bad guys return."

"Doesn't keep me from wishing."

"There may be some blankets with the emergency kit in the back."

"Let's look."

She popped the trunk, and we both stepped out to search. We found flashlights, flares, first aid kits, and an old wool, army blanket.

Back in the car, colder than ever, I offered her the blanket.

"This is no time for chivalry," she said, as she scooted toward me and wrapped the blanket over the two of us.

Cozy.

Warmer.

Dangerous.

I couldn't figure out what to do with my hands.

"Jim Bob, you're as tense as a coiled spring." She said the words slowly. I wondered if she felt a subtle undercurrent, but I didn't say anything. She was right. I was tense.

"It's okay to relax," she said with a smile. "I'm not going to attack you."

"That come with a signed affidavit?" No sooner had the words passed through my lips when I realized that I, too, suggested something else.

"Of course. I keep it in my hip pocket."

"You don't have a hip pocket."

"How would you know?"

"Back at the convenience store, I looked." If I'd stared straight at her, she would have seen a look of guilt. I cleared my throat.

"You licentious slob," she replied with a chuckle. "You were checking me out?"

"I wasn't the only one."

She slid closer, a playful, flirtatious movement that allowed her to rub against me. "You're saying that all men check me out?"

"Yes, ma'am."

"Jim Bob, I have a question."

I could feel her thigh pressing against mine, and I sensed where this was going. "What's the prize if I answer correctly?"

She lowered her voice and in a breathy, expressive tone, one filled with innuendo, asked, "What do you have in mind?"

Chapter 56

Parked in Chris' FBI cruiser,
a block north of the Days Inn Motel, Dumas, Texas

"What's the question?" I asked.

"Here we sit, all alone, pitch black, wrapped in a blanket—" Then she moved even closer, ever so slightly, a sensuous touching of our bodies.

"And—"

"How come nothing's happening?" she asked. She placed her hand on my thigh—a touch so light and casual it could have been accidental.

I felt my pulse quicken and tried to think of a noncommittal response. "Oh, but it is."

"Suppose you enlighten me. What exactly is happening?"

"We're diligently waiting for the suspects."

She chuckled—a throaty, husky laugh, charged with sexual overtones. The blanket came untucked and I should have felt the cold. I didn't. Instead, beads of perspiration lined my forehead and I realized where we were headed.

"Didn't know I was that much of a comedian," I said

"Jim Bob, you must be history's all-time barrel of laughs." Her hand pressed harder as she moved up and down my thigh, utterly obliterating any doubts about her intentions. She moved closer, and the fragrance of her hair dominated my senses.

Our lips touched lightly.

It was a soft kiss. I didn't intend to do it. In fact, when I moved my head toward her, I had planned to say we shouldn't be so close. But there she was, only inches away, and we came together. I'd like to say it wasn't my fault, that *she* kissed me . . . but the truth is, I could have turned away. I didn't.

She pulled back, leaning her head against the seat's headrest. But at the same time her hand on my leg tightened ever so slightly. I felt she was urging me closer. In a nanosecond a thousand thoughts raced through my brain.

Here I sat with the most beautiful woman I'd ever met, my heart pounding like a jackhammer. I could put my arms around her and let nature take its course. It would be wonderful—a night to remember. And who would know?

Things with Maggie were not going well. She constantly nagged me about work, about my efforts to help others in the cattle business, and especially, about my failure to focus on her and her wishes. As little as three weeks ago, she'd asked me to sleep on the couch.

Justification.

But it didn't fit. Something deep inside measured the immediacy of self-gratification against the concept of who I was—who I wanted to be—and an instinctive, emotional response took over. It surfaced in my brain like a flashing, Times Square, neon sign.

One road's *right,* the other *wrong.*

Then a feeling of release, a calmness came over me, and, without thinking, words slipped out, "Maybe this blanket isn't such a good idea."

"Why not?"

"Because I'm married."

"We both know that."

"Happily," I said.

She smiled again. "Then why do I find you studying my anatomy when we go for coffee?"

I didn't answer.

Before I could form the words, a car turned the corner and drove toward us. I yanked the blanket, dropped it on the floor, and scooted away as a Dumas police cruiser pulled up beside us. The uniformed officer rolled down his window.

"Anything happening?" he asked.

"Nothing," Chris answered.

"Want us to take over?"

"No, we're fine."

He raised a hand in mock salute, rolled up his window, and drove on.

Chris and I sat silently for a long time, the cold no longer a concern. Finally, she wadded up the blanket and threw it in the back seat.

"I love my wife, my daughter," I said.

"Hey, this isn't what I planned." A sharpness permeated her voice. It seemed to me that she used the words to cover a hurt, an attempt to maintain her dignity.

I reached out and grasped her hand. "We've made it just fine for these past three weeks. Maybe we can make it for another couple of hours."

After a minute, she lifted her hand and scooted even farther toward the far side, away from me. We sat in silence for a long time, until I noticed a gradual lightening in the eastern sky.

"You remember our agreement?" I asked.

"Nine o'clock," she answered.

"At the airport. Okay if I leave here at six-thirty?"

"I'll get someone to take you." She looked out the window as if to purposely avoid my gaze.

I looked at my watch—6:05. "Paul's probably hanging out at the restaurant parking lot. I can ask him."

"Whatever." There was an edge to her voice. She started the engine, cranked up the heater, and drove back to K-Bob's.

At six-thirty, Chris and I said our good-byes—crisp, formal words exchanged amid a gathering of law enforcement officers.

I threw my suitcase into Paul Edwards' pickup, and we headed to Amarillo.

CHAPTER 57

On U.S. 287, toward Amarillo

Paul and I drove south in light traffic and watched the sunrise. In the flatness of the Texas Panhandle, we could see the horizon for miles as a light glow in the east became a tiny sliver of brilliant yellow, then gradually grew into a blinding, round sphere. But the beauty of the dawn did nothing to soften Paul's sour disposition. A night of frustration and disappointment had left him angry with the world. I decided to forego conversation.

Alone with my thoughts, my mind scrolled through the events of the last fifteen hours. I tried to remember all the scraps of information. I reached into my bag and pulled out my lab notebook to make a list. The old, worn, black leather folder had been lucky for me when I did my research on BSE—what had now become known as The Masterson Test. Just as I had done a decade ago when analyzing the deadly disease, I wrote down a list of possibilities for resolving our present dilemma. Where could the terrorists have gone? What clues did we have?

For thirty minutes I wrote everything I could think of, most of it worthless, unconnected trivia. Then, when I couldn't think of anything else to write, I went back over it—word-by-word, line-by-line.

Midway through, on the second pass, I studied "khaki-uniforms." The two words buzzed my memory like pesky insects in a feed yard. I'm an expert in the Panhandle's cattle business and I'm supposed to know the people, their jobs, and how they dress. I racked my brain, thinking—who wears khaki uniforms?

"Employees at the NTI Animal Nutrition Center," I said, aloud.

"What?" Paul asked.

"Nutrition Technologies Incorporated, NTI, the feed mill on Grand where they make protein supplements for feed yards," I replied.

"What does NTI have to do with taking you to the airport?"

I looked at my watch—7:25 a.m. "Paul, we're going to pass within a mile of the NTI grain elevators," I said. "Why don't we swing by and take a quick look?"

He shrugged. "You're the one with a plane to catch."

"Take a right about three miles ahead, at the Third Street exit."

He shook his head, a puzzled look on his face. "What's up?"

"Probably nothing, but we have plenty of time."

"Damn it, Jim Bob, I don't like to be involved with things I don't understand." Nevertheless, he slowed and made the turn west on Third Street.

Grain elevators loomed on the horizon. "About a mile ahead on the left," I said.

"Yeah, I see it."

"Let's drive through their grounds and look around."

Paul leaned forward a little, both hands on the wheel. "You gonna tell me what you're thinking?"

"Sure, but first I have a suggestion."

"What's that?"

"Try to make it look like we're just early customers. Play it cool."

"Gotcha." Paul sat forward, his back straight, his body tense, as we turned into the feed mill.

We drove slowly past the administration building toward the far side of the tall, white grain elevators.

There we found a single vehicle backed up to the loading dock—a large U-Haul truck.

CHAPTER 58

Nutrition Technologies Incorporated, L.L.C.

"Don't stop," I whispered. "Drive on. Slowly."

Paul nodded.

"Look for a customer parking area."

He found one at the far west end of the NTI grounds, around the corner from the loading dock where the U-Haul was parked. We left Paul's pickup and hurried to a spot where we could see the truck. As we peeked around the edge of the building, two figures in khaki uniforms came out of the grain elevator and climbed into the U-Haul. Even at fifty yards away, I felt sure they were Fahatah and Jabbar.

The truck drove slowly toward the entrance. Paul ran to get his pickup. I stayed to watch the truck go to the NTI entrance and turn south on Grand Avenue.

Paul pulled up. I hopped in. “At the gate, head right.” He did, and we saw the truck, about a quarter mile ahead.

I dialed Chris’ cell phone. It rang and rang. But just as I was about ready to punch off, she answered.

“You at the airport?”

“No, we found the U-Haul. Paul and I are following it.”

She gasped. “Where are you?”

“In Amarillo, turning west on I-40, at Grand.”

“You identified the Saudis?”

“We think so,” I answered.

“Think? You’re not certain it’s them?”

“We were fifty yards away.”

Chris stopped. She went from frantic excitement to stone cold silence.

I waited and heard a door close.

“Start at the beginning,” she said, her voice cold and irritated.

I told her what happened.

“Where are you now?” Chris asked.

“About a quarter mile behind them, driving west on I-40.”

“Do you think they’ve spotted you?”

“No.”

“Paul’s driving?”

“Yes.”

“Let me talk with him.”

I handed the cell phone to Paul. “Chris wants to speak with you.”

“What’s up?” Paul asked, holding the phone close. Then he listened for several seconds.

“I understand.” Paul said. Again, he listened. “Here she is.” He handed the cell phone back to me.

As I took the phone I could see the truck ahead ease into the Coulter Street exit lane. I pointed. “Paul, are you watching?”

“I see him,” Paul replied, his voice tight, as though he resented my questioning his alertness.

“The truck is leaving I-40 at Coulter Street,” I said into the phone.

“Stay with it,” Chris shouted into the phone. “Don’t lose them.”

“Relax. We’ll do better if you don’t yell at us.”

“Sorry.”

“Truck’s heading north on Coulter,” I said. “Wait, they’re turning right into a parking lot.” I motioned for Paul to keep going. A half block farther, Paul turned left into a motel driveway across the street.

“What’s happening?” Chris asked, her voice loud, filled with anxiety.

“How about I hang up, call you back?” I asked.

“Jim Bob, don’t you dare.”

“I can’t converse with someone who’s shouting at me.”

She paused, and I could hear a heavy release of her breath. “How’s this?” she asked in a softer tone.

“Much better. Thank you.”

“What’s happening now?” she asked.

“They’re walking across the street to the Waffle House.”

We paused. No one said anything for a long time.

“What’re they doing now?” Chris asked.

“They’re taking a booth next to the window.”

“Can you confirm a positive ID?”

“Give us a minute.” I handed the cell phone to Paul. Then I got out, walked the short distance to the restaurant, purchased a cup of coffee to go, and returned to the pickup, now parked in front of the Amarillo Inn, a motel about fifty yards north of the Waffle House. Paul handed me the cell phone.

"Hello," I said.

"Where'd you go?" she yelled, her voice rebuking me.

"It's them," I said. "I made a positive ID standing less than ten feet away."

Chris screamed at me, "Damn it, Jim Bob. Did they recognize you?"

"Never even looked up," I said, calmly.

She drew in a series of short breaths, fighting to control her emotions. "Next time you plan to do something crazy like that, let's talk it over first."

"You wanted a positive ID," I reminded her.

She ignored me. "Wyatt Reed is here with me. He's calling APD to circle the truck and standby until we get there. We have four cars leaving Dumas. I'll be in one of those. Keep your cell phone on." She hung up.

Paul and I sat in his pickup and watched the two Saudis having breakfast.

I looked at my watch—8:15—and calculated the latest possible time I could leave and still catch my plane. I estimated it to be an hour from now—9:15—but hoped I could get away sooner.

Minutes ticked by in agonizing slowness. I searched up and down the street, desperately trying to locate law enforcement vehicles. If there were any, they were cleverly hidden.

It seemed my life had come to a standstill. Nothing was happening. I looked at my watch for the hundredth time—9:01. With shaking hands I took my cell phone and punched in Chris' number.

"Where are you?" I asked, anger in my voice causing the pitch to rise.

"Jim Bob, is that you?" she asked.

"Yes, damnit," my voice constricted even more with frustration. "What's taking you so long?"

"We're just a few miles north of Amarillo. We'll be there in fifteen minutes or less."

"Where's the damned APD? You said Wyatt called them an hour ago."

"Stand by. I'll call you right back."

The phone went dead.

Again I searched up and down Coulter Street. No sign of anything resembling a law enforcement vehicle. I thought about asking Paul to let me take his pickup and leave for the airport. But before I could get the words out, two things happened simultaneously. The khaki-clad figures stood and went to the cash register, and my cell phone rang.

I almost dropped the phone. With concerted effort, I willed my hands to stop shaking and found the green button to answer the call. Chris asked, "What's happening?"

"They're leaving," I yelled. "They paid and are now walking across the street to the U-Haul. Where're the damned police?"

"On the way," Chris replied. "They misunderstood Wyatt's directions and went to the Waffle House on Western. They'll be there in five minutes."

"Where're you?"

"We just passed the city limits sign on the way into Amarillo. We'll be there in less than ten minutes."

I made a snap decision.

"Hang on a moment, I want you to talk with Paul." I handed the cell to him. "Paul, you need to take the phone and stand over by the door to the motel." I reached across him and tripped the latch on his door. "Now." As the door came open, I pushed him. "Go!"

Paul half-fell, half-staggered away from the pickup.

I turned the key, and the engine roared to life.

Tires squealed and I burned rubber as Paul's pickup transformed itself into a missile, jumping the curb, flying across the street, and heading straight toward the front of the U-Haul. At the last nanosecond I glimpsed at the two terrorists in the front seat of their truck, staring at me with a look of disbelief.

I have no idea how fast the pickup was going when it collided with the front, driver's-side fender of the U-Haul, but one thing I do know—it was a hell of a jolt.

That truck wasn't going anywhere.

CHAPTER 59

1600 Block on Coulter, Amarillo

Stupid. I had forgotten to buckle my seatbelt.

Thank God for airbags.

Dazed, I sat wondering what to do next, when I heard a glorious sound. A siren. Then another. And before I could gather my scrambled senses, I became aware of flashing red and blue lights. I blinked, used both hands to lift myself off the steering wheel, and eased back in the seat. Looking around I took a slow breath that hurt as my chest filled with air.

Then I heard gunshots.

In spite of my dazed condition I dove for the floor. Hardly a second later the windshield splattered and glass fell everywhere. For the next few minutes, shots rang out, voices yelled, bullets ricocheted, and I felt like I was in the middle of World War III.

Gradually the shooting stopped.

For several minutes, nothing happened. An eerie quiet prevailed. Then voices. At first whispers, then voices growing louder, then shouts of "clear." Someone opened my door, and I heard a familiar voice.

"You okay?" Chris asked, bending into the vehicle to check me out.

I didn't answer right away. "More or less," I sputtered.

"Are you hit?"

I shook my head. "I don't think so."

She climbed up into the cab and looked down at me on the floor. "Here, take my hand."

I did, and she pulled me up into a sitting position. From the floor, I peered out, my eyes just above the dash, and saw an army of law enforcement personnel gathered around the pickup and the U-Haul.

"What happened?" I asked.

"They opened fire before we could give them a chance to surrender."

I cut her a questioning look, dreading the answer.

"They're both dead."

"What about our side?"

"We're checking," she said. "I want you to get out so we can check you."

My chest hurt, but I managed to scoot out the door on the passenger side. A couple of EMTs looked me over and pronounced me bruised and shaken, but otherwise in satisfactory condition.

Paul stood by me, waiting.

"Sorry about your pickup," I said.

"Jim Bob, you ever drive in demolition derby?" he asked with a smile.

Before I could think of a retort, Chris gestured toward an FBI cruiser, and I followed her a short distance to stand by the black Ford Crown Victoria, its motor running, a red strobe blinking on the roof.

"You want to try to make your plane?" she asked.

I looked at my watch—10:05. "It's fifteen miles," I replied, shaking my head.

"We won't know until we try."

"I think you need me to look at what's in the U-Haul," I said.

She nodded. Paul joined us.

They followed me to the back of the truck where the police had rolled up the tailgate. Inside we could see several dozen, black, fifty-five-gallon metal barrels. The three of us crawled up and found the lids marked "grain surfactant."

"What's that?" Chris asked.

"A wetting agent used by feed yards to make grains easier to flake," Paul answered. Together, he and I unlatched the lid on one of the barrels and looked inside. It was empty, but a residue of white power remained.

"Doesn't look like any surfactant I've ever seen," Paul said.

"Don't touch it," I cautioned. "We have no idea what it is. It could be lethal."

Carefully, we reattached the lid and sealed it tight.

"Jim Bob, we need to talk," Chris said.

We climbed down out of the U-Haul, and I followed her a short distance to, again, stand by her FBI cruiser.

"Sure you don't want to make a dash to the airport?" she asked.

I shook my head.

"You might still make it."

"Something needs to be done about these barrels. If that's what I think it is, it must be done immediately."

"BSE?" she asked.

I nodded. "There're two dozen empty containers in that truck. That's enough bone meal to infect every cow in Texas."

Chris and I took the front seat of her cruiser. Paul gathered our stuff from the demolished pickup and climbed in the back seat. Six agents piled into three other cars, and we formed a four-vehicle caravan, speeding toward the grain elevators on Grand. When we arrived with sirens wailing, strobes flashing, the NTI employees gave us their full attention.

The huge feed mill, a heavily automated operation, required only six employees. We had arrived with more FBI agents than they had workers. Chris gathered everyone for a briefing. I gave them my "you get it, you will die" speech. We handed out gloves, facemasks, and then, with fearful caution, we went to look for the deadly white power.

On the drive across town, I had called Ray Underwood. He arrived just as we started our search. I dropped out to brief him, and as we talked, more white USDA pickups arrived. To my relief, Ray took charge, and I gradually felt my responsibility ease.

I began to think of what I was going to say to Maggie and Liz. When would be the best time to call, to break the news?

The feds quarantined the entire NTI grounds.

Ray came to me and reported the terrorists had emptied their white powder into twenty of the feed mill's bins. Whether the protein pellets would be mixed with soybean hulls, alfalfa meal, wheat midds, or any of a dozen other additives, the finished product would contain a heavy dose of BSE. NTI, the largest source of protein supplements for the Texas Panhandle, could have unknowingly spread the lethal disease to virtually every feed yard in the area.

Ray sent feed samples from each bin to his lab—to his pressure cookers—to be tested. He agreed to call me as soon as he had results.

Paul Edwards met me on the loading dock, carrying my bag. He flashed an ear-to-ear smile, the happiest look I'd seen from him in the month since we'd first found BSE in his feed yard.

"Thanks," I said. "Guess I won't be needing this now." With a heavy heart I took the bag and thought again about making the dreaded phone call.

"You haven't talked with Chris?" he asked. He cackled, and his grin spread to the point it threatened to crack the skin on his face.

"What's up?"

"She's arranged for an FBI plane to fly you to New York."

Chapter 60

The General Aviation Gate,
Rick Husband International Airport, Amarillo

Chris and I stood at the gate and watched a Lear Jet taxi in from the runway. It stopped about fifty feet away. The door opened, and the bottom half folded down, forming steps.

"Thanks," I said. It wasn't nearly enough to convey my feelings, but I couldn't think of the right words.

"We made a good team," Chris replied. She held out her arms.

We embraced. She held me a long time, and for a moment, I thought about what might have been. Then she backed away. "I guess this is goodbye."

"You're heading to Los Angeles?"

"As fast as FBI paperwork will allow." She smiled the big wide grin that lighted her gorgeous face, a gesture of radiance I hadn't seen in these last few hours.

I tried to think of something to say. Her eyes turned watery, and she started moving back, small steps. "Your plane is waiting." Then she turned and walked away without looking back.

I boarded the plane, the engines still running. The copilot closed the door.

A Lear is fast, among the fastest of the world's small, private jets. And even though we left Amarillo after one o'clock, almost three hours later than my ticketed American Airlines 10:15 departure, I found that our ETA would be about the same, 5:15.

The cabin of the small plane made it difficult to change clothes. I couldn't stand up with the low ceiling, but I managed. And when we landed at New Jersey's Teterboro Airport, I had on my tux, black tie, and cummerbund. An FBI agent was there to meet me. He knew the fastest way to Lincoln Center, and we arrived a little after seven o'clock. I went to the will-call window and was given a small white envelope with my name on it. Inside I found a ticket and a note from Maggie.

Dear Jim Bob,

Mother is really upset with you. I suggest you give her your best smile and sit between us. She's wearing an expensive new dress, and she had her hair done this afternoon. You might comment on both.

All my love,

Maggie

The coat check girl gave me a hard time about taking my bag. And I'm not sure if it was my winning smile or a green piece of paper with U.S. Grant's picture, whatever, she finally took the bag and gave me a claim check. I found my way down front into the magnificent auditorium's most expensive seats, where in the center of the tenth row, an empty place by Maggie awaited.

"May I sit in the middle?" I asked.

Maggie smiled and moved over.

Katherine winced. I gave her a peck on the cheek before she saw it coming. It startled her. I'm not sure, but I think it was our first kiss since the wedding, twenty-six years before. I settled in between the two.

"Katherine, you look ravishing," I said. "Is that a new dress in honor of the occasion?"

She blushed. "Uh . . . well . . . yes. Thank you, Jim Bob."

"And your hair," I continued, with my best smile. "You look ten years younger."

The blush turned crimson, a full flush. She was speechless.

"Sorry I'm late," I said.

Maggie smiled, took my hand, and squeezed it.

Katherine found her voice. "That's understandable." She patted my arm. "We saw the TV special just before we left the hotel."

I could hardly believe my ears. My mother-in-law excusing my tardiness? I turned to Maggie. "TV special?"

"It's on all the networks," she said. "The FBI is giving you credit for finding the terrorists who were responsible for the infected bone meal."

"Really?"

As the lights dimmed I quickly scanned the program. Just before the auditorium went dark, I saw that there were ten singers—Liz scheduled next to last.

I relaxed and settled in to hear each of the first eight soloists sing three selections. All gave outstanding performances and received long, enthusiastic applause. I began to sweat. This competition was tough, much stiffer than I had imagined. I worried about, and for, my daughter.

Then Liz walked out to center stage and stood in front of the orchestra.

She looked stunning in a white, floor-length dress. She was so poised it reminded me of her performance at the elementary Christmas program almost twenty years ago when she was too young to know about being nervous. When she was six years old, she just sang from the heart. And it wowed everyone.

That night, she did the same in Lincoln Center.

The audience reacted.

People in front of us stood, and so did we.

The applause grew louder, and I looked around to see that everyone was standing. A guy on my left yelled, "Bravo." Others cheered and whistled. I clapped till my hands hurt. Then I hugged Maggie, and she whispered in my ear, "That's our little girl." I kissed her.

I looked around to see that we were the last two standing. I didn't care.

The program continued and the last soloist sang—then the orchestra left the stage. The President of the Metropolitan Opera came out to present the awards.

He called the names of seven performers, asked them to come to the stage to receive checks for $10,000 and contracts to sing at the Met. My first reaction was disappointment that Liz's name was not among those called.

Then I realized, these were the losers. He had yet to announce the first, second, and third place winners.

Next he called the name of a tenor from Bloomington, Indiana. The young man received $15,000 and the promise of a supporting role. The president didn't announce it as third place, but even a slow learner like me could eventually deduce it.

Tension mounted. I grabbed Maggie's hand and squeezed. The president called the name of another tenor, this one from California, and announced that as "runner-up" he was receiving $20,000 and a chance to costar in the coming year.

Of the ten contestants, every name had been called except one.

A hush came over the audience. The President said, "I am honored to announce that $25,000 and the leading role in next season's performance of Puccini's *Madam Butterfly*, goes to—" he paused, then in a booming voice he added, "Elizabeth Masterson of Bushland, Texas."

I knew it was coming, but when he actually said her name a wave of emotion gripped me like a seizure. I couldn't move. Tears welled up and flooded my eyes, rolling down my cheeks like rivers. Another standing ovation—every person in the hall on their feet and clapping.

Except me.

Finally Maggie leaned over and whispered in my ear. "People are looking." She handed me a small pack of Kleenex. In Texas, real men aren't supposed to cry in public. Embarrassed, I used tissue after tissue, trying to wipe my face dry. Finally I gave up, stood, and joined in the applause. It was a glorious moment. One I shall never forget. I let the tears flow.

Gradually, the applause ended. The lights came up. People began to make their way out. I followed Maggie and Katherine backstage where we had a heartfelt, poignant reunion. An hour later, we took a cab to The Tavern on the Green where Maggie had made reservations for four. At midnight we ordered steak dinners—with champagne. The steak wasn't as good as we're used to in Texas, but I didn't complain. Neither did my mother-in-law. A first! And I learned a new principle of familial action—when your kid wins, nothing else matters.

Chapter 61

Room 712, The New York Hilton

The next morning I called room service and, for an outrageous price, we had breakfast in the small suite.

"The panic's over?" Maggie asked.

"I think so," I replied. "At least until the media can think of something else to scare us with."

"Why are you so bitter toward the media?"

"It's their fault," I said. "They created the panic."

"But this was a dangerous disease—they had to report it."

"It's not dangerous."

"How can you say that?"

I paused, trying to think of how I could convince my wife. A comparative analogy might work.

"Name a dangerous disease, one that kills people," I said, as I opened my laptop and turned it on.

She frowned, looked at me suspiciously, shook her head, and then said, "AIDS."

I googled "AIDS, statistics."

Then I read from my computer screen: "The World Health Organization, WHO, states that last year 2.1 million people died from AIDS."

"Honey, that's awful. No, it's sickening, but what does that have to do with what we're arguing about?"

"I'm trying to make a point," I answered. "In the U.K., from 1986 through 2003, the largest documented outbreak of mad cow in history, a total of eighteen years, do you know how many people died of the disease?"

"I guess I don't."

"One hundred and fifty-three."

"One hundred and fifty-three thousand? Million?"

"One hundred and fifty-three people. *Worldwide*."

She stared at me for a moment as the comparison began to sink in. "That's unbelievable."

"The NIH, The National Institutes of Health, has cancelled all their BSE research."

"Why would they do that?"

"The NIH director has said that a person's chances of getting BSE are about the same as winning the lottery and being struck by lightning, all in the same day."

"Wait a minute, I seem to recall a Texas veterinarian who said, 'Cattle or humans, you get it you will die.' Who was that guy?"

"I was reading in *Wired Magazine* about a new word in the

dictionary."

She gave me her big, goofy grin, the one that says *I gotcha*. "No fair changing the subject."

"You want to broaden your vocabulary?"

"What's the word?"

"Ohnosecond."

"What's an ohnosecond?"

"It's that minuscule fraction of time that occurs when your brain realizes you shouldn't have said what you did, right after the words pass from your lips."

She laughed. "So rather than blame yourself, you say it's the media?"

"Hey. They caused the panic."

"What about the terrorists?"

"They caused a lot of mischief, and basically, they made it possible for the media to create the panic."

"What about those dozens of barrels of BSE that they dumped into the grain elevator at the feed mill?"

"What about them?"

"If that had been distributed to all the feed yards—"

"See? You're jumping to conclusions. You're just like the media."

"Don't you think that what those terrorists did, what they were trying to do, was dangerous?"

"No, not really."

"Explain yourself."

"When a feed mill manufactures protein supplements, every batch has to be tested by USDA labs."

"Every batch?"

"Yup."

"In the country?"

"That's the job of the USDA labs. That's why we have USDA inspectors like Ray Underwood."

"America's beef is safe?"

"I'm betting my life on it. I ate steak for dinner last night."

"What about the media? Can we trust them?"

I took my time framing an answer. First, I kissed the tip of her nose. Then I pretended a TV camera was pointed at me, and I was on national television. I screwed up my face in an exaggerated, political satire, and like a 1950s candidate, with booming voice, I said, "You take your chances, ma'am."

EPILOGUE

Texas Panic, like many good stories, is based on factual material. But it is fiction, and it is probably helpful for readers to know which is which.

The single biggest statement of fiction is the so-called "Masterson test," a blood test for BSE that can be administered without sacrificing the animal. At the time of this writing, the only accepted test is the microscopic examination of brain tissue. But research is underway in both the U.K. and the United States to find an alternate test for the disease, one that will not require the death of the animal, and it appears most likely that it will be a blood test.

BSE is real. And the statement attributed to protagonist James Robert Masterson, "Human or cattle—you get it, you will die," is also true. That's the bad news. The good news is that the facts given in the closing chapter are all correct: (1) the NIH stopped all research in 2005, (2) their reason for doing this was (as stated) that the disease is not dangerous, (3) that only 153 people, worldwide, died of the disease during the 18-year outbreak in the closing years of the 20th century.

It is true that our government, speaking through the USDA, says that beef is safe in our country. And they have the scientists and the statistical data to back it up.

It is also true that both print and broadcast media have a natural tendency toward sensationalism. A safe hamburger is dull and boring. Whereas, a hamburger that kills is both interesting and alarming. Anyone who has studied journalism knows that the media business needs exciting news to survive.

The quintessential example of how "shocking material" can be misused is detailed in the Prologue of this novel. All of the information given on pages 7, 8, and 9 is factual.

Obviously there is something to be learned from the rhetorical "what if" of *Texas Panic*. From this story one can see that freedom of the press is not absolute. Journalists must not misuse facts in a way that leads to real panic.

The lesson is that truth must be communicated responsibly—in a way that does not harm.

Credits

I know of no published novel that is the result of a single person's labor. And that is certainly the case for *Texas Panic*.

Doris Wenzel, my editor, comes first in line among the dozens who have made this publication possible. After the success of my first novel Orphan, she asked for another story with the same protagonist and then became the major force in decisions about final editing. Thanks, Doris, for your continued faith in me and my writing.

Andrea Brown, my former agent, had the original idea for the setting, the characters, and eventually, the story. After the manuscript won the NWA contest, she pitched it, unsuccessfully, to dozens of American publishers. In one of the ironies of the publishing world, after Andrea signed off as my agent, the novel sold itself.

But thanks, Andrea, for your help in getting me started.

Paula Silici, the world's most savvy editor, went through the manuscript and made hundreds of suggestions. Paula's eagle eye refined the story and made it shine.

The two biggest influences on my fiction writing have been the Iowa Summer Writing Festival and the Maui Writers Retreat and Conference. I went to Iowa four times and took their advanced novel classes with Mary Helen Stefoniak, Sands Hall, Jonas Agee, and Susan Chehawk. At Maui, Bob Mayer, William Martin, and John Lescroart were my instructors for the three summers I attended. When it comes to point of view, character motivation, or any of the thousands of technical tidbits writers must master to write a publishable story, I have to say I learned it from these great teachers.

Every writer can be helped by a good critique group and I've been lucky to have three that worked on this novel. Janda Raker, Joan Sikes, Diane Neal, and Jarrod Neal met at the church for about three hours every Thursday afternoon and read aloud. I learned from hearing both their manuscripts and mine. On Tuesday mornings I met with Alice Armstrong, Caron Guillo, and Bev Harris—we met in homes, served coffee, and tried our best to help each other. Wednesdays at noon I joined Betty Decker, Scott Williams, and Jodi Thomas for lunch and the trading of criticism. The question was always, "How we could make our stories better?"

This is a story about feeding cattle. Most of what I know about the subject I learned from my neighbors Alan Cansler and Ed Jessup. Alan owns a cattlefeeding operation and did his best to give me all the details. Ed is a nutritionist and an expert in the pellets that are fed to cattle as a supplement for protein. I couldn't have asked for better teachers.

But "the biggie" in technical details are those that relate to Bovine Spongiform Encephalopathy. Dr. Ted Montgomery, head of the department of animal husbandry at WTAMU, got me started. Dr. Robert Sprowls, head of Amarillo's Texas A&M research lab, showed me how they test for BSE and gave me the quote: "Cattle or human, if you get it, you will die." And Charlie Ball, the father of the TCFA, who read the completed manuscript and gave me suggestions about making the story more realistic. Thanks Ted, Robert, and Charlie, I couldn't have written this story without you.

And finally, I owe a special debt of gratitude to the three who labored over the galley-proofs. Gary Garner, Beverly Harris, and Janda Raker went through the manuscript one last time and made wonderful recommendations.

Thanks to all.
Harry, April 2009

2/14-10